Dear Reader,

Home, family, community and love. These are the
values we cherish most in our lives—the ideals that
ground us, comfort us, move us. They certainly
provide the perfect inspiration around which to
build a romance collection that will touch the heart.

And so we are thrilled to have the opportunity
to introduce you to the Harlequin Heartwarming
collection. Each of these special stories is a
wholesome, heartfelt romance imbued with the
traditional values so important to you. They are
books you can share proudly with friends and
family. And the authors featured in this collection
are some of the most talented storytellers writing
today, including favorites such as Brenda Novak,
Janice Kay Johnson, Jillian Hart and Patricia Davids.
We've selected these stories especially for you
based on their overriding qualities of emotion and
tenderness, and they center around your favorite
themes—children, weddings, second chances, the
reunion of families, the quest to find a true home
and, of course, sweet romance.

So curl up in your favorite chair, relax and prepare
for a heartwarming reading experience!

Sincerely,

The Editors

The author of more than sixty books for children and adults, **Janice Kay Johnson** writes Harlequin Superromance novels about love and family—about the way generations connect and the power our earliest experiences have on us throughout life. Her 2007 novel *Snowbound* won a RITA® Award from Romance Writers of America for Best Contemporary Series Romance. A former librarian, Janice raised two daughters in a small rural town north of Seattle, Washington. She loves to read and is an active volunteer and board member for Purrfect Pals, a no-kill cat shelter.

HARLEQUIN HEARTWARMING

Janice Kay Johnson

With Open Arms

TORONTO NEW YORK LONDON
AMSTERDAM PARIS SYDNEY HAMBURG
STOCKHOLM ATHENS TOKYO MILAN MADRID
PRAGUE WARSAW BUDAPEST AUCKLAND

Recycling programs
for this product may
not exist in your area.

ISBN-13: 978-0-373-36449-7

WITH OPEN ARMS

Copyright © 2011 by Janice Kay Johnson

Originally published as THE PERFECT MOM
Copyright © 2003 by Janice Kay Johnson

For questions and comments about the quality of this book
please contact us at Customer_eCare@Harlequin.ca

www.Harlequin.com

Printed in U.S.A.

With Open Arms

CHAPTER ONE

A CHILD SCREAMED, a piercing note of terror that seemed to shiver the window glass.

Kathleen dropped her coffee mug and shot to her feet, tripping over her bathrobe. Even as she raced for the kitchen doorway, heart doing sickening things in her chest, she thought, *Was that Emma? Not Ginny, surely. Even her giggles were soft!*

The scream became a gurgle, a sobbed, "Auntie Kath! Auntie Kath!" and Kathleen knew. Ginny was terrified because she'd found...

Emma. Something was wrong with Emma.

Hiking her robe above her knees, she leaped up the stairs two at a time. "Ginny! What's wrong?"

Their cat hurtled down the stairs, ricocheting off Kathleen's shin before vanishing below. Wild-eyed and wearing nothing but a sacky T-shirt, Jo emerged from her bedroom, the first at the head of the stairs. One of Kathleen's adult roommates who helped pay the rent, Jo was a graduate student and didn't have to get up as early as the others this semester.

"What is it?"

Kathleen didn't answer.

Six-year-old Ginny, the timid mouse in their household, darted from the bathroom. Hiccuping with sobs, she snatched Kathleen's hand.

"Auntie Kath! It's Emma!"

A whimper escaped Kathleen's throat when she reached the bathroom. Her daughter lay unconscious on the floor, blood matting her hair.

"Emma! Oh, no. Emma." She fell to her knees, barely conscious of Jo and Ginny crowding behind her.

A faint pulse fluttered in Emma's throat, but her face was waxen and still.

"She's so cold." Gripping her daughter's hand, Kathleen swiveled on her knees. "What happened, Ginny? Did you see?"

Tears running down her face, Ginny nodded. "She…she was looking at…at herself in the mirror." Another sob shook her small body. "Her eyes rolled back, and she fell over! Auntie Kath! Is she dead?"

Even in her fear, Kathleen spared a moment to shake her head. Ginny had lost her dad to cancer a year ago. Death must often be on her mind.

"No, Ginny. I think Emma fainted. You know she hasn't been eating enough." Understatement, she thought grimly. In fact, sixteen-year-old Emma had been anorexic for the past year, and this spring had managed to stay barely above eighty pounds. An ounce below, she'd been warned, and she was going into residential treatment. "She must have hit her head on the tub."

Jo laid her hands on Ginny's shoulders and gently steered her out of the bathroom. "I'll call 911," she said briskly. "Don't try to move her, Kathleen."

"I won't." Her daughter's hand was icy in hers. "Hurry, Jo. Oh, please hurry."

The wait seemed forever, although Jo must have been back in no more than a minute or two. She was still pulling a sweatshirt over her head.

"I'll stay with her. Go get dressed, Kathleen. You'll want to go to the hospital with her."

Dazed, Kathleen looked up. "Dressed?"

"Hurry." Her dark-haired roommate—and

sister-in-law to be—crouched beside her. "You'll be okay, Emma," she said softly, her hand delicately stroking Emma's cold cheek.

Yes. She had to get dressed. Kathleen stumbled to her feet and backed out of the bathroom, her gaze fixed on Emma's white, gaunt face. She did look dead. And why not? She'd been dying for months, killing herself with her refusal to eat.

Kathleen bumped into the wall and turned, blindly heading toward her bedroom. *Her fault. This was her fault.*

She should have seen it coming, checked Emma into treatment. Her face crumpled. Why hadn't she? Because she'd sincerely thought Emma was recovering? Or because she didn't want to believe she couldn't handle her own child's problems?

In her bedroom, she grabbed clothes from her dresser and scrambled into them without caring what she put on. Not bothering with socks, she shoved her feet into Swedish clogs, yanked a hairbrush through her hair and ran back to the bathroom.

Jo looked up. "Her lashes just fluttered. I think she may be regaining consciousness. I sent Ginny for an ice pack from the freezer."

"Where are they?" Kathleen asked desperately, even as she heard a distant wail.

Jo rose. "I'll let them in." She gave Kathleen a quick hug. "She'll be all right, Kathleen. Just hold on."

The EMTs were actually coming up the stairs when Emma's eyes opened. She stared blankly up. In a slurred voice, she asked, "What happened?"

"You collapsed. And hit your head."

Slow and heavy, Emma whispered, "I was...a...little...dizzy." Her lids sank shut.

"Oh, sweetheart," Kathleen whispered, feeling again how icy her daughter's hand was. "You'll be fine."

For the first time, she knew she was lying.

KATHLEEN PACED THE SMALL waiting room, too scared to sit down or to pretend to read a *Good Housekeeping* or *Sports Illustrated* magazine, as a couple of other people were doing. They watched her surreptitiously, and she saw pity along with kindness in their eyes.

Looking as if she'd been running, Jo appeared in the doorway, Ginny clinging to her side. "How is she?"

"I don't know!" Kathleen wailed. "They're taking X-rays."

Jo opened her arms and Kathleen fell into them, marveling at how natural it felt even though she'd never been comfortable with casual hugs or physical intimacy. It was a moment before she felt movement down by her thigh and remembered that poor Ginny was here, too.

Face wet, she pulled back and said quietly, "You didn't put Ginny on the school bus?"

"How could I? She was too upset. Here, Hummingbird." Jo hoisted the child onto a chair. "Your mom is coming."

"You called Helen?"

Jo looked at Kathleen as if she were nuts. "Well, of course I did! You don't think she'd want to know?"

"Well, I suppose…" Kathleen said uncertainly.

This was new to her, having this oddly assorted family. After leaving her husband, she and Emma had lived for a few months in an apartment, before she decided the arrangement wasn't temporary and they needed a real home. Of course they could have moved in with her father, but she'd been glad to leave her parents' house in the first place, and wasn't about to go back at her age. With Seattle real estate prices and her own lack of job skills, she couldn't afford a mortgage on her own. So she'd advertised for roommates.

She had been amazingly lucky. Kathleen had had her doubts about the wisdom of taking on Helen and small, sad Ginny. Helen was engulfed in grief and Ginny was so withdrawn, Jo admitted to thinking of her as a ghost, drifting insubstantially around the house. The truth was, Kathleen had felt sorry for Helen and offered her a room out of pity, not common sense. Sad though Helen still was, she had become a good friend.

In her late twenties, Jo had seemed like a better choice. Unencumbered with children, she'd gotten tired of being an "acting" librarian and decided to go back to school to get her master's degree so she could be the real thing. She'd seemed to be pleasant, private and quietly ambitious. Better yet, she had turned out to have some construction skills and had been a big help in remodeling first the upstairs and then the downstairs bathrooms in the old house in the Ravenna district.

She had also become engaged in short order to Kathleen's brother, Ryan.

Now, clinging to her hand, Kathleen was intensely grateful that they'd decided to put off the wedding until summer to give his kids time to adjust to the idea of having a stepmom. After all, Melissa and Tyler had suffered enough trauma when their mom decided over Christmas vacation that she couldn't keep them and had sent them to live with Ryan.

Kathleen was dreading having to find a new roommate who would come close to measuring up to Jo.

Especially since the three women and two kids had really come to feel like *family* in such a short time. They depended on each other. How could they replace one member of their household as if she was…was a washing machine that had quit?

"I left a message for Ryan, too," Jo told her. "I don't know when he'll get it."

"Something's wrong," Kathleen decided. "They'd have come back for me if it wasn't." She pressed her fingers to her mouth. "I should go ask. I'm so scared, Jo."

"I know." Her roommate gave her another hug. "But she was already talking to you on the way over, wasn't she?"

"Yes, but her eyes looked funny. And

her voice…" Kathleen had to stop, then try again with quiet desperation. "Her voice was slurred. As if she were drunk."

"She did hit her head," Jo reminded her.

"Yes, but…"

"Mrs. Monroe?"

Kathleen whirled.

A dark-haired, plump woman in a white lab coat, stethoscope around her neck, stood in the waiting room doorway.

Kathleen's heart drummed in her ears. "Yes?"

"I'm Dr. Weaver. Emma wants to see you, but I'd like to speak to you first."

Kathleen nodded dumbly and followed her, leaving Jo and Ginny in the waiting room.

Dr. Weaver stopped in the wide corridor where they were alone, and said quietly, "Emma tells me she's been in counseling for her eating disorder."

"For the past year." Kathleen told the doctor Emma's history, the name of her therapist and internist.

"Ah." Dr. Weaver's face was compassionate. "Well, I suspect she's been conning them somehow. She weighs seventy-seven pounds." The doctor talked about electrolytes, liver and kidney function and the danger of heart damage, concluding, "Emma needs to be in a controlled, residential setting where her food intake is monitored. She should gain as much as ten pounds before she can safely be discharged."

Kathleen seemed able to do little but nod. The lump in her throat made talking difficult, but she said, "We've discussed putting her in a residential program, but she seemed…" She bit her lip, breathed deeply. *Don't cry.* A semblance of control regained, she said simply, "I kept telling myself that she was doing better."

The doctor nodded. "People with eating disorders are some of the best liars and manipulators in the world. They're a little like drug addicts. They'll do anything to protect their habits."

"Has she suffered permanent damage?"

"We'll need to run further tests to have a better sense of where she is. I think she can recover. Her youth is in her favor. The odds of complete recovery diminish the longer someone with her problem goes without effective treatment. You did the right thing getting her into counseling so soon."

"For what good it's done," Kathleen said bitterly.

The doctor gave her arm a reassuring squeeze. "Unfortunately, resisting is also part of the process. Teenagers with this problem don't listen to you or a counselor and say, 'Oh! I see the light.' They kick and scream and dig the trenches deeper. That's what she's been doing. It doesn't mean she hasn't been hearing more than she is willing, yet, to accept."

Kathleen nodded again, teeth worrying her lower lip. "Does she have a concussion?"

"Certainly a mild one. This may be good for her, Mrs. Monroe. A wake-up call even she can't ignore."

Kathleen had to laugh, if without much humor. "Oh, I don't know. Emma can ignore quite a lot."

They agreed that Emma should be checked into the hospital for the night, giving Kathleen time to make arrangements for her to enter a treatment program for eating disorders. Fortunately, Emma's counselor and internist were associated with the program Kathleen had chosen—and hoped never to have to use.

She went out to tell Jo the news and found Helen, her other roommate, there as well. Dressed for work in brown slacks and a cream silk blouse, a rose and brown and rust scarf artfully knotted around her throat, she looked far from the timid and tired woman she had been when she came to look at the house seven months ago.

"Kathleen! Is she all right?"

They all crowded around while Kathleen told them what she'd learned. "I'll need to make some calls, but first I'm going to see Emma. They won't let anyone else in," she said. "I'm sorry."

Ginny slipped behind her mother. Her expression anxious, Helen said, "Oh, dear. Ginny isn't convinced Emma will be okay."

"I'll ask," Kathleen promised. "Maybe they'd let Ginny pop in just for a minute."

Emma lay in a curtained cubicle, a couple of blankets covering her up to her chin. For a moment, Kathleen stood unseen, and her heart seemed to stop. Lying like this, laid out on her back, eyes closed, Emma could have been dead. Her face, once piquant and a little chubby, was marble pale and gaunt. Not the slightest healthy color flushed her cheeks. Even her lips were bluish.

How did I not see how near death she was? Kathleen asked herself in silent despair. *How could I have kept pretending?*

Easily, she knew. Oh, how easily, because the alternative was too difficult, too painful.

The curtains rattled when she stepped forward and Emma's eyes, huge in her thin face, opened. "Mom," she croaked.

Kathleen pinned on a smile. "Sweetie, you scared us."

"I'm sorry. I must have slipped or something. Maybe I spilled some water."

The floor had been bone-dry when Kathleen sat at her daughter's side. "Maybe," she said, smoothing hair from Emma's forehead. Her hair was brittle and colorless, too, a ghost of its former rich gold threaded with gilt and amber and sunlight.

"Can I go home now?"

Here came the hard part.

Kathleen shook her head. "Dr. Weaver wants to check you into the hospital for the night. You do have a concussion, you know."

"But I'm fine!" Emma struggled to sit up. "If they're worried about me passing out or something, you can watch me, can't you? Or Ginny? She always follows me around anyway."

"It's not so bad here." Kathleen hesitated, but didn't have a chance to continue.

"Make them take this out!" Emma brandished her hand, in which an IV needle had been stuck and taped down. In agitation, she exclaimed, "There's sugar or something in that! I'd already had breakfast, and now they're, like, pumping all these calories into me! I'll have to diet for *weeks* to make up for it!"

Diet? The idea would have been laughable if it wasn't so pathetic and even grotesque. How could she cut any more? She barely ate a few leaves of lettuce, nonfat Jell-O and unsweetened herb tea now.

"Honey..."

"I'll take it out myself!" Emma began clawing at the tape.

"Stop!" Kathleen grabbed her wrist and wrenched her hand away, surprised at frail Emma's strength. Holding her arm down, she said, "You collapsed because you've starved yourself. You will not take this IV out!"

"That's not true!" Emma glared at her. "You know I've been eating. You see me."

Near tears, Kathleen shook her head. "No. I don't. You don't eat enough to keep a...a mouse alive. You've been doing your best to kill yourself, but I won't let you. You're not coming home. You're spending the night in the hospital, and tomorrow you're going into residential treatment."

Screaming in rage, Emma tore her hand from Kathleen's grip. "You promised!" she yelled. "You said if I stayed above eighty pounds, I didn't have to go! You're a liar, liar, liar!"

Kathleen drew a shuddering breath in the face of her daughter's vitriol. "I'm not the liar. Dr. Weaver says you don't weigh anywhere near eighty pounds. You've been tricking us somehow. But you knew the consequences, Emma. You're not getting better. You're getting worse."

"I hate you!"

"I love you," Kathleen said, eyes burning, and turned to leave.

Emma threw herself onto her side, drew her knees up and began to sob.

Kathleen's heart shattered into a million pieces. She wanted, as she'd never wanted anything in her life, to say, *All right, you can come home, if you promise to eat.* She wanted to see incredulity and hope and gratitude light her daughter's face, as if her mother could still do and be anything and everything to her. Of course she'd promise.

And then she would lie and scheme to keep

starving. She would exercise in the middle of the night to burn off calories she'd been forced to swallow, she'd take laxatives, she'd hide food in her cheek and then spit it out.

She would die, if she had her way.

Paralyzed, hurting unbearably, Kathleen didn't turn around.

This was harder, even, than leaving Ian, harder than facing her own inability to provide a decent livelihood, harder than facing the fact that she, too, was responsible for Emma's self-hatred. But if she truly loved her daughter, she had to be firm now.

"I'm sorry," she said, pushed aside the curtains and fled.

In the tiny, antiseptic rest room open to family members, Kathleen locked the door, sat on the toilet and cried until her stomach hurt and she'd run out of tears. The sight of her face in the mirror should have stirred horror, but she stared almost indifferently at the puffy-faced woman gazing dully back. She did splash cold water on her face and brush her hair before facing the world again.

At the nurses' station, she stopped. "I'm Emma Monroe's mother."

Quick compassion showed in the other woman's expression. "Are you all right?"

Kathleen nodded, although they both knew she wasn't. "I'm sure my daughter will take out the IV, if she hasn't already. You'd better check it regularly."

"We will. Thank you."

Kathleen explained about Ginny, and the nurse came with her to get the child.

Taking Ginny's hand, she smiled kindly. "Let's just go back and say hi to Emma. You can't stay, because she's getting ready to go upstairs to be checked into the hospital, but I know she'll be glad to see you."

"Thank you," Helen said, watching her daughter be led away. "She's really scared."

Kathleen nodded. Her head felt disconnected from her body. Huge, and yet, eerily, weightless, as if it were a hot air balloon and she were the tiny wicker basket, dangling beneath, swaying in space.

Jo's arm came firmly around her. "You look awful," she said frankly. "Is Emma mad?"

Kathleen nodded again. Her head kept bobbing, as if it didn't know how to stop. "I told her." Her voice sounded far away, too, perhaps because it was being drowned out by the roar of the burners that kept the balloon inflated.

"That she's going into treatment?"

Kathleen was still nodding. A dull throbbing suggested that a headache was building, a storm threatening her sense of unreality.

Jo turned her so that Kathleen had to meet her eyes. "You're doing the right thing. You know you are."

"Do I?"

Once, she had been a confident woman who believed, the vast majority of the time, that she was doing the right thing. She had a perfect life, didn't she? A handsome husband, a smart daughter, a beautiful home, and she worked hard for several charities, doing her share of good. She had glided serenely through life—the life she had chosen, had craved from the time she was a small child and could see the wretchedness of her parents' crummy jobs and shabby house.

Now, Kathleen could see how smug she had been. *Pride goeth before the fall,* she thought bleakly. Perhaps, pride *caused* the fall. With her nose so high in the air, it was easy to trip over an uneven bit of sidewalk, something that should have been right before her eyes.

"I need to make phone calls." She looked

vaguely around. "I didn't bring my cell phone."

"I have mine," Jo offered.

Returning, Ginny raced to her mother. Voice shrill, she said, "There was blood all over! Emma took out that needle in her hand, but they put it back." Her fingers gripped her mother's slacks and she gazed up in appeal. "Why does she have to have it in, Mommy?"

Helen knelt and took her daughter by the shoulder. "You know why, don't you? Daddy had an IV, too, remember?"

Ginny's lip trembled and she nodded hard.

"It doesn't mean Emma is dying like Daddy. All it means is that the doctors want to get medicine or just water into someone's body. Daddy hurt so much, it was the best way to give him painkillers." Her voice wobbled only a little. "But Emma isn't even getting medicine. She's getting water and maybe some vitamins and sugar, because she doesn't eat enough. That's why she's mad. You know how she gets when someone tries to make her eat."

The six-year-old nodded, her expression relaxing. "She yells at Auntie Kath."

"Uh-huh. Well—" Helen glanced up wryly at Kathleen "—this is her way of yelling at the nurses. Right now, she can't stamp her foot or race to her bedroom and slam the door, can she?"

"No-o."

"So she took out the needle and said, 'You can't make me!'"

Creases formed on Ginny's high, arching forehead. "Only, they can. Can't they, Mommy?"

"Yep. They're going to help her get better by making her eat. This is the first step."

"Oh," the child said solemnly.

Helen rose. "Kathleen, why don't you make your calls from home? You can come back later. Emma will be fine. It might be just as well to give her time to get over her tantrum."

Yes. Home sounded good.

Kathleen nodded and let her friends lead her to the nurses' station where she explained, then to the business office where she gave all the information on insurance, and finally to Jo's car.

"See you at home," Helen said, and started across the parking lot with her hand on Ginny's shoulder. Poor Ginny, Kathleen saw, still wore the baggy T-shirt she slept in along with a pair of jeans and sneakers with no socks and the laces dragging. Her unbrushed hair was lank and tangled.

Jo looked better, not because she'd spent more time on grooming, but because her thick, glossy hair seemed destined to fall into place. She wore little makeup at any time, and her sweater and jeans were pretty much what she threw on every day.

Even through her dullness, which she thought must be nature's form of anesthesia, Kathleen remembered uneasily what *she* had looked like in the mirror. Yes, going home was a good idea.

As Jo drove out of the parking lot, Kathleen said, "Thank you."

Jo shot her a startled, even annoyed glance. "You mean, for coming? Kathleen! What did you think we'd all do? Head off to school and work as if nothing had happened?"

"Well, no, but…"

"Then let it rest."

Exhaustion and worry weighing her down, Kathleen gazed unseeing at the passing streets. She wanted to go home and crawl into bed and pretend none of this had happened, that it was Sunday and she could sleep as late as she wanted.

Instead, she should shower and make herself presentable, then start a formidable list of calls. Work, to explain why she wasn't coming. Someone else would have to cover the front desk at the chiropractor's office. The insurance company, Emma's doctor, the therapist, the treatment program...

Her mind skipped. *Please, let there be room.*

Ian. She should at least let him know, although chances were she wouldn't actually have to talk to him. She'd leave a message on his voice mail or with his administrative assistant. He probably wouldn't even call back. Never mind phone his daughter and express concern.

After all, Emma could eat if she wanted. She was just being stubborn. Melodramatic. Ridiculous. Taking her to doctors and therapists was playing her game, pampering her.

He could not, would not, admit that his daughter had a real problem and was thus flawed in any way. After all, he'd had the perfect life, the perfect wife, hadn't he? Kathleen thought bitterly. Why shouldn't he have the perfect daughter, too?

She'd like to believe it was because *he* wasn't perfect. In his rage and intolerance, Ian had made it easy for her to believe he was at fault: his demands, his expectations, his irritation with the tiniest mistake or flaw in appearance or failure in school or on the tennis court or at a dinner party.

What was becoming slowly, painfully apparent was that *her* expectations, her smugness, had hurt Emma as much if not more. Jo had once tried to convince Kathleen that Emma felt free to lash out at her mother not because she was angrier at her than she was at her father, but because she felt safer with her, knew Kathleen loved her. Kathleen hoped it was true.

But she couldn't absolve herself. If she were warm, supportive and accepting, why hadn't Emma been able to shrug off her father's unreasonable criticism? Why hadn't she recovered, after Kathleen left Ian and she'd no longer had to face his sharp, impatient assessment daily?

Would she be lying in the hospital, so perilously close to death, if her mother hadn't failed her, too?

Kathleen didn't say another word on the short drive home. Jo parked right in the driveway instead of on the street, as she usually did, so Kathleen was able to trudge up the concrete steps, stumble on the tree root that had lifted part of the walkway, and make it onto the front porch before she realized she didn't have keys and would have to wait for Jo.

Fortunately, her roommate was right behind her to wordlessly unlock the door and let her in. Once inside, Kathleen glanced at the clock.

"Don't you have an eleven o'clock class? You could still make it if you hurry."

Jo shook her head. "No big deal."

"Go," Kathleen ordered. "I'm fine. Really. I'll take a shower, make my calls and go back to the hospital. Anyway, Helen must be right behind us. She'll be here any time."

Jo hesitated, then said, "Okay."

She bounded upstairs, returning almost immediately with her bright red book bag. "You know my cell phone number. Call if you want me. I'll leave it on even in class. Promise?"

Kathleen produced a weak smile. "Promise."

The moment Jo shut the front door behind her, Kathleen sank onto the bottom step. She *would* shower; she had things to do. In a minute. Maybe in a few minutes. Right now, she needed to sit, be alone and regroup.

Pirate, the seven-month-old kitten they had rescued and adopted the previous fall, poked his fluffy Creamsicle orange-and-white head around the corner from the living room. His right eye, which had been hanging from the socket when Jo and the girls found him, didn't gaze in quite the same direction as the other eye, so the veterinarian wasn't certain how much he saw out of it. They didn't care. The fact that he *had* two eyes was a victory.

Kathleen discovered suddenly that she didn't want to be completely alone. A warm, fluffy, purring cat on her lap would make her feel better.

"Kitty, kitty," she murmured, and patted her thigh.

Pirate took a step toward her.

The doorbell rang. Scared by the morning's events, the kitten bolted again.

Helen must have forgotten her keys, too, Kathleen thought, heaving herself to her feet. But, wait— She'd come from work. She'd been driving. Walking away in the hospital parking lot, she had had her keys in her hand. Kathleen remembered seeing the silly hot-pink smiley face attached to a key ring that Ginny had given her mother for her birthday dangling between Helen's fingers.

Mind working sluggishly, Kathleen was already in the act of opening the door before she had reached this point in her recollections, or she probably wouldn't have answered the doorbell at all. She didn't want to see anybody, even her brother, Ryan.

But the man standing on her doorstep wasn't Ryan. In fact, he was a total stranger. One who...wasn't scary exactly, but could be.

At a little over six feet, he wasn't unusually tall, but he was broad. Big-shouldered, stocky, with strong legs and powerful arms and neck. His hair was dark and shaggy, his eyes some unnameable color but watchful, and his face was blunt-featured, even crude, but somehow pleasing, the only reason Kathleen didn't slam the door in a panic.

He was the kind of man she couldn't picture in a well-cut suit, the antithesis of her handsome, successful ex-husband. This man had to work with his hands. Like her brother's, they were nicked, callused and bandaged, the fingers thick and blunt-tipped. In one hand, he held a gray metal contractor's clipboard.

He seemed to be waiting patiently while she appraised him from puffy eyes.

"May I help you?" she asked finally,

warily, her hand on the door poised to slam it in his face if he lunged for her.

"I'm Logan Carr."

He said his name as if it should mean something to her. Maybe it did, she thought, frowning. Somewhere in the back of her mind, it niggled.

Buying time, she said, "Um...I'm sorry. This isn't a good time."

"We had an appointment." He looked expectant, adding when she didn't respond, "I'm the cabinetmaker."

"Oh, no!" That was it. On Ryan's recommendation, she'd called Carr Cabinetmaking and arranged to dash home during an early lunch hour so that he could look and measure and give her a bid. She, of course, had completely forgotten.

"Are you all right?" He sounded kind.

Somehow this was the last straw. One more thing to have gone wrong, one more thing to think about when she couldn't.

"I'm...I'm..." Suddenly he was a blur, and she was humiliated to realize she was crying in front of this stranger. "Fine," she managed to say.

"No," he said, stepping forward, taking advantage of her nerveless hand to come uninvited into her house and to close the door behind them. "You aren't."

The next thing she knew, she was engulfed in powerful arms and flannel shirt, smelling this stranger's sweat and deodorant and aftershave, her wet cheek pressed to his chest.

And did she, dignified, gracious but reserved, wrench free and demand he leave?

No. She buried her face in that comforting flannel and let herself sob.

CHAPTER TWO

LOGAN CARR MADE SOOTHING sounds while he held the gorgeous blonde.

What? he thought with wry amusement. His face wasn't pretty, but didn't usually inspire women to burst into tears.

When she didn't quiet down, he became worried. Should he be calling the cops? An ambulance? "Can you tell me what's wrong?" he finally asked.

She wailed something about her daughter hating her. Logan assumed she *was* Ryan Grant's sister. There'd been an indefinable something about her that reminded him of Ryan. Logan didn't know her brother that well, but now he tried to remember what Ryan had said about her.

She was divorced, or at least separated. Logan remembered Ryan banging around one day on a work site, growling under his breath about his stubborn sister who was buying a house that would fall down on top of her idiotic head any day. Logan had paused, a screwdriver in his hand, and asked why she was buying the place. The gist, as he recalled, was that she'd left her husband and she claimed this was all she could afford without asking for help either from him—or her own brother—which she refused to do.

"I wouldn't care," Ryan had concluded viciously, "except that the roof will fall on my niece's head, too. Why couldn't she buy a nice condo?" he had asked in appeal.

Personally, Logan didn't blame her. He liked the looks of this place. It was worth a little work.

He kept patting her back and waiting while her sobs became gulps and then sniffles. Logan knew the exact moment when she realized she was crying all over a man she didn't know.

Her body went very still, stiffened, and then she all but leaped back. "Oh, no! I must look…" She scrubbed frantically at her wet cheeks. "I'm so sorry!"

"I invited myself in," he reminded her. Sticking his hands in his pockets, he ostentatiously glanced around, admiring the French doors leading into the living room, the staircase, the arched doorway to the kitchen. "Nice place," he added.

"If you'll excuse me a moment, I'll just, um…"

The doorknob rattled behind them, and the door swung open.

"Helen!" exclaimed his bedraggled blonde. "Oh, good! This is Mister, um… The cabinetmaker. Will you show him the kitchen while I…" She was already fleeing up the stairs.

The redhead who'd come in with the child gazed in surprise after her…friend? Sister? Roommate? He had no idea.

"I didn't beat her," he said, trying to look harmless.

She gave him a distracted look. "No, she's… It's been an awful day. We should have called you, but we forgot you were coming."

"Logan Carr," he said, extending his hand.

"Helen Schaefer." She shook his hand. "This is Ginny."

"Ah." How did you politely say, *And who are you?*

"Ginny, did you want to watch television while I show Mr. Carr the kitchen?"

The waif shook her head hard, her big eyes fixed suspiciously on him.

Helen Schaefer didn't look so hot, either, he noted, which made him wonder anew what had happened to upset both women so much. Her face was too pale under skillfully applied makeup, the shadows beneath her eyes purple. He'd felt the tremor in her hand, saw the gentleness with which she stroked her daughter's head.

"Lead on," Logan said, wishing the classy blonde hadn't skipped. He picked up his clipboard from the step where he'd dropped it earlier.

The kitchen had potential and not much else. The vast floor space was wasted, as was typical for a house of this era. Cabinets had been added in about the 1940s, if he was any judge. Which meant drawers didn't glide on runners, cabinets were deep spaces where you could lose a kid the size of this Ginny, and they stretched to the ten-foot ceiling, the upper ones useful only for stowing stuff that ten years later you were surprised to discover you still owned.

"We can't afford to replace those," the redhead told him. "What we're thinking is that we can make use of this corner." She gestured.

One area held a table, set with pretty quilted placemats. The corner she had indicated currently had a cart and oldish microwave, an extra chair and a lot of nothing.

Logan considered. They didn't want to replace their crappy, inadequate kitchen cupboards. Instead, they had in mind him building something that didn't match in this corner.

Go figure.

"Make use in what way?" he asked politely.

Apparently reading his mind, she smiled with the first spark of life—and amusement—he'd seen in her.

"Kathleen and I have started a business together. We've only made a few sales—this is really at the ground floor—but unfortunately it's taking over the kitchen, and we all have to live here, too."

"All?" he asked, hoping he didn't seem nosy.

"Kathleen owns the house," she explained, "but Ginny and I live here, too, along with another roommate, Jo, and Kathleen's daughter, Emma."

The one who hated her, he presumed.

And who was this lucky Joe, living with a couple of beautiful women?

He cleared his throat. "What kind of business is taking over the kitchen?"

"Kathleen makes soap. I market it."

"Soap."

"Yeah. You know." She gazed expectantly at him. "Bars of it. The good kind. Not the kind you buy at the grocery store."

Personally, he bought whatever was cheap and not too smelly. Speaking of which… He inhaled experimentally. The kitchen *was* fragrant. He'd vaguely thought they must have been baking earlier, but the overall impression wasn't of food, but more…flowery.

"Soap-making," he repeated, and contemplated the corner. "Tell me what it involves."

They both turned at the sound of a footstep. Looking like a different woman, Kathleen came into the kitchen.

Her face was expertly made up, her thick golden hair loosely French braided. She wore a long, black, knit skirt, and over it a simple T-shirt in a vivid shade of aqua. She looked like a million dollars.

"I'm back," she said with a warm but somehow practiced smile. "Ready to beg your pardon for forgetting you were coming, and then weeping all over you."

Her face was maybe still a little puffy, her eyes a little red. Even so, she was the most beautiful woman he'd ever seen, from her high graceful forehead to pronounced cheekbones and a full, sensuous mouth. She had the kind of translucent skin, faintly touched with freckles, that gives a woman an ageless quality. He couldn't tell if she was twenty-five or forty. Either way, her face would have looked fine on the cover of one of those fashion magazines.

"Ms. Schaefer was just telling me about the soap-making," he said. "I gather you work out of the house."

"We both have real jobs, too," Helen Schaefer said almost apologetically, "but we have faith this will take off."

Kathleen Monroe smelled good, Logan discovered when she stopped beside him. The scent was citrus, a little tart but also delicious. He wanted to bury his face in her hair.

Cabinets, he reminded himself. He was here to make a bid. Not make a move on a woman.

They showed him their supplies and the

small pantry, which currently held row upon row of bars of soap, all "curing" according to them. Here was where the smell emanated from. Shelves and the single countertop overflowed, and more circled the floor.

There were long square-edged "loaves" that would be sliced into bars, according to Kathleen. Some of these were clear but vividly colored, sea-green or shocking pink or rainbow streaked. Others were cloudy, dark-flecked and oatmeal colored, another a deep, speckled plum. Some soaps, looking more conventional, had been molded into ovals and rounds, with intricate designs of flowers and leaves pressed into the tops. They were beautiful, he realized, bemused. Not delicate and feminine, but solid and colorful. He resisted the urge to touch or bend over to sniff individual bars.

The fragrance swelled in this tiny enclosed area, a symphony where a few notes strummed on a guitar would have been plenty. Cinnamon and flowers swirled together to overload his nose.

As he backed out, the two women laughed.

"Gets to you, doesn't it?" Helen asked.

"Ventilation," Logan said. "You'll want a

fan out here and maybe another one in the pantry."

"That would be great," Kathleen agreed. "Sometimes it's hard to eat, oh, say, Thai food when what you're smelling are vanilla and cinnamon."

He took out his clipboard and started to make notes: broad, double sinks, a stove top, storage for the tools of soap making; scales, jugs and huge pots and measuring cups and spoons.

"Oh, and molds," Kathleen said, her face animated. She opened a kitchen cupboard so he could see the odd conglomeration of containers used to mold soap, some—he guessed—meant for the purpose, others as simple as ice cube trays, muffin tins and boxes. "A cupboard with nooks designed specifically for the molds would be great."

Her main need, he gathered, was for work and storage space. He took his tape measure from his belt and began making notes while they watched, the kid still clinging to mom and staring as if she thought he was an ax murderer.

"Get my name from Ryan?" he asked casually.

"He says you're the best," Kathleen said.

"Oh, is Ryan a friend of yours?" the red-head asked. "He's marrying Jo."

Joe? The tape measure strung on the floor, Logan turned to see if they were pulling his leg.

Both laughed. *"J-O,"* Kathleen told him kindly. "Short for Josephine."

Ah. Satisfied, he jotted down the measurement.

"So, you didn't put me on your calendar," he remarked.

Out of the corner of his eye, he saw her flush.

"I did. But the day went haywire from the get-go."

The kid decided, at last, to speak. In a loud, clear voice, she said, "I thought Emma was dead. She fell on the floor and there was blood and she didn't talk to me."

"Hush," her mother murmured.

"My daughter fainted and hit her head," Kathleen said. "We had an ambulance here and everything. I just got back from the hospital. It was scary, and everything else just left my mind."

"She okay?"

"Just has a concussion. They're keeping her overnight."

Uh-huh. She'd fallen apart because her daughter had bumped her head.

He wasn't buying.

Writing down another measurement, he asked, "How old is she?"

"Sixteen. Almost seventeen."

A teenager. Well, that explained the "she hates me" part. It also upped his estimate of her mom's age. Kathleen Monroe had to be mid-thirties, at least.

Satisfied with his measurements, Logan turned to them. "Let's talk about wood and styles."

They sat at the kitchen table. Ginny at last became bored and, after a murmured consultation with her mother, wandered away. A moment later, canned voices came from the living room.

He nodded after her. "How old is she?"

"Ginny just turned six. She's in first grade."

He hadn't been around children enough to judge ages. Opening his clipboard, Logan took out a sheaf of pictures.

They discussed panel doors versus plain, maple versus oak, open shelves versus ones hidden behind cupboard doors.

As expensive as Kathleen Monroe looked,

Logan half expected her to choose something fancy: mahogany with gothic panels and glossy finish, maybe.

Instead she went for a simple Shaker style in a warm brown maple. "I want it to suit the era of the house," she explained. "Later, when—if—I can afford it, we'll re-do the rest of the kitchen to match."

He sketched out an L shape of cabinets to fit in the corner, then lightly turned it into a U. "A peninsula there," he said, pointing, "would visually separate your work area from the dining area. Plus, it would give you more counter space. You could have suspended shelves or cabinets from the ceiling, too."

"Um…" Kathleen frowned into space. "It sounds wonderful," she finally decided, "but it may be beyond my means. This may all be beyond my means," she admitted frankly. "We looked at ready-made cabinets at Home Depot and Lowe's, but Ryan thought we could do as well going to you, plus you could configure them more specifically for our needs."

"I'll do my best," he promised, standing. "I'll have the bid to you in a couple of days."

The bottom line would be affordable, he

already knew, even if he took a dive on the job. He wanted to help these women achieve their dream, he wanted to know why Kathleen Monroe had been sobbing—and he wanted to find out what a woman that classy would feel like in his arms when she *wasn't* crying her heart out.

Even if that didn't have a thing to do with building cabinets.

EMMA LAY IN THE DARK, feeling the sugar trickling into her body. It was like…like sipping on soda pop nonstop, all day long, until you ballooned with fat. She could feel it sliding through her veins, cool and sticky. Every time a bag emptied, somebody came and changed it.

She hated the nurses who had put the IV needle back in three times, and even more the ones who had finally tied her hands to the bars of the hospital bed so she couldn't tear it out again.

But most of all, so much it corroded her belly, she hated her mother for letting them do this. For *making* them do it. Mom could have said, "I'm taking her home." She could have told them not to *force* calories on her.

Instead, she was committing her own

daughter to a jail. Just because Emma wouldn't stuff her face.

She was, like, *almost* at a perfect weight. She used to think eighty pounds would be good, but she had still been pudgy when she got there. So she made her goal seventy-five. Or less. Less would be good. It would give her some room to go up a pound or two and not freak so much.

She didn't even know why she was surprised. Mom wanted to control her, and food had become their main battlefield. It was so weird, because Emma *knew* her mother used to think she was fat. Her eyebrows arching disdainfully, she'd say, "Emma, do you really need a second serving?" Or, "Don't you think carrots would be better for your figure than potato chips?"

She liked to give these little mother-daughter lectures, too. She'd sit on Emma's bed and say, in this *friendly* voice, "I know you're only twelve—" or thirteen or fourteen, the lecture didn't change "—but pretty soon you're going to want boys to notice you. It's going to really matter to you if you feel plump or don't like the way you look in cute clothes."

What she really meant was, *You embar-*

rass your father and me. To her friends, she said with a laugh, "Emma still has some baby fat, but she's stretching into this tall beautiful girl." Baby fat, of course, would magically melt away. Real fat was just disgusting and *stayed.*

And Mom and Emma both knew that was the kind Emma had.

Emma had started dieting when she turned fourteen not because she wanted to look good in cute clothes, but to please her mother and father. Mom's face would glow with delight and pride when Emma said no to seconds and dessert and snacks.

When he saw her picking at a salad for lunch instead of pigging out on macaroni and cheese, Dad would say something like, "Keep on that way and we'll have two beauties in this house before we know it." Meaning that Mom already was one, but Emma was plain and fat and he hated it when he entertained and he had to produce his one-and-only child and admit she was his.

For a while, Emma had been filled with hope. Finally, she was doing something right. She was making them proud. She would become beautiful, like her mother. Every morning, she'd look at herself in the mirror, tilting her head this way and that, sucking in her cheeks, lifting her hair in different styles, trying to imagine that moment when she would know: *I am beautiful.* She'd told herself she was the duckling—a plump duckling—becoming a swan.

Only, she stayed a duck. She never saw a beauty in the mirror. And her parents' pride slowly faded as they started complaining about other things. She slouched. Shouldn't she start plucking her eyebrows? Her table manners! The way she hung her head when she was introduced to their friends and business acquaintances. Obviously she needed braces. How could she possibly be getting B's and even a C on her report card, when she was a smart girl?

And she understood at last that she would never be good enough for them. She wouldn't be pretty enough, smart enough, charming enough to be *their* daughter.

Hearing the *slap slap* of approaching footsteps, Emma closed her eyes. The curtain around her bed rattled. A nurse lifted her covers enough to see the needle still stuck in Emma's hand. A moment later, the footsteps went away and Emma opened her eyes again.

She could see only a band of light coming through the half-open door from the hall, diffused by her curtain. She didn't have a roommate, either because the hospital wasn't that full or because they thought she was a bad influence or something. She was glad. What if she had some middle-aged woman having her gall bladder out, or an old lady moaning? They might want to talk!

Of course, she wouldn't be here that long anyway. They were moving her tomorrow. It made her sick, thinking about it. Her therapist, Sharon Russell, used it as a threat: *If you don't eat, we'll send you there, where they'll stick tubes down your throat if you won't eat and not let you alone for a single second in case you try to puke.*

They'd watch her pee and everything!

She wondered if, once they untied her tomorrow and left her to get dressed, she'd have a chance to run away. Emma didn't know where she'd go or what she'd do, but anything had to be better than jail, where some warden stared at you while you sat on the toilet! Energized, she started planning.

She was almost seventeen. She could get a job, maybe, and find a bunch of other kids she could share an apartment with. Or she'd call Uncle Ryan and see if he'd let her come live with him and Melissa and Tyler. *They* never paid any attention to what she ate. Uncle Ryan wasn't embarrassed by her. He didn't want to control her every move.

That was what Emma had finally decided: she couldn't make her parents happy no matter what she did, so she might as well at least be in charge of her *own* life. She didn't want to be fat. It was *so* like them to want to control what went in her mouth. One minute she was fat and disgusting and she was supposed to nibble on green leaves instead of pizza. The next minute, she was getting too skinny and she should stuff her face. The *real* issue was, she should do what they told her to do.

Smile. Try to look dignified, if you know how. When you laugh like that people can see your tonsils. You should be on the honor roll. Your idea is silly—write about this topic instead. Eat. Don't eat. Make conversation. Quit chattering.

Having *her* decide what she would and would not eat drove them crazy. So crazy, Dad didn't even want to see her anymore. Which was fine by Emma. She was *glad* she'd made him mad. When he'd cracked and started screaming at her, she'd felt good. Powerful.

And having Mom choose her over Dad had made her feel powerful, too. For a while. Until she'd realized that Mom was just as bad as Dad. She was as determined as ever to control Emma. Now that she'd failed, she was resorting to force, just like Dad had tried to do. Only Mom didn't shove food in her mouth even though she was screaming. No, she made it look like she was doing the "right" thing. Insisting her daughter get "well." That was her word. Emma wasn't "well" because she didn't want to be a porker like the other girls at school who wore their pants really low but had rolls that swelled over the waistbands.

Emma tried wrenching her hands free again, but they'd tied them too tight. She felt as if she was being poisoned. If she were at home and she'd eaten too much, she would make herself exercise until she thought she'd made up for it. Sometimes it took hours.

Maybe she could exercise even if she was tied down. Emma squirmed and kicked until she got the covers off to one side and her legs were free.

Leg lifts. She could do ten on one side, ten

on the other, then ten with both legs together. She could do it over and over. Or bicycle. Experimentally, she curled her spine, but had a hard time getting her hips high enough to cycle her feet.

Okay, leg lifts. Keeping her toes pointed, she lifted both legs, slowly separated them, then brought them back together, feeling the strain on her belly and back and butt. Pleased, she did it again. And again.

When her legs began to tremble and sweat popped out on her forehead, she smiled.

They couldn't keep her from fighting back. From controlling what happened to her. No matter how hard they tried.

KATHLEEN WOKE TO THE sinking knowledge that today would be dismal. For a moment, she lay in bed, her face buried in her pillow, and tried to remember why. It didn't take long.

Emma. Always Emma.

Kathleen rolled onto her back and noticed dispiritedly that rain was sliding down the window glass and deepening the sky to a dreary gray. Didn't it figure.

She'd taken today off work so that she could accompany Emma to Bridges, the residential treatment center for patients with eating disorders. Emma was not going to be happy.

Yesterday, when Kathleen had returned to the hospital, the sixteen-year-old had been either sullen or in a rage. Her generally sweet disposition had been submerged by the terrifying fear of gaining weight that ruled—and threatened—her life.

Today was unlikely to bring an improvement.

At least the residential program included certified teachers so that the kids didn't fall behind in school. Emma's grades had actually improved this past year and a half, since Kathleen had left Ian, even if she had refused to let go of her obsession with weight. Kathleen didn't know if Emma was studying more because she didn't have anything else to do, now that she seemed to have no friends, or whether she hadn't tried in school just to make her father mad, and now the payoff was missing. Her natural curiosity and intelligence had reemerged, thankfully, resulting in almost straight A's last semester. Kathleen hated to see Emma have to struggle to catch up. Her ego was fragile enough already.

With a sigh, Kathleen made herself get up, put on her robe and shuffle downstairs without even a pause to brush her hair. She needed breakfast and a cup of coffee before her shower. The only plus today was that she'd gotten an extra hour of sleep. The house was quiet, Helen gone to work and Ginny to school, she diagnosed. Jo might still be in bed—no, on Thursdays she had a much-hated 8:00 a.m. class.

Even living as close as they did to the University of Washington, Jo had to allow almost an hour to get there and park in the huge lot down by the football stadium, then hike up the stroke-inducing stairs to the campus.

Kathleen would miss her complaints. Jo and Ryan were getting married in July and taking a honeymoon trip to Greece, while his kids visited their mom in Denver. Then Jo would go home with Ryan, not here.

Which meant she'd be family, but in a different way. Kathleen was going to miss more than the grumbles; she'd miss *her*.

Kathleen and Helen had talked about making a big push to get the soap business earning real money. They were scheduled to have booths at a dozen crafts fairs in the Puget Sound area in late spring and summer, and Helen was spending every spare minute calling on shop owners to try to persuade them to carry Kathleen's Soaps. If they could make enough, maybe they wouldn't have to bring in another roommate. Ginny could have her own bedroom, after Jo moved out. That was their dream: just the two mothers and two daughters living in this ramshackle but charming Ravenna district house that Kathleen had once so optimistically believed she could remodel "gradually."

That was before they'd discovered rotting floorboards beneath the upstairs toilet, corroded pipes and an inadequate furnace.

She shouldn't be spending money on cupboards. She should be spending it on a furnace, she worried, as she poured cereal into a bowl.

At least Ian carried Emma on his health insurance. For Kathleen, it would have been prohibitive and her plan was less comprehensive anyway.

She sliced a banana onto the cereal and wished she hadn't thought of Ian. He hadn't returned her call yesterday, but she couldn't assume he'd heard the message.

She still wasn't convinced that it would be good for Emma to have him reappear in her life, but Emma's therapist had advised her to keep lines of communication open.

"Emma would deny it bitterly, but being rejected by him has further threatened her self-confidence," Sharon Russell had told Kathleen. "If he can be made to see reason…"

That would be a cold day, Kathleen had thought privately, even as she nodded. Ian Monroe exuded confidence and was completely baffled by Emma's uncertainties. He refused to consider the possibility that he had played any part in the development of his daughter's eating disorder. He refused to believe she *was* anorexic. Or maybe he just didn't believe in eating disorders at all. After all, *he* had no trouble disciplining himself to eat well.

Perhaps, Kathleen thought, she was being just a little unfair. After all, she didn't overeat or starve herself, either. It was just that she could understand human frailty. Ian couldn't.

Or didn't want to, she hadn't decided which.

After putting her bowl in the sink, she poured her tea and left it to steep while she called Ian again. She didn't bother trying him at home. He'd have left for the gym for some racquetball hours ago, then been at the office by eight o'clock. He'd curl his lip if he knew at nine o'clock she was still sitting at the kitchen table in her bathrobe and slippers, her hair tangled.

Discipline.

"Crowe Industries, Mr. Monroe's office."

"Patty, this is Kathleen. Is Ian free?"

That was the fiction that allowed them both to save face: most often, Ian wasn't "free." His middle-aged administrative assistant didn't have to say, *I'm sorry, he doesn't want to speak to you,* or lie that he was out.

"Let me check. He mentioned wanting to talk to you."

Kathleen rolled her eyes. *I'll just bet he does.*

But he did come on the phone, an unusual occurrence.

"What's this about Emma being in the hospital?"

"Why, hello, Ian," Kathleen said. "How are you?"

"Just a minute." His voice became muffled as he spoke to someone else, or on a second line. She always had hated talking to him at the office, even when she believed them to be happily married.

He came back on. "Was she in an accident?"

"She has continued to lose weight. Yesterday morning she fainted and hit her head."

"That's all?" he said in disbelief. "She bumped her head, and you're leaving dire messages for me?"

"Which you, of course, panicked about. I noticed you rushed to her side."

"We both know she doesn't want to see me."

"Doesn't she?" Kathleen said quietly.

He let that pass. "Does she have a concussion?"

"Yes, but that isn't the major problem. She's down to seventy-seven pounds."

"What?"

"She's…" Kathleen had to pause and take a deep breath to make sure her voice didn't waver. "She's a walking skeleton."

His voice hardened. "I thought I was the problem."

Unseen, Kathleen flinched. "You are her father. You're not off the hook, just because she didn't magically recover once she wasn't under your roof."

"All those doctors and all that counseling hasn't done anything," he snapped.

"Anorexia is the toughest eating disorder to overcome. Up to ten percent of anorexics die."

"They starve themselves to death." He sounded disbelieving, just as he always had.

"Or they damage their heart or kidneys."

"She's not that stupid."

"Stupid or smart doesn't have anything to do with it," Kathleen said, feeling a familiar desperation. How could she make him understand? "Or maybe it does. Smart girls are the likeliest to develop the problem."

"How could she lose that much weight right under your eye?"

Of course, it had to be her fault. It couldn't be his.

What tore at her was a new fear that he was right. She *was* responsible for Emma's determination to starve.

Nonetheless, she tried to defend herself. "She's been seeing a doctor, a therapist and a nutritionist. They advised me to avoid nagging about food. We've been trying to make it a nonissue between the two of us."

"And failing, apparently," he said cruelly.

She bit her lip until she tasted blood. "It would appear so."

"And what am I supposed to do?"

Shaking from fury and hurt that refused to die along with the marriage, she said, "Nothing. Nothing at all. I just thought you should know," and hung up the phone.

Talking to him had had its usual shattering effect. Once again, Kathleen had confirmation that she and Emma were on their own.

Except, thankfully, for Jo, Helen, Ginny and Ryan. And Kathleen's father, of course. Friends and true family.

Dry-eyed but feeling as exhausted as if she had indulged in a bout of tears, Kathleen slowly mounted the stairs. Time for a shower, and the hospital.

CHAPTER THREE

KATHLEEN SAT ON THE LIVING room couch
two days later, gazing blankly at the opposite wall. A woman who detested inactivity,
she much preferred having a purpose. Tonight she was too tired to even *think* about
Emma, Ian or the myriad of household tasks
that needed accomplishing.

Helen and Jo were picking up the slack.
Even small Ginny had passed a few minutes
ago, gamely carrying a full basket of laundry
up from the basement in order to fold it.

Earlier Helen had wanted to discuss business. A shopkeeper had asked for a larger
discount. Helen still wasn't satisfied with the
label—maybe they needed stronger colors?
She was sensitive enough not to say, *You
should be making soap, we need a huge inventory for the craft fairs.* Kathleen had only
shaken her head and said, "I can't think right
now. I'm sorry," and Helen had backed off.

Kathleen felt useless. Inept. Inadequate.

Incompetent. Unlovable. She could think of a million other words, but those pretty much covered the bleak, gray sensation that swamped her.

She, who had never failed at anything she set out to do, had now failed at everything really important: marriage and parenting. She—once a society hostess, gourmet cook and mother to a delightful, bright and cheerful child—was scraping for a living, cooking in a kitchen with a peeling linoleum floor and a chipped, stained sink and banned for a week from visiting her daughter in treatment for a behavioral disorder that was killing her and seemed to be rooted in anger at her parents.

Yup. Right this minute, Kathleen couldn't think of a single reason to feel positive.

The doorbell rang, and she winced. The cabinetmaker had called earlier to schedule an appointment to present his bid. The timing sucked, if Kathleen could borrow one of Emma's favorite words.

She sighed and dragged herself to her feet. From upstairs, Jo called, "Do you want me to get that?"

"No, I'm expecting someone," Kathleen called back.

When she opened the door, she experienced the same odd jolt she had the first time she saw Logan Carr on her doorstep. Frowning slightly, she dismissed her reaction; he just wasn't the kind of man she usually associated with. He looked so...blue-collar. He undoubtedly went home, and spent his evenings watching baseball on the TV.

A stereotype even she knew was snobbish. After all, Ryan was a contractor, but was also a well-read man who owned a beautiful, restored home and cleaned up nicely.

"Mr. Carr," she said, by long practice summoning a smile. "Please come in."

He nodded and stepped over the threshold, increasing her peculiar feeling of tension. He was too close. She backed a step away, using the excuse of shutting the door behind him. He was so *big,* even though she was sure he wasn't any taller than Ian. But Ian was lean and graceful, with long fingers and shoulders just broad enough to make his custom-tailored suits hang beautifully. Ian projected intelligence, impatience, charm, not sweaty masculinity.

"Unfortunately, Helen can't be here. She was asked to work this evening. Nordstrom is having a sale."

He blinked at what must have seemed a non sequitur. "She's a salesclerk?"

"Children's department."

"Ah." He nodded.

"Come on into the kitchen." She led the way. "Can I get you a cup of coffee?"

"Thanks, if it isn't too much trouble." He did have a nice voice, low and gruff but somehow... soothing. Like a loofah.

"Jo just brewed some. She's a fanatic." Kathleen opened the cupboard and reached for two mugs. "Personally, I'd settle for instant, but she shudders at the very idea."

As if he cared what kind of coffee she'd choose, Kathleen chided herself. She was babbling, filling the silence, because he made her nervous.

"You're not crying tonight."

Mug in hand, she turned to look at him. He wasn't laughing at her. Rather, his expression was serious, even...concerned.

"No," she agreed. "I'm not crying." *Just depressed.* "I'm awfully sorry to have flung myself at you that way. I must have made your day. Nothing like having your shirt soaked with tears."

"I invited it," Logan reminded her. "You looked like you needed a shoulder to cry on."

She hadn't known it, but that was exactly what she had needed. Now, she felt uncomfortable about the whole thing. He was a complete stranger, but he had held her and she'd gripped his shirt and laid her head on his chest and sobbed. The memory lay between them, weirdly intimate.

"I guess I did," she admitted. "Thank you."

"You're welcome." Faint amusement showed in his eyes. The next second, Kathleen wasn't sure, because he continued, "Your daughter, is she all right?"

"Emma's fine," Kathleen said brightly, lying through her teeth, as she'd spent the past several years lying. She would never admit to anyone else that her daughter hated her so much, she was starving herself to death.

"Is she..." the cabinetmaker said noncommittally.

Had Ryan told him something of Emma's troubles? Kathleen wondered, her eyes narrowing. She'd kill her brother if he was spouting her personal problems to casual acquaintances.

"She's, um, not home." As if he'd asked to meet Emma.

"Teenagers rarely are."

His easygoing, I-understand tone made her want to spill her guts. Maybe even cry again, so he'd pull her into his arms.

Shocked at herself, Kathleen stiffened her spine. What was she thinking? He was absolutely not her type, even assuming she had any interest whatsoever in getting involved with a man right now! Which she didn't.

Didn't dare. Emma had reacted with hurt and anger the couple of times Kathleen had dated after the divorce. Right now was definitely not the time to upset the applecart as far as her daughter went.

"Sugar? Creamer?" she asked, in her best hostess voice.

"Black is fine."

She stirred sugar into her own and then carried both mugs to the table.

He'd set that gray metal clipboard, identical to her brother's, on the table. Kathleen nodded at it as she sat down. "Okay, I've braced myself. How much will this cost?"

Logan Carr reached for the clipboard. "I've figured out ways to cut some corners and still give you what you want," he said mildly. "I hope my figures are in the ballpark."

The baseball analogy steadied her, reminded her of the nonstop din of the television. When he slid a neatly typed sheet of paper across the table, she took it, hardly noticing that their fingers briefly touched.

When she saw the figure at the bottom, however, she gaped. "I was expecting twice that much!"

He smiled at her surprise. "Your brother wasn't kidding when he said you wouldn't pay much more for custom. Maybe even less, in this case, because I gave some thought to how I could deliver what you need without adding any unnecessary frills."

She wondered what kind of frills he was talking about, but in her rush of relief didn't really care. She could manage this.

"The amount doesn't include the additional peninsula, does it?" she asked.

"No, I made up a second bid." He slid that one to her as well. The bottom line was less than a thousand dollars more.

"Show me the details again," she asked. There had to be a catch. An unacceptable short-cut. An eliminated frill that was really an essential. "You'll use solid maple, right?"

He patiently got out his notebook and scooted his chair around so that they sat shoulder to shoulder, looking as he flipped pages. He'd drawn a couple of simple sketches of the project, one a crude blueprint, the other three-dimensional, showing slots and cubbies and open shelves.

"The fan will be right above, the switch over here." He indicated the wall by the pantry door with the tip of his pencil. "I can pick one up if you want, or if you'd prefer you can buy your own."

She shook her head. "You do it, please."

Nodding, he made a note. "I'll leave all of this information so that you can discuss it with Ms. Schaeffer."

"That isn't necessary." Feeling more decisive than she had in a long while, Kathleen said firmly, "You're hired."

"Good." He smiled again, turning a face that was almost homely into one that was likable and sexy.

She found herself smiling back, her heart fluttering. Her internal alarms went off, but she silenced them. So what if she felt...oh, just a little spark of attraction. It didn't mean anything. He'd never know. She probably wouldn't even feel the spark the next time she saw him. It was having cried on him that made her aware of him, she guessed. Knowing what it felt like to have his arms around her. Wasn't it natural to stretch that into a small crush?

"Do you have a contract for me to sign?" she asked.

He produced that, too, and went over it line by line. Satisfied, Kathleen signed, and hoped Ryan wouldn't have recommended Logan Carr if he weren't reliable.

"I can't start for a week," he was telling her. "I'm finishing up a project in West Seattle, but I can be on it a week from tomorrow, if that works for you."

"So soon?" she said in surprise. Wasn't spring a busy season for construction? Why wasn't he booked way in advance, if he was so good?

As if reading her mind, he said, "I had a cancellation, and my next job is new construction. They won't be ready for me for a few weeks. This is good timing for me."

She flushed, as embarrassed as if she'd spoken her doubts aloud. "Oh. Well." She forced a smile. "It's good luck for me, too."

He nodded absently and sipped his coffee, instead of standing to leave. "Nice house. Lots of potential."

Her mood lifted. "Do you think so?"

He was looking around, his gaze taking

in the original moldings and high ceilings. "Your brother grumbled one time that you'd dropped your money into a sinkhole. I think he's wrong. This could be a beauty."

"I think so, too." She had this vision no one else seemed to share, but she could see on his face that he saw something similar. "We've actually remodeled a couple of rooms already." She tried to sound casual. "Do you want a grand tour before you go?"

He set down the mug. "Love one."

"You can finish your coffee."

"It'll keep me awake anyway." He gave another of those crooked, devastating smiles. "Lead on."

Pulse bouncing, Kathleen stood, too. "You've seen the pantry."

"You're lucky to have one. They're a smart addition to a kitchen."

She smiled wryly. "Of course, we're back to storing baking supplies in cupboards too high to reach without teetering on a chair, thanks to the soap."

"But what would you do if you didn't have the pantry?" Logan pointed out.

Kathleen made a face. "How true. I'd probably be stepping over bars of soap to go to bed."

He laughed, a low, rough sound, as well-worn as the calluses on his hands.

She showed him the living room, and he admired the arched entry and the built-in, leaded glass-fronted bookcases to each side of the brick fireplace.

"You planning to refinish the floor?"

"Ryan is itching to tackle it, but I've held him off so far. Where would we live while fumes fill the house?"

"That's always a problem," the cabinetmaker conceded. "But without a finish this floor is going to get scratched and stained."

She sighed. "You sound like my brother."

"We both value fine woods."

Ian had valued fine art, she thought irrelevantly. Their house had been a showplace in Magnolia, but it was no more than an appropriate and deserved backdrop, as far as he was concerned. The house had given her pleasure. These days, she tried not to think about the gleaming inlaid floors, stained-glass sidelights and granite kitchen counters.

If she ever had a beautiful house again, she would have earned it herself, and that had come to mean more than the possessing. In his eagerness to help her, Ryan refused to understand that. She had the odd feeling that Logan would.

She led him to the downstairs bathroom, really more of a powder room in the traditional sense.

He stepped past her and, filling the opening, contemplated the tiny room. "Nice," he said finally.

Feeling a glow, she said, "Thank you. We did it ourselves."

He glanced at her, surprise in his raised brows. "We?"

"Jo, Helen and I did the work. Especially Jo," she admitted. "Except for the plumbing. We called Ryan for that."

He took another look. "You did a great job."

They had, if she did say so herself—although she felt a little immodest even thinking as much, given how little she'd contributed compared to Jo. Still...

The floor and walls, up to the wainscoting, were covered with two-inch tiles the color of milky coffee, with darker grout. The sink was a graceful free-standing one, the medicine cabinet an antique Jo had discovered at a garage sale. They'd splurged on a reproduction toilet with an old-fashioned oak tank. A cream, rose and spring-green paisley paper covered the upper walls. Just stepping in here made Kathleen happy. At least they'd accomplished *something,* even if the floors in the rest of the house were still scuffed, the plaster peeling in the stairwell, the kitchen a 1940s nightmare.

"We'll skip our home office," she nodded down the hall. "It's a disaster. That door leads to the basement, which at the moment is our construction workshop, such as it is, and has the washer and dryer. We've all got piles of boxes stored down there, too."

As she climbed the stairs, Kathleen was very conscious of him behind her. She wondered if he was at all aware of her as a woman. Or—she didn't know why it hadn't occurred to her—was he married? She glanced back and made a point of noticing his left hand—no ring. Which didn't necessarily mean a thing. Not all men liked wearing a wedding ring. For one who worked with power tools, wearing a ring might be dangerous.

He hadn't mentioned children of his own, she remembered.

It wouldn't hurt to make conversation, she decided.

"Do you have kids?" she asked casually, as they reached the hallway above.

"Afraid not."

Frustrated, she nodded at the first bedroom door, shut. "Jo's room. Then Helen's."

This door stood half open, and without stopping he glanced in at the high-ceilinged room. "No closets?"

"A couple of the bedrooms have them, but small ones. What would be wonderful, down the line, is to eliminate one of the four bedrooms and create big walk-in closets for the other rooms." She laughed ruefully. "Wa-ay down the line."

"You have to have a plan," he said matter-of-factly.

He believed in dreaming. She liked that about him. Maybe he didn't actually watch sports nonstop on television.

But maybe he had a wife at home, washing up their dinner dishes, wondering why he was taking so long to present a bid for a small job.

She opened the door on the other side of the hall with a flourish. "And the other bathroom."

Every time she stepped in here now, she had a flash of memory—Emma sprawled, unconscious and bleached-white, on the tiled floor. Death was an all too real possibility for Emma, but that morning, it had hit Kathleen like a punch in the stomach.

Emma is dead. I've failed her.

She crossed her arms and squeezed, momentarily chilly. Logan gave her a sharp look but didn't comment. Instead he examined this larger bathroom and gave another nod of approval.

"I could have done a better job on the cabinets, but it looks great."

"They're ready-made," she admitted.

"I know." He propped one shoulder on the doorjamb and smiled. "Sorry. I think I just crossed over from confidence to cockiness."

She found herself smiling back, probably foolishly. "No, no. I'm sure I heard nothing but confidence."

His eyes seemed to darken, his voice to deepen. "Thank you for that."

Cheeks warming, she backed away. "Um… my bedroom is the last—" she flapped a hand toward the end of the hall "—but I haven't done anything except cover the floor with a rug and the peeling wallpaper with pictures."

He glanced that way thoughtfully, then nodded, accepting her unspoken reluctance to show him her private sanctum. Her bedroom. Ryan was the only man to have stepped foot into it, and that was on moving day when he'd helped carry in the garage sale and thrift store furniture.

She found the idea of *this* man in her bedroom disturbing. It wasn't so much the notion of him studying her bed with that contemplative gaze as the fact that he would be out of place. Ridiculously so. She imagined his bedroom as spare, with white walls and beautiful wood pieces and perhaps a simple print hung above the bed. Maybe not even blinds or curtains at the window.

Unless, of course, his wife had decorated their house.

Ian had liked their master bedroom luxurious but modern, the deep plush of the charcoal-gray carpet unadorned, the vast bed the centerpiece of the room, the only other focal point the wall of windows looking out at Puget Sound and passing ferries.

To please herself, and because she couldn't afford luxurious anyway since she'd refused alimony and a split of the possessions she had realized were really his, Kathleen had indulged in a very feminine bedroom for herself, in this house that was her own. Dried

hydrangeas and roses filled cream-colored
pitchers and vases. The cherry bed frame
needed refinishing, but she never noticed,
so heaped was the bed with lacy pillows and
quilts and a crocheted spread she'd bought
for peanuts at the Salvation Army because
it had been stained. Armed with a book on
caring for old fabrics, she had resuscitated it
as well as the pink-and-white pinwheel quilt
the mover had been using as padding, and
the lace that edged several of the pillows.
Whenever she saw an unusual old picture
frame for a price she could afford, she bought
it, and had covered the walls with family
photos dating back to the 1840s and ending
with a laughing Emma, caught only a few
months back in an unwary moment. Kathleen's dresser top was cluttered with her collection of ceramic and wood boxes. A caned
Lincoln rocker that had been handed down
in her mother's family gave her a place to sit
and read by the light of a Tiffany-imitation
lamp that sat on a carved end table, its battered top hidden beneath a tatted doily.

Emma, of course, sneered at the room.
"It's *old* stuff. Dad would say it was all junk
and throw it away."

So he would—which was very likely the

reason she'd decorated the room the way she had.

Kathleen had managed to keep her voice mild. "Old stuff is all I can afford. You know that."

Emma, dear Emma, had flared, "And it's all *my* fault that we're poor! Of course! I didn't *ask* you to leave Daddy!"

She hadn't had to ask, not after the horrific scene when Ian had lost his temper, held her down and shoved food into her mouth.

"Look at it this way," Logan Carr said now. "Not a penny spent on this house is wasted. You'll get it all back if you re-sell. These old houses can't do anything but gain value."

"Even Ryan concedes as much."

Logan gave her a quizzical glance. "I take it you and your brother aren't close?"

"Actually, we are." She smiled at his surprise. "Jo says we squabble like a couple of kids on a family vacation. Insulting, but accurate."

He laughed again, which pleased her. She liked his laugh.

"Well, I'd best get out of your hair," he said, pushing away from the door frame. "You must have a million things to do."

Like climb into bed, pull the covers over

her head and pretend all her troubles would go away. Or cry. She hadn't decided which.

"Well, not a million, I hope," she said with a practiced chuckle. "You probably have plenty waiting for you at home, too."

He opened his mouth and then closed it. She saw the impulse to say something and the instant when he thought better of it.

"Unfortunately," he agreed.

She couldn't help but wonder what he'd been going to say. *Nobody and nothing is waiting for me at home?* Or, *Yeah, the wife insists I fix the leak under the kitchen sink tonight?*

She saw him to the door, chattering about nothing in particular, another skill acquired from the years of entertaining Ian's business associates.

There, she said, "We'll look forward to seeing you a week from Monday."

"Actually, you'll only see me if I need additional measurements. I'll build the cabinets at home and call you when I'm ready to install them."

"Oh." She was embarrassed not to have realized as much, and inexplicably disappointed. "Yes. Of course. I wasn't thinking."

With a shrug, he said, "You figured they

weren't ready-made, they got built here. That's reasonable." He paused, his gaze intent. "Ms. Monroe…"

"Kathleen. Please." Her heart seemed to be pounding.

The cabinetmaker nodded. "Kathleen. I don't suppose…" He stopped, frowned fiercely and shook his head. "Never mind."

"What?" She wanted to stomp her foot.

"No." His expression was stolid again. "It was just a passing thought. Nothing important." He held out a hand. "I look forward to doing some work for you."

What could she do but hold out her hand in turn? His was big, warm and rough-textured. It seemed to her that he released her hand reluctantly before nodding one more time and heading down the porch steps.

Tempted to watch him go, Kathleen made herself shut the front door. She was too old for delusions of romance.

EMMA SAT AT THE TABLE in the dining hall and stared at her dinner tray. They could not possibly expect her to eat all that!

She sneaked a glance around and saw that a few of the other women and girls—right now, there wasn't a single guy here—had matter-of-factly picked up silverware and started to eat. Maybe they had figured out some way to get away from their captors long enough to puke up all this food. Or maybe they had decided eating was the only way out of here. It wasn't like they couldn't lose the weight again.

Emma just didn't want to. Gaining ten or twenty pounds, just so she could go home… She shivered at the thought. She'd be fat!

Reluctantly she picked up her fork and stabbed a few peas. Okay. She guessed she could eat them. They were starchy, but still a vegetable. Then maybe if she stirred some of the other food, made it look like she'd eaten some, they'd let her go.

The peas seemed to stick in her throat. She reached for her milk and gagged when she tasted it.

"It's whole milk," the girl beside her said. "Or maybe two percent. I'm not sure."

"Even my mom buys nonfat!"

"Yeah, but this has more calories."

Beads of sweat stood out on Emma's brow. "I can't eat this."

"You have to. They make you sit here until you do."

"*All* of it?"

"Didn't they tell you?" The girl was really pretty, with shiny thick black hair, and *so* slim, lots slimmer than Emma was.

"They said I had to eat what they served, but I didn't figure they meant, like, every bite." She stared again in dismay at the pork chop, mashed potatoes and gravy and peas.

"I sat here for four hours my first day. The meat was even grosser when it was cold."

Emma took a tentative bite of mashed potato. It slipped down easier than the peas had. "What's your name?"

"Summer Chan. What's yours?"

"Emma Monroe."

"How much do you weigh?"

"Seventy-six pounds." Emma was embarrassed. "I wish I looked like you do."

"But I'm only five-two." She took a dainty bite and swallowed. "You look great. I'm the one who's still fat. No matter what *they* say."

Emma didn't ask what she weighed. She'd end up being totally humiliated.

"Do they ever get so they trust you, and you can go to the bathroom and stuff alone?"

"No." She took another bite. "I've been here before. If you want out, you have to cooperate."

Emma poked at the pork chop. "I'm a vegetarian."

"You had to tell them you were when you checked in. Now it's too late. They'll think you're lying."

Emma hadn't been a vegetarian until she decided meat had too much fat in it. Now… her stomach quivered at the thought. It was almost like being hungry, but more like she needed to throw up.

Summer took a bite of hers and murmured out of the corner of her mouth, "You'd better look like you're eating. Here comes Karen."

Karen was one of the nurses. She was stocky, with chunky arms and shoulders and a thick neck. The idea of ending up looking like *her* scared Emma.

She paused right behind the girls. "How are you doing, Emma? Doesn't look like you've eaten much yet."

"I had some peas. And potatoes."

She laid a hand briefly on Emma's shoulder. "Remember the rules. You have to eat it all. You can't get well if you don't eat."

When she moved on, Emma muttered, "She means, get *fat*."

"Just keep eating," a woman across the table advised. "It's easier if you don't think about it. By the way," she added, "I'm Regina Hall."

"Nice to meet you," Emma said automatically.

Not think about it. Right. How did you do that? She always thought about what she ate! She knew how much fat and calories every bite had, how full it would make her, whether she'd feel like a pig after she was done scarfing it down. To just eat and eat and eat…

"I won't," she said, and put down her fork.

"Suit yourself." Regina, who was maybe in her early twenties, shrugged. "I'd rather watch TV than sit here all night. Even if it is reruns."

"Everybody watches *Friends,*" Summer chimed in. "Monica is so-o pretty. Don't you think?"

"I wish I looked like her," Emma agreed. "I like to cook the way she does, too."

Everyone at the table joined in to talk about *Friends* and whether Phoebe was too fat and how cool it would be to have a job as a chef as long as you didn't have to sample anything and which was the hottest guy on the show.

Joey, most of them agreed, although Summer didn't say anything and Emma didn't think any of them were that hot. They were *old,* for one thing. Her uncle Ryan was better-looking than any of them. Her friends, back when she had some, always said he was super hot compared to *their* fathers or uncles or any of the teachers.

Emma guessed her dad was, too, but now when she thought of him all she could remember was his face contorted with rage and the cruelty of his hands and the terror of not being able to breathe when he shoved food into her mouth until it was smeared all over her face.

It was that moment when she knew how much he hated having a daughter who couldn't do anything right. He'd mostly hidden it until then, but he'd finally cracked. Now she hated him, too, and dreamed about running into him by accident sometime when she was grown-up, and slim, and so beautiful she drove men crazy. And wildly successful, too—maybe a federal judge or mayor of Seattle or a movie star. She'd raise an eyebrow, just so, as if in faint surprise at his temerity in approaching her. Her expression would say, *Do I know you?* He'd mumble something about how much he admired her, or he'd say, "I tell all my friends you're my daughter."

Mostly in these daydreams she was gracious, saying, "How nice," before noticing someone more important she had to speak to. Sometimes, when she was in a bad mood, she'd imagine the scathing look she'd give him. "I have no father," she would say icily, before moving on as if he was nobody.

Right this minute, she wished she had no mother, either. Because then she'd be living with Uncle Ryan, and *he* wouldn't have committed her like a crazy person who needed twenty-four-hour guarding.

Realizing that even Summer was almost done with her dinner, Emma took another bite of mashed potatoes. Her stomach growled, startling her. Two more peas, then a tiny sip of the milk.

"Do you have to drink the milk, too?" she whispered, because Karen was strolling back her way.

Summer stole a glance toward their captor and kept her voice low, too. "Uh-huh."

I can't! Emma cried inside.

She hastily took another bite of potatoes.

"Try your meat," Karen said pleasantly, with another tap on Emma's shoulder.

Regina stood and lifted her tray to bus it.

"It's hard the first time," she said quietly, nodded and left.

Summer left a few minutes later, too, and one by one so did just about everyone else. Only one other girl was left at another table, gazing down in dismay at her plate. Emma saw that her glass of milk was still mostly full, too.

Emma started to stand, but Karen materialized instantly.

"I'm sorry, Emma, but you're not excused until you've finished."

Bubbling with resentment, Emma said, "I was just going to sit with that other girl."

"Oh, I don't think either of you need to socialize when your food is getting cold." Karen smiled, for all the world as if she'd just said something upbeat, like, *You're doing great.* "Finish, and you'll both have a chance to get acquainted."

Three hours and thirty-four minutes later, tears in her eyes, Emma cut her cold pork chop, put a bite in her mouth and grimly began to chew.

CHAPTER FOUR

LOGAN FELT LIKE AN IDIOT, making excuses so he could have a chance to see a woman. A woman, at that, who was way out of his league. It was like being a tongue-tied teenager again, coming up with elaborate reasons for taking a round-about route so he could pass *her* house.

Hesitating, then ringing her doorbell, he hunched inside his coat against the spring chill. It would serve him right if she wasn't even home. Maybe the missing teenage daughter would sulkily show him into the kitchen and sullenly show him out when he was done measuring.

Despite her present circumstances, Kathleen Monroe exuded class and money. He'd bet his entire savings account that predivorce this woman lived someplace like Laurelhurst. With a man who wore a custom-tailored suit and tie every day, read books on how to motivate employees, and had calluses only from gripping a tennis racquet.

Logan didn't want to *be* that man. He liked working with his hands, seeing solid, enduring, beautiful evidence of his craftsmanship and care. But the Kathleen Monroes lived in a different world from his.

Yeah, okay. But he was already here, and he'd heard distant chimes. Footsteps approached.

The door opened, and there she was, a beauty with thick wheat-gold hair loosely braided, a warm, welcoming smile and a tall, leggy body. She looked like she should be seen in the pages of *Town & Country,* striding through the stableyard of her estate.

To her, he probably looked like the groom who watched the lady of the manor from afar.

Maybe, he thought with rueful amusement, it was just as well that he'd shut his mouth last week when the impulse to ask her out to dinner swept over him.

"Hi." He nodded. "Sorry to inconvenience you, but I'd like to get a few more measurements."

"You're not inconveniencing me." Still smiling, she stood back. "Come in."

In the foyer, he cocked his head. "House is quiet."

"Oh, everyone is here somewhere." She waved blithely. "Ginny has homework, even in first grade, Jo has grown-up homework—did I mention that she's in graduate school?—and Helen is researching on the internet, looking for places that might handle our soap and also checking out the competition. I'm the only idle one."

The teenage daughter was conspicuously missing from this recitation, he noticed. The genuine distress in her sobbed, "Emma hates me," kept him from doubting that the girl existed. He was beginning to wonder whether she'd flown the coop, though. A runaway teenage daughter would explain the sadness that clung like a haunting scent to this beautiful woman.

"Can I get you coffee?" she asked over her shoulder on the way to the kitchen.

"Thanks." Any excuse to linger.

"Black, right?"

Pleased that she remembered, he said, "Right. Thanks."

Aware of her behind him, opening and closing cupboard doors and drawers, clinking a spoon against stoneware, Logan methodically rechecked his measurements. All were dead-on. He rarely made that kind of mistake. Although he considered himself easygoing, he was also precise. He liked corners squared, and "good enough" wasn't good enough for him.

When, satisfied, he hooked his measuring tape on his belt and turned around, Kathleen Monroe was just setting two mugs of coffee on the round oak table. Something cramped in his chest. He didn't know what triggered it. A combination, maybe: the table—even at this time of night, set with pretty quilted place mats, a bouquet of bright yellow and creamy daffodils in the center—the quiet of the house, the dark beyond the windows, and the copper-shaded light hanging above the table shining on the beautiful woman smiling at him.

That odd, fleeting, but intense moment of longing made him realize he wasn't as content with his solitary life as he had considered himself.

"Thanks," he said again, hoping he was the only one to notice how hoarse he sounded. Nodding at the mug of coffee steaming on the table, he added, "It's cold outside tonight."

"I noticed." She sat in an easy, graceful motion, tucking one stockinged food under her. "We might even have a late frost."

"Are you a gardener?"

"Not yet." She smiled ruefully. "How can you ask, after walking by those ugly junipers out front?"

"They're easy care."

"And dark and brooding and prickly."

"Well...yeah." And ugly.

"I just don't have time to lavish on digging them out and putting in flower beds. I used to garden..." She stopped herself, her mouth twisting. "I had a gardener. What I did was putter in the garden."

She'd probably had a housekeeper, too, and maybe other staff. He wondered how much she missed that life and why she wasn't still living it. Had the ex-husband lost all his money in some dot-com failure? Otherwise, why hadn't she walked out with half their fortune and possessions?

"You have a funny look on your face," she said.

Chagrined, he stumbled, "I, uh..." Why not be honest? "I was wondering how a woman who looks like money ended up in a fixer-upper with roommates to help pay the mortgage."

"You mean, Ryan didn't tell you?" Kathleen said dryly.

"He only ever said that his sister was divorced."

"And living in a ramshackle money-gobbler of a house."

"Well…" He grinned. "Yeah."

Conflict showed on her face, as she probably debated telling him—politely—that her history was none of his business. To his surprise, she blew out a puff of air and said, "Do you want the short story or the long?"

He shrugged. "Whichever you want to tell me. If," he added scrupulously, "you want to tell me either."

She grimaced. "The short will do. I lived a fairy-tale life with a wealthy and handsome businessman, until our darling daughter developed an eating disorder. He refused to acknowledge as much, displaying aspects to his character that drove me to take said darling daughter and leave."

Logan studied her proudly tilted chin and the defiance in her eyes and knew she disliked admitting to any personal problems.

So why had she?

He took a sip of coffee. "Surely said husband could pay for the floors to be refinished and the kitchen remodeled in this house."

More that was none of his business, but his curiosity was sharp and he figured why not. What was the worst that could happen? She'd crisply, coolly, put him in his place.

Instead she laughed with a noticeable lack of humor. "I had an insane moment of self-discovery and told him to take his money and keep it. *I* didn't need it. I thought it was time I make a life for myself, not take advantage of somebody else's."

"He does pay child support?"

"Oh, of course." She sighed again and cupped her hands around her mug. "He has also instructed his attorney to offer me a settlement on a regular basis. So far I have nobly turned it down. Some winter day when the furnace gives up the ghost, I may succumb." Her smile became more genuine. "Are you sorry you asked?"

"No. I'd only be sorry if I upset you."

She made an unladylike sound. "No! Just about every night when I go to bed, I brood about all of this anyway. Was there a point to turning down his money? Is Emma suffering because of my pride? Is my pride the real thing? I mean, do I truly want to see what I can be?" This laugh was self-deprecating. "Or is it directed at Ian? A way to stick out my tongue and say, I don't need you anyway. So...no. You didn't upset me. I just hope I didn't bore you."

"You're a gutsy lady," he said quietly.

"Oh..." She flushed, the color tinting her ivory skin right where it stretched over finely cut, high cheekbones. "Thank you, but...say it someday when I deserve it. When I've proved myself."

"You don't have to succeed in a worldly way to prove you have guts."

"You know—" her very blue eyes met his "—you're a nice man, Logan Carr. Is this what you do? Make cabinets and listen to sad stories?"

"A jack-of-all-trades." He smiled. "I'm nosy. That's one of my besetting sins. After the way we met..." He shrugged.

"Right." Kathleen took refuge in another slow sip of coffee. "I suppose, since I've told you all my other troubles, I might as well admit that Emma had collapsed that morning, hit her head and been carted away in an ambulance. Despite counseling and weekly weigh-ins, she is still starving herself, and

I've now checked her into a residential program. She is furious at me, needless to say."

Mystery solved. "Anorexic?"

She nodded. "Emma is bright and pretty and talented and sweet. But this, this *monster* has come to dominate her. She clings ferociously to it, and it's all I see anymore." Silent for a moment, she finally shook herself. "Well. That's enough of my life story. What about you, Logan? Are you happily married? Unhappily unmarried? Or something in between?"

He laughed. "Probably something in between. I was married young, we had a good couple of years, and then my wife died when a drunk driver hit her car head-on." He could mention Brynn now, the manner of her death, matter-of-factly, as a piece of his history that no longer carried a great emotional load. Then, he had been stunned, shattered. Rebuilding his life had taken years. Quietly he said, "I didn't know whether to be glad or regret that we hadn't had a baby yet."

"I'm sorry." Kathleen stretched out a hand as if to touch his, then curled it into a fist and withdrew it. "How long ago did she die?"

"It's been almost eleven years. Sometimes I have to look at a picture to remember her face. Time passes." And he sounded like a greeting card.

Tiny lines furrowed Kathleen Monroe's brow. "You must miss her."

"It's been a long time," he said again.

"But you haven't remarried."

Logan shrugged. "It just hasn't happened."

It. That heady, potent awareness that grew into all-consuming need, the liking, the curiosity, the ability to talk for hours, to kiss until you forgot to breathe. He'd dated, enjoyed women's company. He hadn't felt even the faintest tingling of *it*.

Until he stepped into this house and took a crying woman into his arms. A woman who was now chatting with him over coffee in her quiet kitchen because she needed company, needed to talk, not because she felt any answering awareness of him.

"I'd better get going," Logan said abruptly, gruffly, draining the last swallow of coffee and pushing back the chair.

For a moment he thought—imagined— that he saw disappointment on her face before a warm smile took its place. She stood with the lithe ease of a cat, stretched and said, "You'll let us know when you're ready to install the cabinets?"

"I'm going to come and do some prep work first." He still sounded gruff and impersonal. "I'd like to get the fan in, take care of a couple of bumps in the plaster, remove the molding. Say, Wednesday? Will anybody be here?"

"Um…" She glanced toward a calendar hanging near the door. "If you can get here before nine-thirty, Jo should be able to let you in."

"Sounds good."

At the front door, Kathleen said, "Thanks for listening."

Oh, no, she had to go and get personal, when he'd almost escaped without making a fool of himself.

"Listening?" He gave a bark of laughter. "You did notice I was conducting an inquisition, didn't you?"

She smiled. "No, I thought you were politely enduring my whimpers."

"Kathleen." Was he really doing this? "This may be way out of line." *You think?* he mocked himself. "I just thought, uh, well, wondered whether you might have dinner with me sometime." Oh, very smooth.

He braced himself.

She blinked. "Dinner?"

The very concept must be so absurd to her that she had to check: *Are you really asking me for a date?*

"Yeah. Or just coffee. Or we could do something. Go to a movie, or a Mariners game, or…" Men who dated her probably took her to the opera and Brasa or the Seattle Art Museum and Palisades. But, hey, who knew? Maybe she hated wailing sopranos and modern art, and hankered for pizza and a ball game.

He hoped.

"I haven't dated much." Surprisingly, she sounded…tentative. Even timid. "Emma got so upset when I did, that I just…well, figured I should concentrate on her."

Which, he gathered, had not resulted in any noticeable improvement in their relationship.

Or did Emma not care what her mother did evenings? Logan gave his head a shake, realizing he'd been a little slow. Kathleen was letting him down easy, trying to avoid denting his fragile male ego.

"Sure," he said, backing away. "Makes sense, under the circumstances. No big deal. I'll plan on being here at nine Wednesday morning, okay?"

Her quiet, "I didn't say no," took a minute to sink in.

"What?"

"Do you always give up so easily?" she asked, her tone gently teasing.

Stunned, he said, "You will have dinner with me?"

"Why not?" This smile trembled on her lips and failed. "I'm not allowed to visit Emma the first week anyway. In case I damage her progress."

He heard in her voice how much it hurt to be told that she would ever do damage to her child.

"Maybe," he said, "they know you both need a break."

Her mouth curved again, although her eyes remained sad. "Like I said, you're a nice man. And—" she squared her shoulders "—I'd enjoy having dinner with you."

Logan very much feared he was part of the break. She was lonely, bewildered; he was here. Chances were, he wouldn't be anymore, once Emma discovered his existence.

But, hey. He would take what he could get, which was more than he'd expected.

"Friday night? Say, six-thirty?"

"That sounds nice," she said primly. "I'll look forward to it."

Once she'd shut the door behind him, he vaulted down the steps to the sidewalk. There, safely alone in the dark between street lamps, Logan mimicked the motion of leaping to make a jump shot, waiting, hands still suspended in air, for the ball to sink through the net with a whisper.

Yes.

SITTING ACROSS THE DESK from Emma's therapist, Kathleen tried to look assured and even serene. "How is Emma?"

Fingers steepled, Sharon Russell said, "Healthwise, she's doing fine. Her attitude isn't very good yet, however."

"If you'd told me it was, I'd have been shocked," Kathleen admitted, then flushed. "I'm sorry. That sounds negative..."

"But honest." No more than thirty, Sharon was a psychologist who specialized in eating disorders. Emma had seen several therapists before her, but had seemed to respond the best to Sharon. Maybe because of her relative youth, Kathleen had thought. She often wore jeans and T-shirts, and her brown hair was short and disheveled when she ran her fingers through it. Yet she had poise and an indefinable air of confidence that reassured Kathleen. She was firm with Emma.

Now she sighed. "Did I tell you that Emma's jeans had lead fishing weights tucked into the hems? I'm guessing she drank a bunch of water before she came, too. She did often go to the rest room right after weighing-in."

Kathleen nodded. "Is she eating?"

"Yes. Reluctantly, but the staff at Bridges don't take no for an answer."

Kathleen glanced down at her hands, a study in still life atop her purse. "I suppose she's furious at me."

"Well, of course she is." Sharon sounded cheerful. "Did you expect anything else?"

Kathleen gave a wry smile of her own. "No, she offered me the benefit of her opinion at the hospital. I'm cruel and hateful."

"On the upside, at least she'll talk about you. She clams up when I ask about her father."

"Well, since she doesn't see him…"

The therapist leaned forward and put her elbows on the cluttered desk. "But she must be simmering with feelings about him! Kids don't go, 'Oh, my dad's a creep, I don't want anything to do with him.' Rejection is hurtful."

Sharon already knew the back story. Ian probably would have taken Emma every other weekend, or whatever was the norm these days with divorced dads. Kathleen was the one who had said, "Until she resolves her problems, she isn't coming to stay with you. You may call or get together for an outing, but I won't put her in a position to face a repeat of that episode."

She'd stung his pride, of course, so he had chosen to sulk and not call. Rejection, yes. But it wasn't as if he'd told Emma, "I don't want to see you."

"You still think I should encourage Ian to call her," Kathleen said slowly.

Sharon frowned, pursed her mouth, grimaced and finally shook her head. "Not at this point. From what you've said, he wouldn't be supportive or understanding, and she doesn't need that right now. It'd be great if he suddenly swept in and said, I love you, I miss you, what can I do to make up for my ignorance and temper?"

Kathleen snorted.

Sharon laughed, her plain face lighting. "Failing that miracle, I'd say what Emma needs is to concentrate on her responsibility to herself. She needs to ease up, accept life's uncertainties, other people's flaws. The two of you can work on your relationship, which is most central to Emma. No." She nodded more decisively. "For now, let's leave Emma's dad out of this."

"He is...so scathing, I'm not sure he would have cooperated anyway."

The therapist's eyes were sympathetic. "Do you have friends and family to offer *you* support right now?"

"Yes." Her voice firmed. "Yes. I have good friends."

She left with the assurance that she could see Emma on Sunday afternoon, although she was very nearly dreading the moment. Would Emma even speak to her?

How far we fall, Kathleen thought drearily, then brought herself up sharply. What was she mourning? The loss of money and servants? Ian, who was apparently too selfish to even consider putting his daughter ahead of his pride? The friends, who had all disappeared when she left Ian and the privileged world he had given her?

If she was regretting anything, it should be how long she let her own smug belief—

that *her* world was perfect—blind her to the fact that her husband was arrogant and her daughter was miserably unhappy.

But at least she *had* woken up, and she was getting by, even if she was petty enough to hate the stained sink and the yellowing linoleum in the kitchen, the steep stairs to the basement, the cleaning chores she'd once supervised, the cold darkness in the early morning when she left the house for a menial, mind-numbing job that paid peanuts.

And she hated herself for thinking she was too good to live a life that was blessed in so many ways.

She waited at the nearest bus stop with an old man who was talking loudly to himself and a young woman with half a dozen rings through one eyebrow who was reading, of all things, *Beowulf*.

The bus rumbled up and she found a seat by herself. Swaying as the bus started, she was grateful for its relative emptiness. The last thing she wanted was to make conversation or edge nervously from a potential crazy.

She had never ridden the bus when she was married to Ian. That was something left behind with her parents' small, shabby house in West Seattle, along with washing dishes by hand, and enduring the television being on nonstop and her father's puzzlement and exasperation at his daughter's ambitions.

Now, she rode the bus several times a week, saving gas money and the hassle of finding street parking in busy parts of Seattle. She didn't mind it too much on a day like this, when her mind was free to drift.

She should call her father. She hadn't in weeks. He didn't know about Emma's collapse or hospitalization, unless Ryan had told him.

She loved her father, but she had spent her entire childhood also despising him. He was content with on-again off-again jobs, never seeming to care whether his family got ahead financially. It never occurred to him to save so that his kids could go to college. He would have said, "Why would they want to do that?"

When Dad walked in the door every day from work, he slumped in his recliner with the remote control in his hand. He'd grumble if dinner was late, and half the time refuse to come to the table for it. His wife or daughter had to bring his plate to him. Grease seemed embedded under his nails and even in the wrinkles on his big, rough hands. Kathleen had been ashamed of him when he went to school events and parent-teacher conferences, and ashamed of her timid mother who did cheap, at-home dye jobs on her hair and said "ain't."

It seemed she had been born envying the kids from privileged families where the moms looked chic and drove BMWs and the dads had clean hands and wore business suits.

She was *different,* she used to declare when she was mad enough to yell at them. She didn't belong in this house.

Ryan sarcastically called her a princess. She secretly thought maybe she was, that two babies had been switched at birth in the hospital and she was really...a princess's daughter, or at least some rich attorney's child.

Except, she had to grudgingly concede as she got older, she and Ryan did have a strong familial resemblance, and she looked a lot like her grandmother on her mother's side when *she* was a teenager.

But Kathleen didn't get over her hunger to leave their working-class neighborhood and find a life that fit *her.* At the University of Washington she met Ian Monroe, who was everything she'd ever dreamed about: hand-

some, charming, ambitious, smart, athletic—
and from a family with money. She finished
her degree, but never considered going on to
law school the way she'd intended. She was
too madly in love, too thrilled with the life
Ian gave her.

Too smug.

She got off the bus on Roosevelt near
Whole Foods, went in and bought milk and
bread and then walked home. Bulbs were in
bloom everywhere, primroses peeked from
cracks in stone retaining walls and candytuft
spilled above the top. An old crab apple tree
rained fairy-tale pink petals to the cracked
sidewalk.

Kathleen's mood should have lightened,
but didn't. She had spent the past year and a
half discovering that she didn't like herself
very much. She had tried, slowly and painfully, to change. Sometimes she thought she
was succeeding.

Today wasn't one of those days.

How did you…well, find the parts of yourself that were likable and keep them, while
discarding whole chunks of standards and
beliefs and motivations that were snobbish?

One of Emma's favorite lines was, "Just
because *you're* so perfect!"

It used to irritate her. More recently, she'd begun a self-examination: *Did* she think she was perfect? Was it something in her attitude that Emma so resented, or did she somehow have to visibly manifest imperfections? Leave dirty dishes in the sink and go to work without makeup and…and…

Her imagination failed her. Was it so *bad* to like order and cleanliness? To want to project a certain image to the world?

Maybe not—unless she'd put them ahead of listening when Emma needed to talk, or just needed *her.*

Or maybe she'd just conveyed her chosen image too well. Maybe Emma didn't believe she could ever match it.

And Kathleen had not the slightest idea how to convince her that her mother was just as uncertain and scared and confused and afraid of rejection as anyone else.

Because Emma no longer listened to her mother. No longer believed her.

And whose fault was that?

Wearily Kathleen started up the steps from the street to her front porch.

CHAPTER FIVE

EMMA MISSED HOME SO MUCH.

She huddled in bed, covers pulled tight around her, the lights out, and felt muddled and alone.

Mostly she was resentful and horribly conscious of the fat that was probably swelling on her butt even as she slept. She'd eye the other girls and wish she could be as slim as they were. Summer was delicate, like those paper snowflakes kids cut out in school. In comparison, Emma felt like an ugly lump of clay.

But once in a while in a group session or just talking during craft time, something would be said that made her remember the days before she had to think all the time about food. When she could just eat, or not eat, when she tried makeup and studied herself in the mirror and secretly believed she was pretty, even if she was fatter than her friends.

Turning her face into the pillow, she thought wistfully how nice it would be to go back, to be like Ginny, who stared at her with those huge, amazed eyes when she turned down an ice-cream cone or just a glass of milk. To not *care* whether spaghetti had ten calories or ten million, just to be able to suck each noodle in and savor the slippery texture and the rich flavor.

But then she caught herself, like she did each time, and rolled over angrily to stare at the ceiling. Sure, she could just eat and eat, but then she'd be fat again, so fat she'd have to wear tent dresses and waddle and her arms and legs would dimple and her chins wobble! Was *that* what she wanted? If she let herself eat, she wasn't sure she could stop. Maybe she never would. Goose bumps rose on her arms at the thought, and she hugged herself under the covers.

She did miss Ginny. Sometimes, with Ginny, Emma could be a kid herself again. She even played dolls with her, and they had tea parties, or played hide-and-seek in the backyard, both shrieking with laughter. Those were the times Emma *didn't* think about food, or how hungry she was, or how full, or whether she should exercise for *hours* tonight to make up for the graham cracker she'd eaten.

The staff pretended this place wasn't a hospital. The hallways were painted bright colors, and the rooms were decorated and had nice comforters and posters, but nothing could make it really feel like home.

In her bedroom at home, Emma could smell whatever soap Mom was making downstairs. Vanilla and cinnamon would make her stomach rumble, or odd spicy scents made her imagine she was in a Middle Eastern bazaar, or flower essences smelled like Hawaii, where they had gone on vacation a couple of times. This place smelled like cleansers.

And Pirate. He mostly slept with Ginny, but sometimes he'd be waiting in Emma's room when she went to bed, and he would paw at the covers until she let him under, where he would curl against her waist and purr, making her think he was crooning her to sleep. He was so warm, she would wrap herself around him and even snuggle her cheek against his soft head.

If Pirate was here, she wouldn't be so lonely and cold and scared.

Sometimes she told herself she was glad

they wouldn't let Mom visit, but other times she missed her mother with a fierceness that hurt, as if her chest was being crushed. One minute she hated Mom, and another she loved her. Going back and forth wasn't an easy shift; it was more like getting your hand wedged between the bars of a wrought-iron gate, then yanking and squirming and yanking some more until you freed it, terror flooding you at the *idea* of being trapped. Only, it wasn't her hand that she had to wrench free. It was something inside, in her chest or stomach.

She *liked* it when she and Mom could be friends or talk or laugh together. Even though she pretended not to, Emma was glad that Mom still insisted on tucking her in every night. Mom smelled good, like her soaps, and her hand was soft when she smoothed Emma's hair back and her lips were warm on Emma's cheek.

Emma rolled over again and buried her face in her pillow. Her eyes burned, as if she was about to cry. She didn't *want* to miss her mother, who had put her here. Mom probably didn't miss her at all! Without her problem daughter weighing her down like a school bag bulging with books from every single class of the day, she was probably having fun.

Maybe she had even had lunch with Dad this week, or dinner. Emma knew they'd still be married if it wasn't for her. They were so perfect for each other. Emma had watched them talk to each other without words across a crowded room, dance together as gracefully as stars in those old movies Mom preferred, get dressed up to go out and *look* like those stars, Dad in his tux and Mom in a long dress with diamonds sparkling at her throat.

It was Emma who had ruined everything. From the time she could remember, she had known that she disappointed Dad, at least. She wasn't athletic, like he was, or beautiful like Mom. He hated that she was just okay at most things she did. Like, when she got a chorus part in the school play, he sat and fidgeted in the auditorium and afterward said irritably, "If you keep hiding behind your hair, you'll never be the lead."

Mom and Dad had started fighting when Emma was in sixth grade, and at her fattest. Emma would creep to the top of the stairs when she was supposed to be in bed and listen. She couldn't always hear every word, but the bite in Dad's voice and the anger in

Mom's carried. Mom said Emma would out-grow her "baby" fat, that he'd damage her self-esteem if he kept saying things at the dinner table like, "Don't you have any self-control?" or, "Have you *looked* at yourself lately? And you can still eat cake?"

Of course, Mom said things, too, but more gently. Emma could tell that she was worried her kid would always be fat, that she was lying to Dad about the baby fat melting away when her body stretched out in puberty.

When Emma started to diet, for a while things got better. They both smiled in approval. Until Mom decided she should stop. *Then* Mom would look at her dinner plate with puckered brow and say, "Please try to eat a little more." And Dad would snap, "You want her to go back to stuffing her face?"

But he got mad, too, when Mom insisted that Emma should see a counselor. That's when they really started fighting.

Over her.

She'd liked knowing that Mom was taking her side. But sometimes she thought her dieting was ruining everyone's lives. Only, she was pretty sure *she* was the problem, not her eating. She had always been one big disappointment. Dieting was the first thing she'd ever been really, really good at. Better than the other girls. Better than anyone she knew.

Denying herself when she desperately craved a bite of lasagna or a slurp of a root-beer float or even just a nibble of lettuce made her feel strong. Proud of herself.

If she let that go, she would hate herself completely. She knew she would. But nobody seemed to understand what she was talking about.

Except the other girls here. She bet most of them felt the same.

Today, one of them had said something interesting. It was in Group, when six girls were slumped in their chairs, ignoring the counselor's efforts to get them talking, Maria chewing on her fingernails and Rochelle looking so spacey Emma wondered if she was really in there. Then this eighteen-year-old named Lauren said suddenly, in a loud voice, "I think my mom is anorexic, too."

The counselor, a guy who was, like, thirty but already going bald and developing a paunch around his middle, made that humming sound therapists used to indicate interest.

"Why do you say that?" he asked.

"It's obvious!" Lauren sat up, her face

intense. "She takes maybe a bite or two at dinner, then moves the food around on her plate so nobody will notice she hasn't eaten more. She loves to cook and tries to get everyone *else* to eat. She claims she samples it and that's why she isn't hungry, but I've never seen her. And she, like, *freaks* if she thinks her pants are tight or something."

"Has she always been this way?"

Lauren nodded.

They talked about how people maintained a sense of control over their environments and relationships with family and friends. Emma got to thinking about *her* mom, and how super picky she was about tons of things. She couldn't stand it if anyone left shoes lying around or empty cups or pop cans, and the dishes had to be washed right after dinner. Her closet was like something in a magazine, with shoes arranged by type and color and clothes hanging perfectly spaced like in a store, dresses here and pants there and shirts color-coded.

The kitchen cupboards at home were just as weird, by most people's standards. Mom alphabetized the soups!

So, while she was pretty casual about her

diet, she controlled her environment in other, really obvious ways.

They also talked about whether these attempts at control actually worked, and mostly everyone agreed they didn't. Alphabetizing soup cans hadn't kept Mom and Dad married.

In the end, Emma's dieting had made her father even more disgusted with her than he had already been. It didn't make either of her parents proud of her.

"Maybe," she had said tentatively, "we're trying to prove something to ourselves, not to other people, even if that's what we believe when we start dieting, or whatever we do."

The counselor clapped his hands. "Bravo, Emma! I think you might be right. How about the rest of you?"

They hadn't all agreed. One girl said her boyfriend *hated* fat girls and she loved him so much she wanted to please him. Another one admitted that partly she wouldn't eat because it made her mother furious, and that was her goal. Lauren and Maria had looked thoughtful.

The discussion pretty much died there.

Emma pushed the little call button on her headboard and, with a sigh, turned on her lamp and swung her legs over the edge of the bed. She fumbled for her slippers and waited for one of the attendants. The thing she hated absolutely the most about being here was having somebody watch her pee!

Only once or twice had she ever tried to puke after she thought she had eaten too much, but the feeling was horrible. She'd rather exercise. Besides...she liked knowing she had the self-discipline to refuse food. If she stuffed it all in her mouth and then puked it back up, she'd feel like a pig! She might be slim, but she wouldn't feel good about it.

After visiting the bathroom, she kicked off her slippers and got back in bed. It was time for her leg lifts. She always felt better once she was sweating and her stomach and thigh muscles hurt. Secretly exercising was the only thing she could get away with here that still gave her any feeling of control. They could make her eat, but they couldn't stop her from burning off *some* of the calories.

Without that...well, she didn't know. The whole idea was scary. She got this desperate, clammy feeling, like when she saw a picture of somebody like Christopher Reeve and imagined losing absolute, complete control over her body, and having everything done *to* and *for* her. What if you were getting water therapy, and the attendants started to laugh about something and didn't notice that water was washing over your face and you couldn't breathe? How could you ever trust somebody that much?

But what if you didn't have any choice?

Well, she wouldn't *let* them decide everything for her! She'd fight, Emma decided. Like now.

She lifted both legs together, felt the strain on her belly and lower back, counted slowly to five, then lowered them. Again. Again.

She concentrated so fiercely, she hardly noticed that tears joined the beads of sweat on her face.

"YOUR BROTHER HAD a funny expression when he saw me," Logan said with amusement. "Is he going to beat me up the next time I run into him?"

Kathleen laughed. "I hope not. I think he was just surprised. Like I said, I haven't been dating. Besides, he's a brother. He probably can't figure out why anyone would want to ask me out."

"Oh, he must know his sister's a looker." Logan opened the menu.

"Why, thank you!" She seemed pleased, as if she didn't get told constantly that she was stunning.

Tonight, when she came down the stairs in drapey black slacks and a simple but elegant white top that bared plenty of shoulder and throat, he'd gaped. Without the strain on her face and the tired shadows under her eyes, Kathleen was spectacular. Sitting across the table from her at Stella's, candlelight playing with the fine, strong bones in her face, highlighting, shadowing, deepening the blue of her eyes, Logan felt a lurch in his chest every time he looked at her.

"Made up your mind?" he asked, nodding at the menu.

"Mmm." She smiled. "I always get the pasta with the marinara sauce when I'm here. It's wonderful."

"I'm a fan of their lasagna." He closed his menu, too.

After the waiter left with their orders, Logan asked, "Do you have a picture of your daughter?"

"Need you ask? I'm a mother." She bent to pick up her small handbag.

Plenty of mothers of troubled teenagers would just as soon forget they existed. He reached for her wallet as she handed it across the table.

"There's Emma in, let's see, seventh grade. And this one is her school picture for this year."

There was no mistaking the mother-daughter resemblance. Her Emma was a blue-eyed blonde, too, with a face that had still been gently rounded and unformed in seventh grade, and was now gaunt. The sparkle she'd had when younger had been replaced by a kind of blankness in the more recent photo.

"She's pretty. She has your cheekbones and eyes."

A shadow crossed her face. "Do you know, she doesn't believe she's pretty?"

"Teenagers are famous for thinking they're ugly," he pointed out. "Didn't you spend time staring at the mirror, convinced that pimple in the middle of your forehead was the most hideous zit ever, or that your nose was too long or your teeth huge or *something?*"

She had such a peculiar expression for a minute that he was afraid she'd say no. Maybe she'd never had an awkward stage or a single doubt.

But she gave an odd little laugh and said, "What terrified me was that an 'ain't' would slip out of my mouth, or I'd say something like, 'He don't go to this school,' because that's the way my mother talked. I wanted so desperately to look like someone whose family popped over to Greece in the summer or went skiing at Aspen in the winter. I just knew that everyone could tell I was a fake. I *agonized* over what were the right clothes, or how to laugh or flip my hair back or raise an eyebrow to wither the unworthy." She shook herself. "The sad thing is, I *was* a fake. Maybe I still am. The truth is, my mom was a waitress and my dad a welder. We never had any money, my mom had a sixth-grade education, and my dad's idea of a good time is sitting in a boat on a lake with a hook in the water."

He shrugged. "So, you're self-taught. What's so bad about that?"

"Maybe nothing." Her smile was crooked. "I don't know. I just regret feeling so ashamed of where I came from."

"You know," Logan said musingly, "the first time I saw you, I figured you belonged somewhere like Laurelhurst or Medina. You look expensive. Classy."

"Then, apparently I succeeded," she said with deceptive lightness.

The waiter appeared with their mineral waters. When he was gone, Logan lifted a glass. "My suspicion is, everyone fakes it some of the time. Some people, most of the time. The few people who are genuinely self-satisfied are jerks."

This laugh was a delighted gurgle. "Wait a minute!" she protested. "Aren't there a few people out there who have learned to like themselves, flaws and all? Isn't that a good thing?"

Gaze holding hers, he grinned. "Those are the ones who fake it only some of the time."

"I see." The laugh lingering in her eyes, she sipped her water. "Which category do you count yourself in?"

"Oh, I'm a some-of-the-time guy. For example…" Why not hang himself out to dry here? "When I asked you out, I thought about suggesting the symphony or a performance at Meany Hall of that dance company I saw advertised the other day. But that would have been dishonest and unproductive fakery. You'd have seen through me in no time. I'd have probably fallen asleep in the middle of the performance and humiliated you with my snores."

She laughed again, making him feel witty.

"To tell you the truth," she confessed, "I like country-western and folk music. I'm afraid I just don't have the ear to appreciate classical."

"That'll teach me to make assumptions."

"I look like Tchaikovsky, instead of George Strait?"

Laughing himself, he said, "Something like that."

Her gaze shied from his, and color touched her cheeks. "I made a few assumptions myself."

"Like?"

She said it fast. "That you're a baseball fan."

Her stereotype wouldn't have stung so much if she hadn't already told him about her father.

Logan set down his glass. "And you agreed to have dinner with me anyway?"

Kathleen gave a crooked, apologetic smile that didn't last. "My father would never have held a sobbing stranger and told her everything would be all right. He'd have mumbled apologies and retreated, like any sane man."

His eyebrows rose. "So now I'm insane?"

"Nice," she corrected. "You're nice."

"Ah." His jaw muscles bunched. "What if

I told you I do watch sports, and I follow the Mariners?"

She lifted her chin. "I'd ask what you think their chances are this year."

Logan managed a laugh that rumbled in his chest, but she'd hit him where it hurt. Okay, so he wasn't college-educated. He'd never been to Aspen or Greece. That didn't mean he was a dumb redneck.

"Poor," he said, and made a few pithy remarks about the manager and last year's trades, to which she responded intelligently.

Okay, so she at least read the sports page. Or...

"Your dad keep you up-to-date on the Mariners?"

"What?" she said in surprise. "Oh. No. I only talk to him every few weeks. No, I turn on the games sometimes while I'm making soap."

"Ever go to games?"

She shook her head. "I haven't in years. Not since they blew up the Kingdome."

"Nice sunny day, it's fun to watch a game, eat your Cracker Jacks, maybe stand up during the seventh inning stretch."

She cocked her head. "Is that an invitation?"

Was she flirting with him? "Maybe," he said cautiously. Then he thought, *why not?* "Sure. What do you say? Shall we take in a game some Saturday?"

"Maybe." A shadow crossed her face. "I don't know. Let me see how Emma is, and how she feels about…" She hesitated.

"Me."

"No, not you." She bit her lip. "Her mother dating."

He was tempted to say, *The kid is sixteen. Almost an adult. You're entitled to a life.* But he didn't, because he wished his own mother had cared enough to make sacrifices for him.

Assuming, of course, that Kathleen wasn't using her daughter as an out. *Oh, I had such fun tonight, but Emma says no. I'm so sorry!*

His gut told him that Kathleen Monroe wasn't coward enough to take that route, but he couldn't be sure. Not yet.

While they ate, they talked about music, movies and traffic, a favorite topic—or rant—of Seattleites these days.

"I've got a book in my truck," he admitted. "I spend so much time not moving at all on the freeway, I read."

"I only come north a couple of exits on my

way home from work, and it can take me half an hour. Especially when it's raining."

He snorted. "You'd think we'd never seen a drop of rain, the way traffic snarls when the road is a little slick."

She nodded. "I hate standing at the bus stop when it's pouring, but, do you know, once you're on the bus it's so much faster than driving yourself."

She told him about her job as a receptionist at a chiropractor's office. "I was so grateful to get it, and I hate every minute."

"What would you rather be doing?"

"Running a nonprofit. Raising money for a good cause. I think, if I'd been able to take some time to get a job, I could have gotten hired as a fund-raiser or even director of a small nonprofit agency. I was on the boards of half a dozen when I was married to Ian. I can't tell you how many events I've put on! I'm good at it." She made a face. "That sounds immodest, but it's true. I am."

"I believe you." He studied her. "So why aren't you doing it?"

"Initially, I needed a paycheck fast. Last fall, I was just starting to look around when Helen had her brainstorm about us going into business with my soap. The idea of working for myself, of having something I love doing become profitable, was irresistible."

When he prodded, she told him about their dreams and plans. "We already have eight outlets in Seattle and three stores on the Eastside that carry our soap. We're going to be doing a dozen or more craft shows this summer and selling directly to the public. We're thinking of trying for internet sales with a website, too." She lifted her glass in a mock toast. "Who knows? Sales may dribble along and not be worth the time we're putting into it, or I may become a business tycoon."

"I'll bet on success." Logan lifted his glass, too. "You look like a determined lady."

She seemed bemused at the idea, but after a moment she gave a small nod, as if arriving at a conclusion. "I suppose I am," she admitted. "Emma might put it less kindly."

She asked about his business, as well, and how he'd become a cabinetmaker. He told her about the uncle who had raised him, a silent man who could say more with a squeeze of the shoulder or a clap on the back than most could with effusive praise.

"Someday I'll show you his work. He can do inlay you'd swear is seamless. When I was seventeen or eighteen, I helped him inlay a floor with leaves and twining stems." Logan shook his head, remembering. "The house was featured in one of the big magazines. *Home,* I think."

"Really?" She looked suitably impressed, maybe just out of politeness. "Is he still alive? You did say 'can' and not 'could.'"

"Yeah, Uncle Pete is retired, but he still builds furniture for fun. Remind me to show you my dining room table."

How was that for cocky? he mocked himself. *When you're at my house... Uh-huh. Sure.*

But she nodded, instead of looking coolly down her nose at him. He wondered again why she had agreed to go out with him at all.

Maybe just to talk, but she hadn't spent the evening telling him her troubles. She'd actually been pretty restrained when mentioning Emma or her ex. She had either really wanted to learn more about him, or she was good at faking it.

But if she was faking, that opened the question again: Why was she sitting across the table from him?

Was there any chance at all she was attracted to him? That if he kissed her tonight, on her doorstep, her lips would soften and she'd sigh and clutch his shirt.

Then he thought, *sports fanatic*. Her assumptions about him did not suggest that he'd stirred any yearnings. She clearly despised her father and her roots, and Logan knew his own roots plunged right into the same soil.

Maybe he'd just been handy. Her daughter was away and she could kick up her heels, but had no partner to lead her onto the dance floor. He'd asked, and she'd thought, *Why not?*

Relaxing his frown, he saw that she was watching him with open amusement.

"What?"

"You haven't heard a word I've said in the past five minutes."

"Sure I have," he lied.

"I just told you I thought I'd run for governor and asked if you'd vote for me."

"Ah…" He felt himself blush and laughed. "Okay. I remembered a phone call I should have made today. Sorry."

Over coffee they wandered onto the touchy subject of politics, and discovered they basically agreed.

"Ian loved to tell me masterfully who was

worthy of our votes. It frustrated him to no end when I canceled out most of *his* votes." She smiled. "I'm still canceling out his votes. My modest revenge."

At last, reluctantly, Logan said, "I suppose I should get you home."

"Mmm. Helen and I have an appointment to talk to the owner of a day spa in Edmonds tomorrow morning at ten, so I do have to get up."

Tossing bills on the table, Logan said, "I don't see you sleeping in until noon anyway. Am I wrong?"

Kathleen sighed. "Unfortunately, no. I'm too…" She hesitated.

"Disciplined?"

"That sounds much nicer than 'set in my ways,' or 'uptight.' I just don't like feeling lazy." She made a sheepish face. "Have I administered a mortal insult? Don't tell me you like nothing better than lounging in bed until two in the afternoon every Saturday and Sunday."

Logan held her coat as she slipped her arms into the sleeves. "No, you're safe. I'd get bored. Eight o'clock is sleeping in for me."

"Me, too. I like being up before everyone else. The house is so quiet and peaceful."

"Mine is all the time." That sounded bleak. He nodded his thanks to the maitre d' and held open the outside door for Kathleen.

The sidewalk and street were busy with couples arriving for eleven o'clock or eleven-thirty showings at the Metro, a movie theater next door to Stella's. The University district didn't shut down early, even on weeknights. A panhandler was working the corner, and headlights flashed as a steady stream of cars passed on 45th.

At the car, Logan let Kathleen in first, then went around to the driver's side.

"Do you have a workshop in your home?" she asked out of the blue.

"Yeah, I bought my place because it has a big daylight basement that opens into the garage, so I can carry cabinets straight out to the truck."

"Where do you live?"

"Ballard. House built in the forties, with nowhere near the charm yours has."

"Oh."

Okay. Had she been hinting that she'd like to see his house sometime? he wondered hopefully, but couldn't believe it. She was sitting a little too stiffly, not looking at him, as if she was starting to get nervous.

The drive to her house didn't take five minutes, which was maybe just as well. He couldn't think of a thing to say.

Will you go out with me tomorrow night, too? Too desperate.

He kept stealing glances her way when they passed under streetlamps or paused at red lights and tried to imagine scenarios. Him bending his head and her stepping quickly back. Her accepting a kiss with the enthusiasm of a transplanted Californian facing another rainy Seattle morning.

Her kissing him back.

He stole another look at her classic profile and soft mouth, and had to wrench his gaze back to the road. Looks had never been really important to him. Brynn had been pretty, but not spectacular. He'd fallen in love with her sweetness, her spirit, her sense of humor, not the sway of her hips or the regularity of her facial features.

But Kathleen Monroe's elegance and beauty got to him. Represented something, maybe, that he'd yearned for. Whatever. He didn't altogether like the feeling, or himself for responding so powerfully to something so shallow.

Assuming that *was* what he was responding to.

A Volkswagen sat in her driveway, and there wasn't a place on her block to park. In fact, there was barely room for him to maneuver his big pickup down the middle of her narrow street, with cars parked on both sides.

He hesitated, then set the emergency brake and said, "I'll walk you up."

She reached over, covering his hand with hers and giving a soft squeeze. "Don't be silly. Somebody might want to get by. I can make it safely to my front door."

But she hadn't reached for the door handle yet, which gave him hope.

He said quietly, "I enjoyed tonight."

She sounded just a little breathy. "I did, too."

"Can we do it again?"

"I'd like that."

Was she feeling shy? he wondered in amazement.

"Kathleen…"

"Yes?" she whispered.

He reached out and wrapped one hand around her nape, feeling smooth skin and the delicate jutting of vertebrae. A quiver ran through her, but instead of grabbing for the door handle and babbling her good-nights, she only waited, her eyes big and dark in the dim lighting.

Logan bent toward her, hesitated and then touched his mouth to hers. Her breath sighed against his lips. He brushed hers again, then deepened the kiss.

When he lifted his head, she made a tiny, ragged sound. They stared at each other for a moment. Then her lashes fluttered and she withdrew, physically and in every other way, and opened the pickup door so hastily she nearly fell out.

"Good night, Logan." Her voice was high, hurried. "Thank you, I had fun."

"I'll call," he said, just before she slammed the door.

She lifted a hand and hurried away, slipping between the bumpers of parked cars and up the stairs to her house, built high above the street. She waved one more time from the porch before letting herself inside.

Well.

Unless she kissed every man that way, and from her startled reaction he rather doubted it, it would seem that he'd been wrong.

A pleased grin tugging his mouth...

He'd stirred her coals, all right, and the heat was enough to warm his hands.

CHAPTER SIX

TENSION TIGHTENING HER shoulders and squeezing her temples, Kathleen walked down the hall to Emma's room. The visit was not off to a winning start, considering that Emma hadn't been waiting in the lobby for her.

She passed a big room where a bunch of girls lounged on couches and chairs watching television. Almost all were perilously thin, hair dull and lank like Emma's, the fuzz on neck and cheeks a testament to the body's resolve to protect itself. Yet when something funny happened on the show, giggles erupted. Normalcy and tragedy entwined.

Others gave her wary glances when she passed the open doors of bedrooms. None of the doors were shut, she saw. Apparently closeting yourself in was against the rules. A couple of nurses chatting in doorways or wandering by smiled and nodded.

Emma's door, with a poster of Rob Pattinson on it, was ajar. Kathleen knocked.

After a moment of silence, her daughter said in a low voice, "Come in."

Taking a deep breath for courage, Kathleen pushed open the door and walked in, smiling. "Hi."

"Hi." Face averted, Emma sat cross-legged on the room's single twin bed, her feet bare and her hair in a loose ponytail. Her T-shirt bared stick arms and a bony collarbone and neck, but her cheeks had a faint flush of color instead of a waxen pallor for the first time in a long while.

Kathleen's chest filled with anguish and happiness so acute, it hurt. She bit her lip hard to stop tears that burned the backs of her eyes.

"Do you mind if I sit down?"

Emma shrugged and picked at a chenille flower on the bedspread.

Sitting at the foot of the bed, Kathleen asked softly, "How are you?"

Emma still didn't look up. "What difference does it make? I'm stuck here anyway."

Kathleen reached over and covered Emma's restless hand. "How you are *always* makes a difference."

Her daughter flung up her head, eyes flashing. "I hate it here! It's like...like prison!

They watch you all the time, and they put tubes down your throat if you won't eat, and lots of the girls are prettier than I am, and..."

Kathleen scooted over and gathered Emma into her arms. "None of them," she said firmly, "is prettier than you. I saw a whole bunch of girls when I was coming in, so I'm competent to judge. And Sharon told me they didn't have to put a tube down your throat. Did they?"

Rigid in her mother's embrace, Emma shook her head and sniffed. "But they serve all this gross food, and you have to eat every bite even if it's something you hate! And it's like I'm a baby here! I can't decide anything for myself."

Tears escaped Kathleen's eyes. "I know, sweetheart. I didn't want to have to send you here…"

Emma wrenched away, her expression wild. "Then why did you?"

A lump in her throat, Kathleen said, "Because you didn't leave me any choice. You say you can't decide anything for yourself, but you did decide. You lied, and you conned Sharon and Dr. Tisdale, and you lost more weight than we'd agreed on."

Emma spat, "Eighty pounds is too much! I was fat."

A huge weariness pressed on Kathleen's shoulders. "I won't have this argument again. You're not seeing yourself as you really are. Until your eyes are opened, all I can do is keep you from killing yourself."

Defiantly, Emma leaped to her feet. "What if I want to die?"

Kathleen didn't touch the tears dripping down her cheeks. "Please tell me you don't." Her voice was thick, barely more than a whisper.

After a frozen instant, Emma's face crumpled and she threw herself at her mother again. "I don't want to die," she sobbed. "I just...I just..."

Clearly she didn't know what she wanted. She only knew she was trapped in an obsession she didn't understand and couldn't escape. *Kathleen* didn't understand it; things might have been easier if she did. Anorexia truly was the monster under the bed, lurking in the closet, hiding in shadows—invisible yet terrifying, real no matter what anyone said.

"I love you," Kathleen whispered against her hair. "I love you."

"Then take me home!" her daughter wailed.

Rocking, rocking, her heart squeezed in agony, she said, "I can't. You know I can't."

Once again, Emma tore herself away. Face wet with tears, she screamed, "Then you don't love me!" Leaping from the bed, she raced from the room.

Kathleen gave a small, unheard cry of pain and sat without moving for a very long time.

LOGAN CALLED THAT NIGHT to find out how the first visit had gone. Kathleen had already been wondering how she'd come to reveal so much of herself to him over dinner. But the moment she heard his deep, slow voice, so calm, she crumbled without a fight.

"Terribly." She clutched the phone and huddled under an afghan in the overstuffed chair in the living room. After dinner, the others had all gone about their business. She'd retreated to pretend to read a book that lay open on the end table. Half-grown Pirate, rakish with the one eye askew, lay purring on the back of the chair as if he knew she needed him. His orange plume of a tail wrapped her neck. "She told me that I don't love her or I wouldn't leave her there."

He gave a comforting chuckle. "Teenage hyperbole."

Kathleen blinked. "Well…yes."

"Isn't that about what you expected?"

"Yes, but…"

"It hurt anyway?"

She let out a long breath, somehow releasing pain with it. "Yes," she said simply. "Where Emma is concerned, I can never seem to…gird myself sufficiently."

"I'm told that just letting go in the normal way is hard. Having her try to tear herself away must be a thousand times more painful."

Kathleen let the afghan slip a few inches and her knees relax against the arm of the chair. "How did you get so wise?"

Again she heard that comforting rumble of a laugh. "Maybe I'm faking it."

"I hope not." She had to blink away tears. "You always make me feel better."

"Good." Warmth infused his voice. Not just the comforting kind: steaming, fragrant cups of tea and thick quilts and hand-written notes on thick lilac paper. But also something more, the smoldering glow she occasionally saw in his eyes, before he veiled it.

How could she be responding like this,

when she was racked with so much fear for Emma and so deep a sense of her own failure?

"Do you have time to get together this week?" he asked.

She wanted to say, *Come over now. Wrap your arms around me and hold me while I cry and then kiss me again.*

Swallowing the lump in her throat, Kathleen said, "I start counseling with Emma this week. Monday and Wednesday evening, then Saturday morning."

Tone expressionless, he said, "That won't leave you much time at home. It's okay. Just give me a call if…"

Laughing despite being on the edge of tears, Kathleen interrupted. "You never let me finish. I was going to say, Tuesday or Thursday if you'd like to come over and join us for dinner, or go out for pizza or just for a cup of coffee, I'd like that."

There was a long moment of silence. She almost thought he'd already hung up. Then he said, "I don't seem to be very secure where you're concerned."

"I've noticed. I just don't know why."

"I think you must be my dream girl." He

made a sound in his throat. "You know. The one who's always beyond reach."

"I'm...I'm not that..."

"Yeah. Yeah, you are. At least in my eyes."

"Oh," she whispered, not knowing what to say. She couldn't possibly make any kind of declaration, if that was called for.

"Tuesday it is," he said more briskly. "Why don't we go out for pizza or whatever you'd like?"

"Just so I can wear jeans and clogs," she told him, "anything is fine."

Knowing she was going to see Logan Tuesday night was a warm glow she hugged to herself. She desperately needed something to look forward to, as low as she felt about herself and her life.

Monday night was the first counseling session with Emma and Sharon. Before, Sharon had seen Emma alone and talked occasionally to Kathleen.

"Now," she said, smiling at both as if they were in for a treat, "I think it's time we work together."

Plainly Emma was not enthusiastic. She sat in the straight-backed chair with her head bent and her spine curved, her hair a curtain to hide her face.

Kathleen tried to look cheerful and attentive.

"Emma, you know why you're here," Sharon began.

Emma began chewing on a fingernail.

"I'm pleased to see that your weight is up by two pounds. How do you feel about that?"

Emma said intensely, "I *hate* gaining weight."

"You do understand that you collapsed because your body was weakening from malnutrition."

She slumped lower in the chair. "I slipped and bumped my head. Big deal!"

"You scared us," Kathleen said, with what she thought was admirable understatement. "I didn't know Ginny could scream like that."

Emma looked interested. "She screamed? Really?"

Kathleen had to grit her teeth. Her charming daughter's tone suggested that she was about to say, *Cool!*

"I suggest," Sharon interjected, "that we not spend this time together arguing about your weight, or whether you need to gain or lose. Let's talk instead about your relationship with each other. Who'd like to start?"

Emma muttered something. Both the women looked at her.

"Can you say that so we can hear?" Sharon prodded.

The teenager's chin shot up. "Why does everything have to be about *her*?"

Kathleen felt as if a knife had just slipped between her ribs. She couldn't breathe, could only sit still enduring the pain that radiated from the wound.

Sharon leaned forward. "Why does discussing your relationship mean we're talking about your mother? Aren't we talking equally about you?"

"I don't want to talk about me, either!" Emma declared sullenly.

"Then what do you want to talk about?"

"Nothing!" she cried.

"I see." Sharon turned to Kathleen. "Is there anything you'd like to say?"

Kathleen's fingernails bit into her palms as she chose her words with care. "I would like to know why Emma is so angry at me."

"You put me in here!"

"You put yourself in here," she retorted.

"I was fine!"

"You weren't fine."

"Now, now," Sharon interrupted. "We're

wandering back into old battlefields. Can we talk about *before* you entered the Bridges program, Emma? Were you mad at your mom then?"

Emma shrugged.

"Is that a yes or no?"

"I wasn't mad. Except when she, like, *spied* on me."

"Spied?" Kathleen echoed in surprise. "What are you talking about?"

"To see if I was eating, or puking, or exercising, or... It's like you wanted to know what I was doing every minute!"

Take a deep breath. Stay calm. "I worry about you."

She mumbled something else.

Sharon spoke up. "Louder, Emma."

Abruptly straightening in the chair, Emma all but yelled, "I know you worry! I know you love me!" Fists clenched, she stared with burning eyes at her mother. "I just...I wish... Sometimes I wish you'd be mean or stupid or do something awful, like other people. But you always do the right thing."

Stunned by the attack, Kathleen whispered, "The right thing?"

"You're nice! You're perfect! *I'm* the stupid one with the problem."

There was a moment of silence. Emma ducked her head and stared down at her lap.

"So you do believe you have a problem," Sharon said gently.

Emma wouldn't say any more.

After Emma had hurried out to go to her room, Sharon walked Kathleen to the lobby.

"I think that was very productive," she declared.

Kathleen rubbed her temple. "Really."

"You sound doubtful."

"Yeah. I am. All she did was repeat her usual litany. She's dumb, bad, ugly, stupid and everything is her fault."

The two women paused in the lobby by the double glass front doors. "But she did concede she has a problem."

"Maybe," Kathleen said with a sigh. "Or was she just conceding that we all *think* she does?"

The plump therapist ignored her reservations. "I'd love to get her to open up more about you. She never wants to say anything bad about you. That's not normal for a troubled girl her age."

Kathleen gazed at her wavery reflection in the glass, eerily indistinct with the lamplit parking lot on the other side of the doors. "I am terribly afraid," she said in a low voice, "that she has me on some sort of pedestal. Her favorite line at home is, '*You're* so perfect.' You know, with that scathing note only a teenager can add. Once, Ian told her that if she'd lose weight, he'd be lucky enough to be living with *two* beautiful women. I think Emma is still trying."

"And you're her ideal. Yes, I can see that. You've suggested something like this before, but Emma mostly talks warmly about you, so I guess I didn't take you seriously. But if you're not just her mother, but also her...oh, *standard,* and maybe in a way even a sort of competitor..." Her cheeks flushed and she nodded vigorously. "Yes, that's an interesting idea. We can explore it further with Emma on Wednesday."

"I can hardly wait," Kathleen said dryly.

Sharon laughed. "She's doing fine. Did you notice how much better she looked? She won't admit it, but I can see her energy level rising, and the aides tell me she's eating with less reluctance. Sometimes that's the big hurdle, you know. Just getting someone like Emma to actually put food in her mouth and chew it and swallow it, day after day. Once she's done it for a few weeks, the whole idea isn't such a barrier. We hope to get her comfortable with eating small but wholesome meals."

"She did look better." Giving a twisted smile, Kathleen held out a hand. "Thank you, Sharon."

Sharon responded with a quick hug instead. "You're welcome. We'll get her through this."

Kathleen wished she could be as sure.

SHE AND LOGAN ENDED UP going out for Chinese food, choosing several dishes to share. It being a weeknight, the restaurant was almost deserted. The nearest diners besides them were a couple of Asian men talking intently over tiny cups of tea half a dozen booths away.

Sipping his wonton soup, Logan listened as Kathleen told him an abbreviated version of the counseling session.

"At least that suggests she admires you."

"Resents me is closer to it, I think."

He made a "maybe" motion with his head. "The way we feel about our parents is probably always complicated."

The way she'd felt about her own parents certainly was. She, of course, had been sure she could do a better job raising her own child. She'd give her all the advantages, including a mother who didn't have to work full-time and leave her kids with a neighbor or, later, as latch-key kids, Kathleen responsible for her little brother.

"You haven't mentioned your parents," she said. "Are they alive?"

"My mom is. My dad...who knows?" Logan almost succeeded in sounding indifferent. "My parents broke up before I was born. They were just kids themselves, and my father wasn't up to the challenge. Mom tried, but she wasn't, either. Eventually she dumped me on her big brother. Uncle Pete raised me from the age of eight or nine."

"And you let me whine about my parents?" she exclaimed. "Why didn't you tell me to shut up and count my blessings?"

Logan laughed, an easy sound. "Just because your parents were there doesn't mean they were perfect. I love my uncle Pete, but I've been known to grumble about him."

"For instance?" Kathleen challenged.

"He's..." Logan hesitated, setting down his spoon. "He doesn't have much to say. Or maybe, it's that he doesn't say much."

"There's a distinction?"

"He conveys most of his opinions with a grunt, a raised brow, a nod. When you've disappointed him, you know it. When you've pleased him, you know that, too. What Uncle Pete was never much good at is giving advice."

"You mean…he really *doesn't* talk much? Or, I mean, um…"

Logan laughed again. "Oh, he can talk. He's not mute or anything like that. I remember my mother telling me that he had a speech impediment when he was a kid, and people made fun of it, so he pretty much just shut up. As he'd put it, he's not much for chattering."

Kathleen nodded, fascinated by this glimpse into Logan's childhood. "Your mother—do you ever see her?"

"She has another family now," he said matter-of-factly. "She'd like to include me more, but…" His big shoulders shrugged.

"But?"

"It's too little, too late."

"You won't forgive her."

He raised one eyebrow, rather, she guessed, as his uncle Pete might have. "I don't know that forgiveness is the issue. She's a stranger. I don't care."

"Are you sure?" Kathleen asked shrewdly. Little as she liked her father, little as they had in common, she couldn't just cut herself off. In his own way, he loved her. Maybe, in her own way, Logan's mother loved him, too.

When she suggested as much, he shrugged again. "Maybe. I speak to her. I'm not rude. I just don't go over to join the family for Thanksgiving or Christmas."

"How does Uncle Pete feel about her?"

Kathleen realized she was being nosy, but for some reason questions kept slipping out.

Logan gave a crooked grin. "He's okay with her. *He* goes over for Thanksgiving dinner sometimes. My uncle Pete is a philosophical man. He figures people do what they can do, and if they don't measure up to someone else's standard, well, who set the standards anyhow?"

Kathleen winced at the parallels with her troubles with Emma. When Logan noticed, she said weakly, "I suppose we each set our own. Or maybe our parents do it for us."

Oh, dear, she thought in dismay. Had *she* somehow held herself up as an ideal to her small daughter? Or, worse yet, had she held up as the shimmering, never-attainable ideal the person she had always so desperately wished she'd been, the one she'd spent twenty years or more trying to become? The rich girl, the princess, the snob?

Logan seemed to read her mind. "You're trying to think of a way to blame yourself, aren't you?"

"Who else is to blame?" she asked, with bitterness she couldn't disguise.

"Your ex? Your parents? Their parents?" He spread his hands. "Maybe nobody. Schizophrenia used to be blamed on somebody, too, before doctors figured out that the causes are physical or chemical or something. We're beginning to accept that alcoholism is a disease, maybe hereditary, but probably not caused by the way your mom raised you. Who's to say eating disorders aren't the same? Would you be blaming yourself if Emma had early on-set diabetes, or leukemia?"

Tears filled her eyes. "No. Maybe. Every parent looks for ways she's failed her child. But..." Her smile wavered. "Maybe you're right. Maybe it isn't my fault."

"Good girl," he said, eyes warm with approval. "Now, eat."

"Is that an order?"

Once again he managed to steer conversation to entertaining if innocuous topics while they ate Mongolian beef and chicken with pea pods and heaps of rice. He insisted on trying to eat with chopsticks, absurdly small in his big hands.

They argued amiably about a growth management initiative that was to be on the fall ballot, about how the Seattle mayor had handled a near-riot at a Mardi Gras celebration, about the merits of vitamin C in cold prevention, and whether the state effort to produce a standardized test that all students must pass to graduate from high school was a boondoggle or a praiseworthy objective.

On the way home, in the darkness of Logan's pickup, he reached out and took her hand. "The Mariners are at home Friday night. What do you say to that game?"

She turned inward for an instant, expecting a complex internal battle, and found no antagonist. She couldn't see Emma every day, even if the sixteen-year-old wanted or needed her mom's presence. They had a counseling session Saturday, but there wasn't a reason in the world that Kathleen couldn't go out with him on Friday night.

"Okay." She realized how tentative she'd sounded. "Sure," she said more strongly. "That'll be great."

"Dinner first?"

"Yes, but I feel guilty when you keep insisting on paying. Why don't we have dinner at the house first?"

"Okay," he said agreeably.

"I wonder…" She stopped herself.

His thumb made a circle on her palm. "You wonder?"

"What Emma would think of you," Kathleen said in a rush.

He was silent, and she realized she must have offended him. *Will* think of you, was what she should have said. But they'd only gone out twice! She didn't know if this had even a short-term future. It might be weeks before Emma came home. She and Kathleen had enough to fight about without adding a man who might have vanished from the scene in a couple of weeks to the mix.

"I'm usually considered inoffensive," Logan said, with so little inflection she realized that she *had* hurt his feelings.

Kathleen turned her hand in his to squeeze

back. "I didn't mean it like that. Only...only that everyone else will be there, but not Emma. I'd like you to meet her."

He gave her a look, unreadable in the darkness now that he'd turned onto her street, overhung with big old trees. "The time will come."

Would it? Did she really want Emma to meet Logan? How would he compare in a teenager's eyes to her father? Would she think the idea of her mother dating this... this carpenter, with his calluses and high-school education and shaggy hair, was ridiculous?

Feeling a hot flush of shame burn her cheeks, Kathleen turned her head quickly to look out the side window.

Emma would never think those things. She, Kathleen, was the one thinking them, and trying not to. She hated the idea of running into Ian, say, and having him eye Logan with disdain. Expensive suits and haircuts and intense, high-paying jobs shouldn't be the measure of a man, but for her they always had been.

If she hadn't been...oh, reexamining herself lately, she never would have considered going out with some guy who'd happened to show up, sweat under his arms and dirt under his fingernails, to build kitchen cabinets.

And that was why she was ashamed of herself.

Ashamed—and not sure she could really let go of her old prejudices and stereotypes. What if she and Logan were ever in a situation where she was embarrassed by him, or for him?

What kind of shallow person was she? she wondered unhappily. He was a nice man, sensitive, patient and caring. He was intelligent, articulate and he liked her. How could she be worrying about how he'd compare to Ian if the two men came face-to-face?

"What are you thinking?" he asked.

Kathleen started. They were pulled up to the curb in, wonder of wonders, a spot only one house down from hers. The neighbor's teenager, who usually parked here, must be out for the evening.

"I'm sorry!" she exclaimed. "My mind was wandering." She gave a laugh she hoped didn't seem faked. "Obviously."

"Question is," he said quietly, "where?"

"Oh, Emma, of course," Kathleen lied, with compunctions she hadn't known she would feel. "How our session tomorrow will go."

He studied her with unreadable eyes. "If you want to talk afterward, call."

Despising herself in the face of his kindness, she tried to smile and failed. She felt like crying again, out of grief she hardly understood.

"Hey." He rubbed a thumb across her cheek, and she realized that she *was* crying. "Stop that," Logan murmured, voice a soft burr. "I have faith your Emma will be fine."

Kathleen nodded. She took a swipe at her own tears. "I don't know what's wrong with me. I'm sorry!"

"Quit apologizing." For a moment he sounded angry, bringing her head up. The next instant, he was kissing her.

She made a shuddery sound, melted and thought, *This is why.*

Why she'd gone out with an uneducated cabinetmaker, why she'd felt that warm glow at simply knowing she was to see him again. For some unknowable reason, she responded to him as she hadn't to anybody. Ever.

He was overmuscled and not altogether graceful and not really handsome, but she didn't care.

Shocked by her feelings, she gasped when he lifted his mouth.

"I'm sorry. That was…" He swallowed. "I don't know where it came from."

"I…" She moistened her lips. "It's okay. I actually, um…" On the verge of chickening out, she made herself say it. She owed him that much, after her snobbish thoughts. "I like it when you kiss me."

He reached out and cupped her cheek.

"Good night," she whispered, and fumbled for the door handle.

"I'll walk you up…"

"Don't. Please." Scrambling to the ground, she turned back to give him a shaky smile. "I might want to sit on the porch swing and stay up with you all night, and then somebody would be sure to get the wrong end of the stick. Maybe we can take this up Friday night."

"Count on it," he said softly, just before she slammed the door and hurried up the sidewalk.

Inside her house, she locked up and then, knees weak, leaned back against the door.

Well!

When she had so many doubts, so many

fears, when life was so complicated, did she really want to start something like this?

Eyes closed, Kathleen gave a shaky laugh.

The answer seemed to be a resounding, *Yes*.

CHAPTER SEVEN

KATHLEEN HAD had a seriously lousy day. She had set out for work ten minutes late, after discovering a run in her panty hose on the way out the door and rushing back to change. She'd gotten wet just hurrying to the car, with rain pouring from a charcoal sky. Not three blocks from home, the car had lurched and begun thump, thump, thumping. A flat tire, of course. Kathleen couldn't remember the last time she'd even *thought* about checking her tires.

Naturally the block was as deserted as the tumbleweed-strewn street in a ghost town, which meant no chivalrous male rushed to her aid. After a minute, she remembered that she had a can of the mysterious stuff you could squirt into a tire that was supposed to reinflate it. She popped the trunk, thought longingly of her umbrella, in the closet at home, and leaped from the car.

Only to discover that she hadn't unloaded

the soap-making supplies she'd bought two days before. Muttering under her breath, Kathleen dug under bags and boxes, feeling the slanting rain drenching her nylon-clad legs and wool skirt. By the time she found the can, crouched beside the tire and connected it to the valve, hearing a hiss as the tire mysteriously inflated, she was soaked to the bone and shivering.

In the car she debated between home and a hot bath, work and the service station. The service station won, given that she had no idea how long the tire would hold what air—or gas, or whatever—was in it. They informed her that the tire was punctured and they *could* fix it—but it wasn't worth fixing. The tread was all but gone.

Several hundred dollars poorer, she drove home on four new tires. From there, she phoned work, found out someone else had called in sick, threw away yet another pair of panty hose, took a rushed and unsatisfactory shower, dried her hair, dressed and started out again.

Because the office was understaffed, she never took a lunch break. The bagel and latte she had stopped for on her way to Bridges wasn't curtailing her growling stomach. Her patience was in short supply.

Emma was being sulky again. What else was new? Kathleen thought wryly. The teenager was shrugging at everything Sharon asked, her entire attention seemingly fixed on plaiting a stringy strand of her hair into a thin braid.

"Emma," Sharon prodded, "I thought we had agreed that tonight we were going to explore further your seeming anger at your mom."

Emma rolled her eyes, reached the end of the braid and let it drop, then reached for another strand.

Kathleen stood. "You know what? My day has sucked. If you're not going to talk to me, I'm going home to take a nice long bath."

Even the counselor looked startled. Kathleen didn't care. She marched toward the door.

"I didn't say I wouldn't talk to you!" Emma cried.

Kathleen turned. "No? Well, you aren't, which is the same thing."

"I just…" Emma was halfway to her feet, too. "I don't like all these questions!"

"Sharon wouldn't be asking them if you and I had done so great on our own."

"What would you say to your mother if I weren't here to ask questions?" the therapist interjected.

"That's a question!"

"Yes, it is," Kathleen agreed mildly. "But I'll ask it, too. Is there anything you do want to talk about?"

Emma's huge blue eyes widened, and she sank back into her chair. "Um...not really."

Frustration and hunger weighed heavily on Kathleen. She sighed. "You know, you make constant, biting remarks." She mimicked her daughter. "'*You're* so perfect.' But when I call you on them, you'll never tell me what I'm doing wrong. We both know I'm not perfect. So what am I?" When there was no immediate answer forthcoming, she shook her head. "You know what? I'm going home."

Sharon didn't say a word. Emma let her mother get halfway out the door before she cried, "You're too perfect!"

Kathleen froze, then slowly turned. "What?"

Her daughter's elfin face was alive with a tangle of emotions that included grief and resentment. "You never make mistakes! You're always, like, organized and pretty and you never gain weight and everybody likes you." In a rush Emma finished, "And I'm really scared I can't be like you!"

In the thundering moment of silence that followed, mother and daughter stared at each other, both stunned in different ways.

Then, aching, stiff and feeling old, Kathleen returned to her chair. Groping for the right answer, or perhaps just for honesty, she said slowly, "I have two things to say. The first is, you don't have to be like me! You shouldn't even try. You're a different person."

Emma's expression of anguish didn't alter. She wasn't convinced, maybe never would be.

Her weariness deepening, Kathleen said, "And second, I make plenty of mistakes. If I didn't make any, why are we here?"

"Because I screwed up!"

Kathleen shook her head. "No. Maybe. Maybe we both made mistakes and poor choices. But the truth is, I've spent so many years polishing my image, I never let you see how flawed I am inside, and that was *my* big mistake."

Sharon, wisely, stayed silent, her head turning as she listened.

Emma hugged herself. "What are you talking about?"

"You know Granddad. And you remember Grandma pretty well, don't you?"

The teenager nodded.

Kathleen told her then, for the first time, what she'd told Logan: how she had seemingly been born dissatisfied with her place in life, how she had cringed at her mother's ungrammatical speech and been ashamed of their weedy, shaggy lawn and exhaust-spewing car and tiny dark living room with dingy shag carpet and worn recliners.

Mouth twisted, she said, "I wanted so badly to be popular, and I thought that meant I had to be rich and well-dressed and have a great house. Ryan and I fought about it all the time. He called me a princess and a snob." She was quiet for a moment. "He was right."

"But...it's not so bad..." Emma said haltingly.

"It is if you deny the people who love you and pretend you're something you aren't." Kathleen sat very still, her hands folded on her lap and her back straight, saying all these things that were so hard to admit. "Mom—Grandma—was a waitress. She worked really, really hard so that Ryan and I could have decent clothes and money to buy year-books and go out for sports and to dances. I lied to my friends about what my parents did. I was too good for them."

"But…maybe…" Emma tried again.

"Grandpa has his own flaws. He irritates me and I irritate him. But he does love me." She hesitated again, then stripped herself bare. "Did you ever wonder why he came to the house so seldom, and never when other people were there? Even then, as an adult, I was ashamed of him. I had perfected," she mocked herself, "my snooty rich persona, but he was a crack I couldn't cover with makeup or an amusing story. So I just didn't invite him."

"Did…does he know?" Emma whispered.

"How can he help it?" Kathleen heard the self-loathing in her voice. "Either that, or he assumes I just don't want to see him. I'm not sure. I never let myself wonder. I never let myself *care* about what he thought or felt." She tried to smile, felt it waver. "What does that make me?"

Her daughter gaped. "But…you're always so nice. I don't believe you."

"Believe it," Kathleen said harshly. "Your

mother is a fake. What you see is a mask disguising someone ugly behind it."

Emma jumped to her feet. "I don't believe you! Don't you love me?"

Kathleen stood, too. Tears in her eyes, she said, "Of course I love you! So much that I wanted to be the perfect mom in your eyes. So I kept on pretending. Until…" Her voice faltered. "Until the day I realized you were killing yourself trying to be perfect, too. And I saw what a sham my whole life was. So I took you and started over. Only—" this smile twisted, too "—I'm discovering that changing the outside isn't good enough. And changing *me* isn't easy." She knew she was crying openly. "I'm sorry, Emma."

Emma's face crumpled, but she dashed away the tears. "You're lying," she cried. "It's me…I'm the one…"

Kathleen took a step toward her, hand out. "You're the one who has to get well. But maybe we both need to learn to like ourselves again."

Emma lurched back to avoid her touch. "You've made all this up! You want me to think…to think nothing is my fault. But I don't believe you!"

The next moment, she ran for the door.

Both women heard the thud of her footsteps racing down the hall.

Kathleen closed her eyes, tears seeping from beneath the lids.

She was still standing there, eyes closed, hands dangling helplessly at her side, when she felt a gentle touch on her arm. She blinked and, through the blur of tears, saw Sharon nod.

"I'm proud of you. What you did couldn't have been easy."

"But it didn't do a speck of good," Kathleen said hopelessly.

"Oh, yes, it did. Chances are, she's going to get really mad at you because you're *not* perfect. She can take you off the pedestal, as every other normal teenager does her parents. And, especially for Emma, that's really important. Just give her time, Kathleen."

Time.

Well, time marched on whether it was helping or hindering, so she might as well hope.

She nodded, gave an unhappy smile and said, "Why not? What else can I do?"

HER MOTHER WAS LYING. She had to be lying!

Emma slammed the door to her room, then

angrily opened it a few inches so the hall Nazis would leave her alone. Flinging herself onto her bed, she punched her pillows into place and lay against them with her arms tightly crossed over her chest, glaring at the wall.

Mom had never said any of that before! Sharon had probably coached her into coming up with some story. Emma could just see it.

"We need to show her you have feet of clay. What can you say?"

Thrumming with rage and shock, Emma still faltered on this scenario. Mom hadn't seemed rehearsed. She'd looked really tired, and almost *old.* Mom never went anywhere without her makeup perfect and her hair casually styled but *chic* and her clothes put together as if she hadn't given it any thought but made everything look elegant. Today, her shoes hadn't matched her suit. Emma had noticed that. They were blue, and Mom had worn them with a brown skirt and blazer. And her hair had been kind of stringy, and maybe she hadn't even put on eye makeup.

When she stood up and started to walk out, she seemed...not mad, but fed up. That had scared Emma. Her mother had never given up on her before, and today, for a minute, she'd looked like she was going to.

She wouldn't, would she? Emma tried to scoff at her own fear. If Mom had left Dad and her perfect marriage for her own daughter, she wouldn't give up. How could she? That would be like admitting that she'd made this huge mistake, and Mom didn't make mistakes.

Except, today Mom said she did. Big ones.

And Emma couldn't help wondering whether Mom wasn't thinking that leaving Dad was one of them.

Only... Emma felt a surge of hope. Dad wouldn't exactly have been dazzled if he'd seen Mom today. Maybe, if he and Mom *had* had lunch this past week, he'd be the one who wouldn't be interested in them getting together again.

Fear clutched her chest. *Face it,* she thought in despair, *they're perfect together. If Mom hadn't chosen you... If she doesn't keep choosing you...*

Emma couldn't even think about going back to live with her dad. Not after he'd grabbed her with rough hands and shoved food into her mouth and kept shoving and shoving, while she gagged and tears and snot ran down her face and she was choking. Her vision had been going funny, and she wondered if she would have died. Whenever she thought of him, before she could blank it out she had a flicker of remembrance of his face—all contorted with rage because *she* wasn't good enough to be his daughter.

Mom wouldn't go back to him! She must remember, too. She'd beaten on his shoulders with her fists, screaming at him, until he'd let Emma go and she'd fallen from her chair to her hands and knees, food falling from her mouth as her stomach heaved and she fought for breath.

Through streaming eyes, Emma had looked up and seen this look of revulsion on Mom's face as she turned on Dad.

"What you just did," she had said in an oddly quiet voice, "is unforgivable." She'd knelt by Emma and whacked her back, helping her get chunks of bread up, then hoisted her to her feet and led her from the room.

The very next morning, they had moved out.

Emma hadn't seen her father again, and she didn't want to. Not ever.

Mom wouldn't abandon her, Emma knew that.

She thought she knew that.

But if it was true and Mom had, like, ignored Grandpa and not invited him over and stuff because she was ashamed of him, what if she got so she was ashamed of Emma?

Emma flipped over and hugged her pillow. No! Mom had to be lying. She was too... too *nice* to be that mean to Grandpa! Emma didn't like her grandfather that much, either. Mostly when they went over he ignored her and kept watching baseball on TV and sometimes he'd belch and this *horrible* smell would waft to Emma. He'd bellow at the TV or at some other driver if he got mad when he was behind the wheel and he used words Emma's parents never said, especially around her.

But she'd also seen the way he looked at her mother sometimes, as if he did love her. His face, for just a minute, would soften. Other times, when Mom made an excuse, Emma had seen an expression she hadn't understood. Now she thought it was a kind of bewilderment, as if he didn't know what he'd done wrong.

So maybe it was true, that Mom was ashamed of him and had not invited him to Christmas or Thanksgiving celebrations because she and Dad had friends over, and she didn't want them to meet him.

Emma's stomach churned. If Mom could be that mean, then maybe she wasn't anything like Emma had always believed her to be. Maybe she *was* a fake.

The idea was too weird. It was scary and disorienting and also exhilarating, in a strange way. She had spent years watching her mother with a kind of despair, because Mom was so pretty and had such a wonderful smile and laugh and everybody liked her the minute they met her and she was never stupid or graceless or unkind.

All the other kids at school rolled their eyes when they talked about their mothers. "What's *her* problem?" they'd mutter, or, "Can you believe it? My mother wants to take me shopping! Like *she* knows how to pick out clothes."

Emma had always rolled her eyes, too, but she didn't mean it. *Her* mother had better taste than she did. When she picked Emma up somewhere and chatted for a minute with the other kids, the next day they'd be saying, "Your mom is *so-o* cool! I wish *my* mom was like her."

Emma had always been filled with pride

mixed with despair, because nobody ever told her she was cool, or they wished they were like *her*, and she knew in her heart they never would. If she grew up and got married and had kids, their friends wouldn't be saying, "Your mom is so cool!"

But now, she knew her mother was a big fat liar. Sometimes, maybe she could let herself hate Mom, not because she was jealous, but because Mom *deserved* it for letting her think she was so perfect.

Emma squeezed her pillows in her arms, feeling angry and giddy at the same time. She was glad she knew.

Aloud, she said, "My mother is a fake."

She loved the ring of it.

KATHLEEN SOUNDED BREATHLESS when she answered the phone.

"Did I get you from something?" Logan asked. He sat in his recliner, the remote control on his lap. First he'd muted the Mariner game, then turned it off. He couldn't call her while he watched baseball on the television. Not after her tale about her father.

"I just walked in the door," she admitted. "Okay, ran."

"Counseling," he remembered.

"Yes, another wonderful hour spent confronting my daughter. Except it wasn't an hour. As usual, she tore out in the middle."

"I'm sorry," he said quietly.

"No, it's okay. Tonight I asked for it, I guess. I got...frustrated and almost walked out myself. I've had a really lousy day."

"Do you want to tell me about it?" he asked. Only half joking, he added, "I could come over, if you need a shoulder to cry on."

There was a moment of silence, and he feared he'd taken too much for granted. She had friends, housemates, who would be happy to hear her troubles. Why would she choose him?

"Do you mean that? You'd go out in the rain, so I could blubber on you?" she asked.

His hand tightened on the receiver, but he kept his tone light. "I kinda like it when you do that."

She gave a funny, choked laugh. "I would love it if you'd come over. Jo is over at Ryan's, and Helen and Ginny went to a school open house. They just left. The house seems awfully empty."

"I don't mind being a stand-in," he said, meaning it.

"I brought home a pizza. I forgot everyone

else was going to be gone, so there's plenty. I can at least feed you."

He didn't have the heart to tell her he'd eaten. If you could call a sandwich slapped together in his kitchen eating.

"Deal. I'll be over in fifteen minutes."

Thanks to the rain, it actually took longer than that. Normally a patient driver, he got downright irritable when Seattle drivers panicked at rain-wet roads. It wasn't as if it never rained in the Pacific Northwest! But half the drivers slowed to a terrified crawl, and the other half didn't slow down at all, which meant that accidents blocked the freeways and clogged city streets. It took him ten minutes to get half a mile up 15th. Then he had to park two blocks from Kathleen's house.

"Sorry," he said, when Kathleen let him in her front door. He shoved his wet hair off his forehead. "Accident in Ballard. Bunch of idiots rear-ended each other. And now I'm dripping on your floor."

"Just a minute." She disappeared toward the downstairs bathroom, coming back with a plush towel. "Here. You are soaked."

He stripped off his slicker and then gave his hair a quick rub with the towel. "Thanks," he said, hanging it on the coatrack on top of his slicker.

"Come on into the kitchen. Let me reheat the pizza in the microwave."

Logan followed her, noting with amusement the fuzzy slippers and faded, sacky sweatshirt she wore with jeans. She hadn't dressed up for him tonight. Good sign or bad?

"Can I help?"

"No, it'll just take me a second." She waved toward the table. "Sit down. Iced tea? Milk? Pop?"

She set the microwave to humming, then got them both a pop. While she brought plates and silverware to the table, he took in her bare face and damp hair pulled carelessly back. The funny thing was, she looked more beautiful than ever to him. It was like a house just going up, the clean lines not yet cluttered with shutters or foundation shrubs or curtains fluttering in windows. She had the kind of face that would still be striking when she was eighty.

As she shuffled back to the table carrying a huge pizza on its cardboard tray, he decided he liked her better this way. She didn't intimidate him so much.

"Here," he said, standing and divesting her of the pizza. Sniffing, he came to the conclusion that he was hungry after all. "Smells great."

They ate, making minimal conversation. She did tell him about the first part of her day: the flat tire and the four expensive new ones.

"I forget to check tires or oil." She waved her slice of pizza, then had to take a quick bite to rescue the toppings. When she'd swallowed, she said, "That kind of stuff. I never do it. I go out and get behind the wheel and stick in the key. I just don't *think*. I've got to learn to. I'm lucky I wasn't on the freeway when I had a blowout."

"Yeah." Not liking the idea, he frowned. "Do you know how to check the oil?"

She made a face at him. "That much, I can manage."

"But you don't."

"Getting it on my schedule is another story," she admitted with a sigh.

Pushing away his plate, he said, "So what else went wrong with your day?"

"I had to throw away two pairs of panty hose." She laughed at his expression.

"They're expensive. Two pairs in one day i a minor to major glitch in the budget."

"O-kay."

Kathleen laughed again. "No, that's not th main reason my day stank. It was the tire and spending money I didn't have, and the we were short-staffed at work and I didn' get lunch, so I was cranky, and finally ther was Emma."

"No more cooperative than ever?"

Looking plainer than he'd ever seen her she said wearily, "No." Then she bit her li and jumped up. "I'll make coffee."

They took it to the living room, where sh curled up at one end of the sofa and he sat a the other. A half-grown orange kitten leape up to sprawl on the back of the sofa and con template Logan. The two eyes didn't seen to be quite pointing in the same direction which he found mildly unnerving.

"His eyes are a little odd," he said, nod ding at the kitten. "Was he born that way?"

Kathleen told him about Jo, Emma and Ginny stopping to pet kittens when they saw a Free Kitten sign and discovering that tiny Pirate had been attacked by a dog and had an eye hanging from the socket. "We spen a small fortune to save it," she said ruefully "and we don't even know if he can see out of it. He refuses to read an eye chart."

Logan chuckled. "I've heard cats do fine with only one eye."

"Yes, but the girls were both so upset, we thought we had to try." Her voice became slightly husky. "Emma hugged me. I figured it was worth every penny."

"More rewarding than new tires."

Her laugh came more naturally. "No kidding." She reached out and scratched Pirate, who began a deep rumble and leaped to her lap.

"So, did you get anywhere tonight, before your kid stomped out?" He figured she needed to tell him.

Kathleen gave him a look that echoed the cat's, curious and doubtful. "You don't even know Emma. You can't possibly want to hear every gory detail."

He was actually looking forward to meeting the infamous Emma. He had a feeling she was going to turn out to be a lot like her beautiful, stubborn, smart mom.

On the spot now, Logan shrugged and said, "She's important to you."

Kathleen's eyes suddenly brimmed with

tears and she dashed at them. "Every little thing sets me off."

Feeling useless, Logan said, "Including me. I'm sorry."

"No! You say the nicest things. Nobody…" She stopped. "It's been a long time…" Letting out a huff of breath, she tried to laugh. "Oh, dear. That sounds pathetic."

"I have a hard time believing men haven't said nice things to you in the past couple years. Probably a lot more gracefully than anything I've said to you."

This smile glowed, lighting her face in a way no makeup job could. "You're the only man I know who wouldn't have run as fast as he could in the other direction when I started sobbing that first day! You were my knight in shining armor."

"An unlikely-looking one." He rubbed a hand across his jaw, feeling a day's stubble. "I'm probably the troll."

"No." Her eyes were soft. "You're a good-hearted man, Logan Carr. I don't deserve to have your friendship."

Friendship wasn't what he was feeling. He hoped it wasn't all she wanted from him. Her kisses said it wasn't. Her common sense, though, probably dismissed any idea of romance with a homely working man. *His* common sense told him the knight-in-shining-armor luster would wear off once she didn't need someone to lean on.

But he wasn't willing to walk away without trying. Not given the emotions she stirred in him. With his record, he would probably never feel these things again. He might as well go for the ride.

He took a swallow of coffee and grabbed for a casual tone. "So, tell me about the session."

Stroking the kitten who wallowed on her lap, she kept her gaze downcast as she said, "I was tired, bedraggled and hungry." She half laughed. "The bedraggled part is obvious, right?"

He hadn't touched her yet tonight. Now he couldn't resist. He moved a cushion closer and slid his fingers into her hair. It felt… crunchy.

He must have looked his surprise, because she laughed. "That's what happens when you use gel and then get your hair wet over and over. I was heading for a nice hot bath when you called. I probably should have taken a quick one anyway, so I didn't shock you."

He traced her jaw. "Fishing for a compliment?"

She gave another snort of laughter. "This is not the moment when I'd fish, I assure you."

"Funny," Logan mused, "I was thinking earlier that I'd never seen you look more beautiful."

Her mouth actually dropped open. "What?"

"I figure this is how you'd look in the morning, when you first wake up and smile. You're a beautiful woman. You don't need fancying up."

She had another peculiar expression on her face. "See? There you go again, saying something so sweet, I can't even politely argue and say, 'Oh, no, I'm not.'"

His hand slid to her nape, which felt more delicate than seemed reasonable.

"Would you mind terribly if I kiss you, before everyone else walks in the door?"

"Speaking of polite," Kathleen murmured, as she turned her head so she could kiss his arm. She got out the, "Yes, you may," just as he lifted her chin and bent his head to capture her mouth.

Squished between the two people, poor Pirate thrashed and then shot away.

When Logan lifted his head long enough

to look down at her, his heart tightened like a fist in his chest. Color flagged her cheeks and her eyes glowed a deep blue, while her mouth was soft and rosy. "You're so pretty," he said roughly. "Why are you letting me kiss you?"

Hurt that he didn't think he'd inflicted flitted across her face. "Am I pretty? If so, it's just the outside. If you look deeper... No!" she cried, and pressed her mouth to his. Against it she whispered, "Don't look deeper. Please don't. Just kiss me, Logan."

What could he do but oblige, even though he knew he'd lie awake that night as he tried to puzzle out why this beautiful, classy woman disliked herself so much.

CHAPTER EIGHT

RESTLESS ON THURSDAY EVENING, unable to settle to a book or dreaming up a new soap, Kathleen finally realized that she missed Logan. She was tempted to call him, just to talk, but refused to let herself. This was ridiculous. She'd seen him three out of the past five days! Two weeks ago, she'd never met the man.

She did call Emma, who said sullenly, "How am I? How do you *think* I am? I'm in jail!"

Kathleen refused to lose her temper. "You knew the rules."

"Yeah, yeah. Do not pass go," she jeered. "Nobody asked me what *I* thought of the rules."

"That's because if you were given your way, you might have died by now." Kathleen sighed. "Let's not have the same argument again."

"I don't have anything else to talk about," Emma said disagreeably.

I do. I'm thinking of a wonderful man who has calluses on his hands and drives a big pickup truck. I must be crazy, but I can't seem to help myself.

Not the kind of thing you told your teenager under the best of circumstances. *I'm* dating *a wonderful man,* now that was something she was going to have to admit to sooner or later, unless she planned to drop him like a hot potato the day before Emma was released from Bridges.

"Ginny went home with a friend after school today," Kathleen said. "The girl's mother dropped her off afterward and said the two did a lot of giggling."

"Really?" In her surprise, Emma sounded like herself for a minute. "I didn't know she had a friend."

"Shelly just got transferred into Ginny's class. Somehow or other, the two hit it off."

"That's cool."

"Shelly is coming over to play on Saturday, apparently. Ginny can hardly wait to introduce her to Pirate."

Emma was quiet for a minute. "I miss Pirate."

"Last night, he started with Ginny, then visited all the rest of us for a few hours each. I woke up with him." Actually, she'd woken up *because* of him; he'd wrapped his long body around her head and was purring like a buzz saw in her ear.

"I wish I'd…" A stifled sound might have been a swallow or even a sob. "Can you bring him to visit me?"

"Unfortunately, I don't think he'd be allowed."

"I was joking!" snapped Emma, back to form. "He'd be scared anyway."

"Yes. He would." *Just like you are,* Kathleen thought sadly. She cleared her throat. "How's your studying going?"

"I don't get my math. The tutor here can't explain anything."

"Oh, dear. Shall I see if your teacher can call you?"

"It doesn't matter," her daughter muttered.

"Of course it matters. I'll leave him a message at school."

There was a long silence. "Well," Kathleen said heartily, "I guess I should say goodnight."

"Are you coming tomorrow night?"

Guilt swamped her. Tomorrow was Friday.

She was having Logan over for dinner and going to a Mariners game. She wasn't going to visit Emma.

Unless she canceled with Logan. She should cancel. He'd understand. She wasn't ready yet anyway. If Emma wanted to see her... Relief and disappointment warred within her.

"Not that I care," her oh-so-charming daughter declared.

"I'm afraid I'm not," Kathleen admitted. "I'll see you Saturday."

Another moment of silence. At last, sounding reluctant, as if she'd waged her own internal war, Emma asked, "Are you doing something tomorrow night?"

She cared about her mother's activities! Kathleen might have been more curious why Emma *had* asked if she weren't still conducting her own battle.

She could say, *Helen asked me to...* To do what? Kathleen thought frantically. Go to a movie? Sure. That was it. Make it casual. *Helen and I made some plans.*

Or...no. *I'm horribly behind on making soap. I just have to make a batch.*

No. Emma would think she was saying, *You've taken so much of my time, now you should feel guilty because I have to scramble to catch up.*

"Mom?"

"I'm going on a date," she said in a rush, then almost clapped her hand to her mouth. What had she done?

"A date?" her daughter repeated, on a rising note.

"Is that so awful?"

"You just never…" She skidded to a stop so fast the screech was all but audible. "You're going out with Dad, aren't you?"

Stunned, Kathleen said, "Your father? What on earth would make you think that?"

"'Cuz I'm the only reason you left him. And now I'm not around!"

Hearing the near-hysteria, Kathleen said hastily, "No, I'm not seeing your father. I will never date your father, I promise you. After what he did to you—" She bit off the rest. The therapist wanted her to let Emma remember good times with her dad, not just the bad. But she was horrified that Emma would ever, for a single second, think her mother would get back together with him.

Emma was quiet for a moment. "You're not lying?"

"No, I'm not lying!" Kathleen protested indignantly.

"Then…" The sixteen-year-old's voice was small, even scared. "Who are you going out with?"

"His name is Logan Carr." His name sounded respectable. New England, upper crust. The kind of man who had frequented the world in which Emma had grown up. "He's a cabinetmaker," Kathleen admitted. "You remember my plans for the kitchen? He's building those cabinets for us."

Trust Emma not to say, *Like I care what he does.* No. She felt compelled to jump right into her mother's deep pool of doubt and snobbery and splash right around.

"But…you're always saying stuff about Uncle Ryan. How he shouldn't have to work with his hands, if he's smart and ambitious, he should be running his business and telling other people what to do. And this guy just hammers wood together?"

"Cabinetmakers are considerably more skillful than that!" Kathleen snapped. "They don't 'hammer wood together.'"

"Neither does Uncle Ryan," her daughter pointed out, inarguably.

"I'm not marrying Logan! He seems nice,

and I thought we'd have fun. I don't care what he does for a living!"

"But…"

"Enough! I'm going on a date, whether you like it or not." She couldn't resist adding, "So there."

"Mom. You sound…"

Childish. That's what she sounded. Flushing with embarrassment, she said, "I remember how much you hated me dating before. I just figure I'm entitled."

In a stiff little voice, her daughter said, "Sure. Have fun. I gotta go. 'Night."

The click came before Kathleen got, "Good night," out of her mouth.

"YOU REALLY LIKE THIS GUY?" Jo asked seriously.

The two women were preparing dinner together, Kathleen tearing lettuce for a salad and Jo stirring an enormous pot of stroganoff.

"Oh, I hardly know yet…" The doorbell rang, and Kathleen jumped.

Jo laughed. "I think that's Ryan. I heard his truck."

Logan's probably sounded the same, Kathleen thought but didn't say. After all, she was dating a guy with a lot in common with her brother, who she had always secretly thought should be making more of himself. The trouble was, the secret contempt wasn't all that secret; Emma had caught her out a long time ago.

Kathleen wished she could loudly tell the world that she'd changed her mind about her brother, but how could she? She didn't want him to know how much she'd looked down on what he did in the first place—if he hadn't figured it out himself. Realizing how wrong she'd been was particularly galling now that she had to ask him for help on a regular basis. *And* now that she was dating a man in the same line of work.

Hearing voices in the front hall, Kathleen reached for a cucumber. If Logan was here, he'd find her. Why get nervous?

"It's the first time you've dated since I've known you," Jo continued. She dug in a lower cupboard for a pan, then ran water into it to boil for noodles.

Cucumber peels curled and dropped to the cutting board. "Emma," Kathleen said concisely. "She was jealous. Also..." She dropped the peeler and picked up a paring knife. "You're younger than I am. Decent, single men in their mid-thirties and forties are about as common as—" she groped for a comparison "—as snowy owls. If they're not married, they're jerks, or they're self-pitying. Temptation does not trip me up often, believe me."

Jo threw back her head and laughed. "I may be a little younger than you are, but not *that* much younger. I could hardly believe somebody hadn't already snapped up Ryan."

"Well, somebody did. She was just idiot enough to let him go."

"Yes, but again." Jo lifted the lid of her stroganoff and peered in. "Wouldn't you think women would have lined up to ask Ryan out, the minute they knew he was divorced?"

"They probably did." Kathleen added chopped green onion to the salad. "He's always been…oblivious." She shook her head. "Even I, big sister, could see that he was a hunk. Girls swarmed him, and he hardly noticed. You should be big-time flattered that he *really* noticed you."

"Oh, I count my blessings." Jo gave a soft, dreamy smile. Then her expression became considering and she cocked her head. "You know, I don't hear the kids. Maybe that wasn't Ryan."

Nervousness fluttered again in Kathleen's stomach, and she realized with astonishment that she was fussing over what everyone else would think about Logan. Never mind that they'd all met him! But this was different. He was here for dinner as her date. This was like bringing a guy home for your parents to inspect.

The doorbell rang again, and Jo laughed. "Well, I guess it doesn't matter. Sounds like everyone's here now."

"And my salad is done." Kathleen frowned. "I wish the table was bigger."

"We'll be cozy." Jo gave her a quick, unexpected hug and murmured in her ear, "I like him." Then, more loudly, she said, "Logan, hi. And Tyler. Where's your sister?"

Salad bowl in her hands, Kathleen turned. Logan looked…well, not handsome, but almost, his hair damp from a recent shower and slicked back, his long-sleeved navy polo shirt emphasizing the power in his shoulders.

"Hi," she said, a little shyly.

He gave her a smile that stole her breath. Maybe he was handsome.

"Aunt Kathleen!" Nine-year-old Tyler,

small for his age, gave her a hug. "Dad says Emma is in the hospital. He says maybe we can go see her."

"On Sunday there's open visiting, if you want to go." She smiled crookedly at her brother when he came into the kitchen. "I know Emma would love it. Right now she'd enjoy seeing you guys a lot more than me."

Her nephew's forehead furrowed. "Why?"

"She's mad at me for checking her into the hospital," Kathleen explained. She looked over his head. "Where's Melissa?"

"She went looking for Ginny."

Melissa, almost a teenager, could be a brat, but like Emma she seemed to feel real affection for six-year-old Ginny, the mouse.

Or, hummingbird, as Ryan called her.

Eventually they all sat down to eat at the table. Even with its one leaf in, it sat only six and here there were eight around it. Elbows bumped and Ginny promptly knocked over her mother's water. Kathleen and Jo played waitress and then jumped up to offer seconds, because there wasn't room in the middle for serving bowls.

Kathleen was very conscious of Logan, so close beside her that his thigh pressed against hers. Initially he nodded and smiled and let the conversation wash by him, but gradually, she noticed, he joined in, his laugh becoming more spontaneous.

He remained seemingly unfazed when, midmeal, Ryan began not so subtly to grill him.

"Kathleen tells me you're building her cabinets right now. That was mighty quick."

With the fork partway to his mouth, Logan said briefly, "Had a cancellation."

"Uh-huh." Her brother's tone wasn't unfriendly, but it was definitely suspicious. "Do you have kids?"

"Nope." Appearing placid, Logan continued eating. Apparently the two men hadn't gotten personal when they worked together, as he didn't seem surprised by the question.

"Divorced?"

"Wife died."

Everybody momentarily froze. Glances at Helen, who had blanched. But she looked steadily at Logan and said in a soft voice, "I'm sorry. My husband died last year. I know how hard it is."

When Helen and Ginny moved in last August, Kathleen had wondered if she'd made a mistake agreeing to rent to Helen. She hadn't planned on a child, for one thing.

Especially not one who was a sad shadow of a normal six-year-old. Ginny had clung to her mother, even waiting in the hall outside the bathroom when Helen went in. Helen had seemed perpetually exhausted, her eyes often puffy from crying. She couldn't make decisions and was so meek Kathleen wanted to shake her.

But over the fall and winter she had slowly emerged from her grief. Becoming the marketing partner in Kathleen's budding soap business was building her confidence in amazing ways.

And Ginny... Well, shy Ginny was blossoming, too. At the moment, she whispered something to Tyler beside her and then giggled. The reference to her father's death had apparently passed by her, thankfully.

Ryan must have figured the pause had been of a decent duration, because he resumed the attack. "Business good?"

"Considering the economy."

Kathleen began to enjoy the mounting frustration she saw on her brother's face. Logan's terse but civil answers were failing to either satisfy Ryan or provide fuel for his suspicions that Logan was somehow unworthy of Ryan's sister.

Kathleen wasn't all that certain who was seducing whom. After all, she'd been the one to fling herself into a strange man's arms, hadn't she? Of course, he'd taken the voluntary step across the door jamb.

But she wasn't offering any of those details to Ryan, either.

Jo had baked blueberry pie earlier, and after they'd all had slices, Logan lifted a brow at Kathleen.

"If we're going to catch that game, we'd better get going."

"Oh, right." Guiltily Kathleen looked at the mountain of dirty dishes. "I should…"

Helen, collecting pie plates from the table, saw her expression. "Don't be silly. Go. You and Jo cooked, the kids and I'll clean."

Tyler and Melissa groaned.

Their father cleared his throat and they subsided. Then he grinned. "I didn't cook, either. Sign me up."

"See?" Jo said to Kathleen, to everyone else's puzzlement.

"I did train him right, didn't I?" Kathleen responded smugly.

Her brother elbowed her on his way by. To Logan, with the first trace of friendliness he'd shown, he said, "Watch it with her. Give her half a chance, and you'll be mumbling, 'Yes, ma'am, no, ma'am,' before you know it."

"You *needed* bossing!" she declared tartly, sticking out her tongue.

Laughing, Logan took her arm and steered her toward the front door. "Thanks for dinner," he said over his shoulder, for probably the third time. "Jo, that was great."

At the front door, Kathleen pulled a cream-colored, Shaker-stitch cardigan on over her T-shirt and watched while Logan shrugged into his jacket. Butterflies fluttered in her stomach again.

You're not committed to anything but a baseball game, she told herself sternly.

But when their eyes met, a tingle ran through her. She was ready for more kissing. So ready. If he suggested skipping the game...

But he didn't. He was somewhat quiet during the drive, but once he'd parked the pickup, he tucked her hand securely into the crook of his arm as they started across the huge parking lot. "I like your family."

"My family?" His forearm was thick and strong under her fingers. She matched her steps to his and let their hips bump. "Oh. You mean Ryan and the kids."

"And Jo and Helen and Ginny. They're family of a kind, aren't they?"

She remembered thinking in the emergency room how much like family they'd become. "Mmm," she agreed. "It's hard to believe sometimes that I didn't know any of them a year ago."

"Now Jo will be your sister-in-law, and Helen's your business partner."

She made a face. "If the business goes anywhere."

"Oh ye of little faith…"

Surprised, Kathleen looked up at him. "How funny. My mother said that. Every time I'd doubt my ability to do something, she'd say, 'Oh ye of little faith.' It didn't sound like her, so I asked her one time and she said she guessed *her* mom had said that when she was growing up."

"I take it she encouraged you to make something of yourself?"

She felt an odd pang. "Yes. Yes, she did. She wanted me to have better opportunities than she'd had. She never knew how to do anything but waitress. I remember her taking off her shoes one night and showing me how swollen her feet were, and how she was getting varicose veins. 'Sit behind a desk,' she said." Kathleen fell silent, ashamed as she was every time she thought of her mother's love and support and her own embarrassment at what her mother was.

"How did she die?"

"Heart. She ignored symptoms until she had a massive heart attack. She was only fifty-eight."

The couples and families pouring toward the stadium converged in a line at the gate. Half the crowd wore Mariner hats or sweatshirts; a few boys and men carried baseball gloves in hopes of snagging a home run or foul ball.

With the rain having let up today, the roof was open to a black sky. High clouds kept even the moon from peeking through. The steep banks of seats and the field below were lit so brightly, Kathleen imagined the space shuttle crew peering down at the burst of white light and speculating on the cause.

The crowd, good-sized with early season optimism, rustled and murmured expectantly, then roared with approval when their team ran onto the field.

The season before, Kathleen had actually

listened to enough games on the radio to know who was who and why this pitcher was on the mound and who was probably warming up in the bullpen and why the crowd exploded with pleasure every time the right fielder waved good-naturedly.

In Logan's company, she settled back to enjoy the game. His occasional commentary and knowledgable answers to her questions made her suspect he was more of a fan than he'd admitted.

"Have you ever played?" she asked, between innings when the teams were trading places on the field.

"In high school. I, uh, play on a slow-pitch team now, just for fun." He sounded embarrassed admitting it, as if a grown man shouldn't play games.

"Really?" She should have guessed that he must be active in some way, to keep muscles as impressive as his. "What position?"

"Catcher. That's what I was in high school, too." He gazed down at the field, expression reflective. "I was actually drafted by the Angels, but I knew I didn't have what it takes to make it to the big time. I'm too slow."

"Catchers usually are solidly built, like you," she realized aloud.

He gave her a rueful glance. "You mean, built like a fireplug."

"You're too big to compare to a fireplug. You're more like, um, a Mac truck. Or a draft horse."

"Right. Stocky and slow."

"Strong," she corrected, bringing a glint to his eyes and a quirk to his mouth that showed appreciation and awareness.

"Is it fun? Playing slow-pitch?"

"Yeah." He grinned. "We're good friends, competitive in an easygoing way." His hand closed around hers. "You'll have to come to a game someday."

She loved the way he took her hand, so naturally, and then held it clasped on his thigh. "I'd like that."

She imagined herself in the bleachers with a few other girlfriends and wives, cheering on their men. She'd never done anything like that. Ian's sports were tennis and racquetball, played at his club.

"Our first game is a few weeks away. We just started practice last month."

At the roar of the crowd, she looked down at the field where a Texas Ranger had popped up a foul ball. The Mariner catcher flung off his mask and backed up, glove in the air. The ball dropped neatly into it.

The Mariners won easily, fueling hopes that this season would be different than last. Joining the exodus, Logan led the way. When they reached the stairs, he reached behind him and put Kathleen's hand on his belt.

"Don't lose me," he ordered, using his big shoulder to wedge his way into the thick clot of humanity climbing the steep concrete steps.

She liked the way he kept glancing back to check on her, and the fact that his arm closed snugly around her the minute they reached the concourse and she could come up beside him.

Ian hadn't been much for touching. He'd held her close on the dance floor, where she'd enjoyed some of her favorite moments with her husband. He was graceful, masterful and occasionally dramatic, dipping her outrageously or suddenly kissing her with deep, demanding passion.

But he'd never taken her hand when they walked side by side. If he laid a hand on the small of her back or put his arm around her at a party, it was because he thought another man was flirting with his wife and he wanted to assert possession. He didn't like to snuggle on the sofa to watch TV or read. In the first flush of marriage, Kathleen had expected to sleep with their limbs entangled, his heartbeat beneath her ear, his breath warm in her hair.

All it had taken was an irritable, "How can I sleep with your elbow in my ribs?" for her to learn to lie quietly on her own side of the huge bed.

She'd never thought of herself as missing anything as simple as casual touches. That wasn't the kind of need she allowed herself. She had worked too hard, for too many years, to project an image of herself as cool, sophisticated, well-bred. In her circle, not many marriages seemed happy at all. She hadn't known a woman who cuddled openly with her husband, or walked hand in hand with him. Any craving she had for affection was satisfied by her relationship with her small daughter, who snuggled with complete confidence into Mommy's arms at any excuse.

Where had that child gone? Kathleen wondered with sudden despair.

And how had she deceived herself for so long that she loved Ian and was loved by him?

Kathleen felt as if she and Logan walked alone in the midst of the crowd, a bubble separating them from the people jostling toward the exits. Within it, they were quiet.

At the truck, he unlocked her side, closing the door when she was inside and circling the hood.

"That was fun," she said brightly, the minute he got in.

"I'm glad you enjoyed it." His voice was deep and *comfortable*. As he inserted the key, he asked, "Do you want to come to my place for coffee?"

The caffeine coupled with her already jangled nerves would send her through the roof. "I don't dare have any this late."

Logan nodded and turned the key. The engine started with a throaty roar. But he made no move to back out and join the stream of vehicles creeping toward exits.

She looked directly at him for the first time. "I don't know how I ended up here, with you."

He turned his head and gave her a crooked smile. "For once in my life, I got pushy, I guess. Maybe lately you've been a little easier than usual to push around. Seems that's what your brother's afraid of."

Kathleen laughed. "He did come on strong, didn't he?"

"If I had a sister, I'd do the same." He hesitated. "So, shall I take you home now? There's no hurry, you know."

On an impulse that was foreign to her, she unbuckled her seat belt, leaned over and pecked him on the cheek. "I know there's no hurry. But I think I'd like to go home with you for that cup of coffee."

His big hand left the steering wheel to close around hers, strong and comforting.

His house was built on a quiet side street. The driveway led between retaining walls into a basement level garage, just big enough for his pickup. The house, which he'd told her was built in the 1940s or '50s, was much smaller than hers.

"My panel truck is out back," Logan said, turning off the ignition. "I have an alley entrance."

"Can I see my cabinets?" she asked.

"Sure." He pushed a button and the garage door whirred shut behind them as they both got out.

His workshop took up most of a basement that must be a thousand square feet, Kathleen guessed. It was scrupulously neat and brightly lit. Steel gleamed and even the floor was swept clean, the only sawdust in an open plastic garbage can.

Verging, she knew, on obsessively tidy herself, she appreciated the order he maintained, tools on pegboards in spots sized specifically for them and no other, saw blades oiled and wood satin smooth.

Her cabinets were unfinished but taking shape, the wood pale when she stroked it, but almost silky from sanding, the joints clean and the proportions balanced.

"They're going to be beautiful," she said, admiring.

Leaning against a vast table saw—at least, she thought that's what it was—Logan watched her. "I do my best."

His voice was a little husky. She met his eyes. He straightened, and she took a step. Then maybe another, and another, she didn't know, but they met, his arms closing around her, his mouth coming down on hers sweetly.

CHAPTER NINE

KATHLEEN KNOCKED ON EMMA'S door and got in return the familiar, grudging, "Come in."

It was three weeks later, and the teenager had made the room more distinctly hers in that time. Pictures of guys she considered "hot," cut from magazines, were taped to the walls, along with others that seemed random: a photo of a rosebud, a Bart Simpson poster, an art-style portrait of an anonymous woman sitting with head bent and arms and legs crisscrossed. All were from her room at home, brought by Kathleen on demand. Emma's schoolbooks littered the desk and bedside table, and she hastily shoved a journal out of sight under a binder as her mother entered.

"I didn't know you were coming today." Her tone was an accusation.

"I've been talking to Sharon and Dr. Tisdale." Kathleen sat at the foot of the bed. "They think you're ready to come home."

Emma's face lit. "Really?" Then a mask covered the bright light of happiness. "Whatever."

Why, Kathleen wondered, was she so determined to be unhappy? Emma looked so much better than she had a month ago, her hair shinier, her skin flushed with color. Her hands weren't so icy cold. She was still frighteningly thin, but she might pass in a crowd as a pretty, delicately built girl.

Kathleen watched her daughter's face. "Do *you* think you're ready?"

"To be good?" Emma mocked.

"To continue eating without a monitor. To live," Kathleen said quietly.

The teenager rolled her eyes. "It's not like I don't have *you* to tell me what I'm doing wrong all the time."

Once, Kathleen had enjoyed every minute spent with her daughter. Now, she had an ache in her chest that only became more painful with each barb.

"No." She made herself stay completely calm and in control, giving away no indication that the barbs had drawn blood. "I won't monitor your eating, Emma. You know that. Sometimes I couldn't hide my worry. Probably I'll slip again in the future. I'm your

mother. How can I help it? But these are
choices you have to make for yourself."

"Sure."

Ignoring the sullen taunt, Kathleen continued, "I won't let you become dangerously
thin. I'll check you back in here in a heartbeat, if you start losing weight and Sharon
recommends it. But day to day, I'm going to
do my best to pay no attention to your eating.
If we fight, it'll be about other things."

Emma looked at her sidelong, betrayed by
curiosity. "Like what other things?"

"Your tone when you talk to me. I don't
think asking you to be polite is unreasonable."

Emma bent her head, so that the curtain
of fine blond hair shielded her face.

"I don't want you stomping out anymore
without telling me where you're going. It
scares me when hours go by and I have no
idea where you are."

"I just go for walks," her daughter muttered.

"Seattle isn't a small town. It's not safe for
you to wander for hours by yourself."

Emma flung her head up and stared defiantly at her mother. "So now I'm going to be
under house arrest?"

"No." Kathleen willed herself to gaze back without letting frustration or anger show. "I'm asking you to show some common sense and some consideration for me and for Jo, Helen and Ginny."

Eyes dark with resentment, Emma said, "And *him,* I suppose."

"You know, you might like Logan."

"What difference does it make?"

"Quite a bit, to me." Kathleen dared to reach for her daughter's hand, feeling its fragility but also renewed strength and warmth. "I love you, Emma."

Emma sat unmoving so long, on a sharp bite of grief Kathleen let go of her hand.

"I love you, too, Mom."

For a moment, Kathleen thought she was hearing things. "What?"

Emma's eyes were huge and blue and pleading. One crystalline tear trembled on a lash. "I do love you. Even when I'm all mixed up and mad."

Feeling the sting of tears herself, Kathleen leaned forward and gave her daughter a quick hug. "I'm glad," she whispered. "If I was always sure of that, it would help."

"Sometimes I think maybe you wish you didn't have me."

Kathleen sat back, disentangling this hasty, mumbled sentence. "What on earth would make you think something that silly?" she asked in amazement. "I love you more than anybody or anything in the whole world."

Emma stole a glance at her. "Even when I'm not very nice?"

Kathleen gave a tremulous smile. "Even then."

"When I was fat, I embarrassed you."

"You never embarrassed me."

She wished she could be sure that wasn't a lie, that she could honestly say she'd been proud to introduce Emma as her daughter no matter what. She thought it was the truth, even if she'd had a few pangs when friends' daughters were prettier or more graceful or accomplished at some given age.

Why had she wasted so much energy on unspoken, perhaps even one-sided competitions? Was she so insecure that she always had to win, always had to be part of the in-crowd, had to be the best, had to *have* the best, whether it was husband, child or home?

Kathleen wished she'd channeled all that drive into something more fruitful. When younger, she could have attended law school or gone into business. She could have accomplished something, instead of spending her days worrying about image.

The sad thing was, she didn't know if those inner battles had been won. Did she still care?

Enough that she would turn her back on what she had with Logan?

She shelved the self-doubt and smiled at Emma. "So? Are you ready to come home?"

"Like...*now?*"

"Why not?"

"Cool!" Emma flung herself at her mother, gave her a quick, hard hug, then leaped to her feet. "Let me take my stuff off the wall. And I have to pack."

Kathleen stood. "I need to go down to the office and do some paperwork. Take your time. I'll help when I get back."

Emma must have spun through the room like a whirlwind, because her suitcase and book bag were bulging when Kathleen returned, and Emma sat waiting at the foot of the bed.

Picking up the suitcase, Kathleen asked, "Any goodbyes you need to say?"

"I already did. There are only a couple girls I liked that much."

"Will you be glad to be back at school?" Kathleen asked, as they walked down the hall.

Emma's brightness dimmed. "I like class, but..." Her voice flattened. "Yeah. Sure."

"Well, Ginny can hardly wait to see you."

"Really?" The light came back on. "That's cool. I'll be glad to see her, too."

A few girls and women nodded or smiled and said, "Bye, Emma," or, "Good luck."

Emma's standard response was, "Yeah, see ya."

Kathleen hoped she wouldn't, not if that meant she had to check into Bridges again.

On the drive home, Emma studied the passing buildings and pedestrians as if she'd never seen them before. "Just think," she marveled, "what it would be like if you'd been in jail for, like, twenty *years,* and suddenly you were out?"

"Very, very weird."

"*I* feel weird." She was quiet for several blocks. "Is he coming over tonight?"

Kathleen's stomach knotted again. "I didn't ask him. This is your homecoming. I figured I'd let you choose the dinner menu, and we can even go to a movie or something if you'd like."

"Can I cook dinner?" Emma asked eagerly. "I haven't cooked for ages."

Kathleen had never been able to understand how Emma could spend several hours preparing dinner and not eat a bite, but she claimed to love to cook. The therapist had said this wasn't uncommon, that anorexics were, despite—or because of—their reluctance to eat, obsessed with food. They thought about food, dreamed about food, worried about food. Cooking was a way to handle it, look at it, smell it, without partaking. It was also a way to disguise how little they ate.

"I sampled so much I'm not hungry," was Emma's standard excuse, as she avidly watched other people eat.

Kathleen didn't know if her eager desire to cook dinner tonight was a good sign or bad. But she had resolved to let Emma take responsibility for her own problem, so she said after only the briefest hesitation, "If you really want to. As long as you'll let me help. Do we need to stop at the store?"

"I want to make spaghetti. Also—" Emma sounded hesitant "—maybe I could pick out some stuff just for me? I mean, not that I wouldn't share, but you know. Food I'll eat."

"Sure. Whole Foods?"

"Cool!" Emma declared happily.

Kathleen didn't go there often for general shopping, because the prices weren't the lowest, but the produce was luscious and the selection unusual. Emma loved the store, which specialized in organic and vegetarian foods and toiletries.

In harmony, they pushed the cart around, Emma frowning in long concentration over cereals and soups before making selections. Kathleen assumed she was studying the caloric and fat contents, but she didn't comment or try to hurry her.

"Can I make the spaghetti with soy instead of hamburger?" Emma asked. "I especially hated eating the meat. I think I'm going to try to be vegetarian."

"You know, you'll have to work at getting enough protein and the right nutrients—"

"I know, I know!" Emma interrupted. "I talked to the dietician at Bridges about it, and she gave me a book to read. But I really like the idea."

It would give her an excuse all too often not to eat dinner, unless the whole household went vegetarian, but Kathleen figured the first day was too soon to break her resolve.

"Fine," she said mildly. "It'll mean you making your own dinner sometimes."

"That's okay. I thought I'd pick out some frozen stuff here."

Kathleen gulped at the total the checker rang up, used her debit card and waited apprehensively for Approved to appear on the small screen. Ian's child-support check would be welcome this month.

The remainder of the drive home was short. They'd barely pulled into the driveway when the front door flew open and Ginny came racing down the porch steps.

"Emma!" she cried.

Emma met her partway up the concrete stairs carved through the retaining wall. The two girls hugged and, chattering, came down to help carry groceries.

With big eyes, Ginny gazed at the sea of grocery bags. "Ohh," she said happily, peering in. "I like angel food cake."

"I thought we'd celebrate," Kathleen said. "Here. Is this bag too heavy for you?"

The six-year-old shook her head and, accompanied by Emma carrying her suitcase, began trudging up the steps. They were met by Jo, coming down.

She hugged and kissed Emma, too, then

arrived at the car to blink in surprise at the contents of the trunk. "Wow! You went to town."

Kathleen sighed. "It seemed like the thing to do. Emma wanted to pick out food she's comfortable eating, and everything looked so good. You may have to buy the toilet paper this week."

Poking inside a bag, Jo said, "If I can have some of these cookies, toilet paper is a small price to pay."

"Needless to say," Kathleen confessed, "Emma didn't pick those out."

Jo laughed. "I guessed."

As the two women, fully loaded, climbed the steps, Jo asked, "Is Logan coming to dinner?"

Tartly, Kathleen said, "Why does everybody assume...?"

"Everybody?" Jo glanced over her shoulder. "Oh. Emma."

"Yes, Emma! I haven't even told her that much about him, and she's braced for a wedding! It's not like I'm that serious."

"Aren't you?" Jo murmured, just as they crossed the threshold, ensuring that Kathleen couldn't argue.

Helen had appeared from the bathroom,

hair wrapped in a towel, to greet Emma. Now they all put away the groceries and talked. Emma had already found Pirate, who draped contentedly across her thin shoulders.

"He missed me," she declared, when she and her mother found themselves briefly apart from the others.

"Looks that way," Kathleen agreed.

Emma looked around at her bustling "family" and said, "Everybody is acting like they missed me, too."

"They did." Kathleen hugged her carefully and kissed the top of first Emma's head, then Pirate's. "*We* did."

"Good." The teenager nodded with blatant satisfaction. "It feels just like always. I don't want anything to change. Not *ever*. Except I guess Jo can marry Uncle Ryan, 'cuz then she'll be family and that's okay. But Helen and Ginny and us can stay like this forever. Right?"

Kathleen knew a pointed message when she heard one. She also recognized the frightened desire to hold on to the familiar.

"I don't know about forever," she said lightly. "You, kiddo, will be graduating from high school in two years and going on to college. Life doesn't stand still. But for now, I think we're all pretty happy with the way things are."

It wasn't a lie, not quite. She *was* happy, when Emma was being her sweet self. But Logan was part of "the way things are" for her now, and Emma didn't want to acknowledge it.

And what if Logan wanted more?

Quelling a small burst of panic, Kathleen grabbed empty grocery bags and stuffed them in the drawer where they were kept.

She was worrying much, much too soon, she reassured herself. He might not want more. She might not. She probably wouldn't.

The "probably" made her stop, her hand on the drawer handle.

Why "probably"? Because she wasn't in love?

Or because a mere cabinetmaker was okay for a boyfriend, but not a husband?

Wishing she didn't even have to ask herself such questions, she buried the creeping shame and self-doubt.

"Well, Chef Emma, shall we get started with dinner preparations?"

THIS FIRST MEETING would be interesting, Logan figured. Not since he was sixteen himself had he cared what a teenager thought of him. This particular teenage girl, though, might eventually cast a deciding vote. Since the outcome of that vote had begun to matter a whole lot to him, it would have been nice to know if there was anything at all he could do to sway her opinion.

Or would Miss Emma Monroe hate any man her mother dated?

It was Tuesday night and a dinner invitation had been tendered. Logan had talked to Kathleen several times since Emma was sprung on Saturday, and she'd sounded… lighter. Excited.

"She actually is eating! Not just when someone's watching. The other day, I came down and I know she didn't hear me. She was eating a bowl of cereal just like anyone else. I had to back out and get a grip on myself before I went in the kitchen and pretended I didn't notice."

"Good for you."

"Do you think?"

What did he know about raising a kid? Nothing. Nada. Zip. But he did know that compelling someone else's behavior was difficult. And kids seemed programmed to rebel, from the Terrible Twos to the teen years.

"She's being so loving," Kathleen had said, during another conversation. "So sweet. It's like all our arguments never happened. I worry this is…oh, a honeymoon period. You know? Things don't turn around that fast."

He didn't know what to do but advise her to enjoy it while it lasted. Logan just hoped he wasn't the cause of the first rupture.

Tonight he had to park a block and a half away from the brick house the three women shared. On his walk back, he stumbled several times when the sidewalk buckled over tree roots. The streetlights seemed far apart, the drizzly night dark. He hunched inside his coat against the dampness.

The house was brightly lit and welcoming. Looking up at it, he realized ruefully how eager he was, how long these past four days had seemed. His own house felt cold and empty now when Kathleen wasn't there. He wondered how he'd endured years of solitude. Even aside from how hungry he was to be with Kathleen, he liked coming here, with the lively talk, laughter, smell of lavender and cinnamon and kiwi all mixed together, the shy little kid and the clatter of feet on the old staircase. It felt homelike.

Ringing the doorbell tonight was the first time since that introductory dinner that he'd been nervous. He braced himself when he heard the dead bolt unlatch and the door opened, but it was Jo, wearing sweats and fuzzy socks, who let him in.

"Hey," she said with a friendly smile. Over her shoulder, she called, "Kathleen! Logan's here."

Kathleen called back, "Send him into the kitchen."

"She's cooking," Jo told him.

"Smells good."

Seeing right through his lie, Jo laughed. "She was experimenting with some bizarre combinations of essential oils last night. Helen and I nixed the idea the minute we got home. Unfortunately, it lingers. Dinner really does smell good, when you get close enough."

"Ah," he said in relief. "I thought maybe we were having squid or seaweed or…" His imagination failed him. The smell was both pungent and distinctly unpleasant.

Kathleen looked cute with an apron tied around her neck and waist over a long-sleeved pink T-shirt and chinos. She wore clogs. "Hi," she said, coming to kiss him on the cheek, one hand in an oven mitt and the other holding a spatula. "Dinner will be ready in just a few minutes."

"What is it?" he asked, trying surreptitiously to look past her.

"Southwestern wraps. Black beans and rice and jack cheese. They're good."

He nodded. "Emma home?"

"Up in her room." She made a face. "I'm sure she knows you're here. She has excellent radar. She's just waiting to make a casual, I-don't-care entrance."

She had her daughter pegged. Exactly five minutes later, Emma sauntered into the kitchen.

Logan was leaning against the kitchen counter, sipping a glass of iced tea and contemplating his own cabinets, installed in the far corner. They looked good, if he did say so, as long as he zeroed in on them and didn't widen the lens to include the rest of the kitchen with shabby, painted cabinets and peeling vinyl.

Kathleen was spooning rice onto tortillas when the teenager walked in.

"You look just like your mother," he exclaimed, startled by the resemblance. The minute the words were out, he wished them back. Maybe that was the wrong thing to say to a teenager with mixed feelings about her mother.

A flash of…something showed on her face. Pleasure? Irritation. Whatever it was, she shut it down right away and gave him a cool look.

"You don't have to say that. Mom likes you anyway."

He felt Kathleen turning and hoped she wouldn't jump in to rescue him even if he did already feel like a dumb oaf.

"I'm sorry. Don't you like the comparison? Your mom is beautiful, and you are, too."

The girl sneered. "Right. Sure."

"That's not very polite," Kathleen said mildly. "'Thank you' is always an appropriate response to a compliment."

"He's complimenting *you,* not me."

"Actually, I was talking to you." Logan looked levelly at her. "I mean what I say."

"Whatever."

He could feel tension radiating from Kathleen, who mechanically continued dinner preparations, the spoon whacking the bowl.

So much for making conversation with

Emma. He couldn't think of a thing to say *So, do you like school?* He'd seem like any other idiot adult.

"What do you think of my cabinets?" he asked, nodding at them.

She gave them a disdainful glance "They're okay."

Now he was ticked. "Okay?" he repeated "Have you really looked? Come here."

He'd caught her by surprise. She actually did follow him to the soap-making corner.

"Feel this wood," he ordered.

She hesitantly reached out and ran her fingers over the satiny surface.

"Open and close a few doors. Try the drawers."

Arms crossed, he loomed over her until she did. The drawers floated, the cabinet doors sprang silently shut.

"Study these joints," he said, running his own finger over a dovetailed corner. "These cubbies are exactly the size and shape your mother ordered."

Clearly she felt his pricked pride, because her sidelong glances had become wary.

"Did you know the kitchen floor slope slightly? Half an inch from here to here." He pointed. "A marble would roll away. Ceil ing isn't level, either. They never are in old houses. Can you tell, looking at these cabinets?"

Wordlessly she shook her head.

"Have you ever tried woodworking?"

"No-o," Emma admitted.

"That isn't true," her mother said behind her. "Jo let you make some cuts with the jigsaw when we were doing the downstairs bathroom."

"Oh." Her face flushed. "Yeah. It was, um, hard."

"Compare these cabinets to the ready-made ones in your bathrooms."

"I remember we had to cover the crack around the outside with molding," she admitted. "'Cuz it got really wide near the floor. Like the wall, um, bowed."

"It probably does. Have you ever used a level?"

"Yeah, Uncle Ryan has let me."

"You ought to wander around with one. You'd start to think you're in one of those carnival houses, where mirrors make everything you see deceptive. Here, you think you're seeing straight, but you're not."

She actually looked interested. "Really?"

"It's why working on old houses is such

a challenge. Replacing a window, for example. You find out the right top corner is two inches lower than the left corner. What do you do? Put the new one in the same way? Carve up the wall, even if it means replacing siding or crumbling plaster? Or figure, Oh, well, and live with it?"

Her brow puckered. "I'd go, Oh, well."

"Mmm-hmm. Except then, the blinds you install don't work right, because they're not hanging straight. Or you've chosen a wallpaper with stripes, and are those going to make it obvious that something's off."

"Pick flowers," she decided.

He grinned. "Actually, that's what I'd do, too. Part of the charm of an old house is the inconsistencies. One bedroom door is taller than the others in the hall. Why? You pull up vinyl and carpet. Are you going to find the same kind of wood floor throughout the house? Probably not. Rooms have weird nooks that seem to serve no purpose. Doorknobs don't match."

"But it means your house, and your bedroom, are special," she said, obviously intrigued with the idea.

"One of a kind," he agreed. "Unless your old house was once company housing."

She'd never heard the term. He explained how large companies had once provided housing for their workers, rather like the military did on bases, and built row upon row of identical houses.

"For example, have you ever gone over to the Peninsula? Port Gamble is a perfect example. Great old houses that are all exactly alike, if you look past the paint jobs, a few added porches or gingerbread." He shrugged. "Even with those, carpenters were more seat-of-the-pants than they are now. Your materials didn't all come from a factory. You might even be planing boards yourself."

"I hate to interrupt," Kathleen said a little dryly, "but dinner is served."

He blinked. "Oh. Sorry. I got carried away."

"That's okay," Emma surprised him by saying. "It was interesting."

He gave her a rueful grin. "Thanks. Shall we go eat?"

She wrinkled her nose and said in a low voice, "I hope it tastes better than that... *smell.*"

"Me, too," he murmured.

They exchanged conspiratorial smiles and went to the table.

The wrap was good. So good, he had a second one. Kathleen carefully didn't look her daughter's way, but Logan did, and saw that Emma was nibbling. By his standards, she didn't eat much before she declared she was full, but then she was a tiny thing.

Conversation ran the gamut, as usual, from teasing about Kathleen's noxious soap experiment to grumbles about tomorrow's Spanish test—that was Emma—to Ginny's awe at a substitute teacher who said he skydived for fun.

"He says floating down is the best feeling ever," she reported. "Once, he said he met an eagle prac'ly eye to eye." As if somebody had expressed doubt, she added firmly, "That's what he said."

"I've skydived before," Logan said.

Heads all turned. "Really?" Kathleen asked.

"Yeah, a friend talked me into it. To tell you the truth, it scared the—" he cleared his throat "—it scared me. Stepping out of that plane was one of the hardest things I've ever done. I don't think I could have made myself if I hadn't been so depressed about my wife's death, I didn't care all that much if something did go wrong." Maybe he shouldn't have admitted that, Logan thought, seeing the way the girls' eyes widened. He hurried and said, "But once the chute opened, it was pretty incredible. It's just you and the wind and the world spread out below. You feel like you're moving so slowly—floating—until you wham down on the ground. I ended ingloriously by spraining my ankle."

They all laughed, but continued to gaze at him with gratifying respect.

"I don't think I could make myself do that," Helen said. "I don't even like flying in a 747."

Emma said, "*I* think it would be cool."

Kathleen opened her mouth, then closed it.

"I actually think it would be, too," Jo said, not so surprisingly. "What I've thought about doing is a ride in a glider. Somehow that seems a little safer."

Logan pictured the fragile-winged gliders he'd seen banking above the Arlington Airport up north, and wasn't so sure about the safe part.

"Maybe," he said.

Jo laughed. "Coward."

"That's me," he said amiably.

Later, while they were cleaning up, Emma asked if he knew her uncle Ryan.

"Yeah, he's the one who recommended your mom call me." What was she was getting at?

"You, like, *work* with him?"

"I've done jobs with him a couple of times. He's more of a general contractor, and since I met him a year ago he's called me a couple of times if cabinets have to be replaced or built to match existing ones."

She looked incredulous. "Mom knows that?"

Baffled, he said, "What I do for a living, you mean?"

"I guess." Emma frowned. "I mean, I know she does, because you built those. It's just…" She shook herself. "Never mind."

Logan crossed his arms. "Do you know how infuriating it is when people do that? Just when they're getting to the interesting part, they look mysterious and say, 'Never mind.'"

Emma giggled, an airy sound. "It is *so-o* irritating, isn't it? But…" She turned her head and lowered her voice. "Here comes Mom."

"Are you going to tell me later?" Logan asked, voice low, too.

"Maybe," she murmured, just as Kathleen stopped in front of them.

"You two sure have your heads together. Just what are you whispering about?"

"Nothing," they said in tandem, then laughed together, too.

When she looked at her daughter, Kathleen's expression might have been funny if it hadn't also been sad, made up as it was with delight, suspicion and yearning.

"We're not conspiring against you," Logan assured her. "Just, uh, exchanging a few notes."

"Ah." She planted her fists on her hips. "How about you help clear the table instead?"

He kissed her cheek. "Will do."

Emma watched interestedly. When her mother raised her brows at her, she said, "Okay, okay," and grabbed some glasses.

Logan left shortly thereafter, since he had to drive to Bellingham to look at some wood in the morning.

Kathleen slipped out the front door and pulled it shut behind her. When he wrapped his hands around her waist, she clasped hers behind his neck.

"You got on with Emma like a house afire."

"Yeah," he said thoughtfully, "I did, didn't I? She seems like a nice kid."

Kathleen fought a visible battle with herself, a mother's pride against a mother's frustration. "She is. Sometimes. I just didn't think tonight would be one of those times."

"You thought she'd hate me."

She made a face. "Emma hasn't been enthusiastic when I talked about you. Honestly, I'm surprised."

He waited for her to add, *And glad.*

She did. Eventually, and almost grudgingly. "Of course, I'm pleased."

He'd never understand women. Why *wasn't* she pleased? Or, at least, why did she have mixed emotions about her daughter's apparent capitulation where he was concerned?

Logan knew better than to ask. Events would unfold; the truth would out. Or so experience suggested.

"Forget Emma," he said with sudden impatience. "Kiss me."

She did. Not at all grudgingly.

CHAPTER TEN

"YOU'RE WATCHING ME!" Emma glared at her mother.

Mom flushed; she always did when she felt guilty. But of course she claimed, "Don't be ridiculous! Why would I watch you?"

Furious, Emma snapped, "Because I'm eating, and you want to count how many bites I take or something!"

She'd made herself soup for lunch, and—what a surprise!—Mom had just *happened* to wander into the kitchen and say, "Lunch. What a good idea. Maybe I'll make myself a sandwich." Emma *never* got to eat out here by herself. Mom was always oh, so casual, like she was fooling anyone.

"It's lunchtime!" Mom snapped right back. "I can't eat until you're done?"

Emma stood up, carried her soup to the sink and dumped it. "There. That's what you thought I was going to do, isn't it? Why won't you just *trust* me?"

"I wasn't watching you!" Mom yelled, her face really red now. "Why won't you believe me?"

Emma stared in frustration, then shook her head. "I can't talk to you." She walked out, even though Mom was saying, "Emma, you come back here right this minute!"

Yeah, so they could have a *talk*. Emma hated their talks.

She'd promised not to go for long walks, but she grabbed a school sweatshirt, tugged it on over her head and went out the front door. She could go around the block, couldn't she? Unless she found out Mom had locked one of those electronic ankle things on, and the police would roar up the minute she got twenty yards from the house or something.

She stomped down the sidewalk, mad that it was drizzling—again! this was the *worst* spring ever—and at her mother for being so suspicious.

Mom had *promised* she wouldn't try to monitor what Emma ate. But she was anyway. Emma could tell. Every meal, Mom kept eyeing her plate and watching the fork go to her mouth. If she said, "I'm full," Mom would say, "Oh, but this is so good! You've hardly had any." Or she'd ask questions when Emma was on her way out the door to school, like, "Did you have a chance to make a lunch? Or do you need money?" Emma bet Mom was dying to dig through her pack and see what she'd packed for lunch.

She *was* eating. Sometimes it was really hard, but she did like feeling stronger, and not so cold. She tried not to look in mirrors, because she knew she was getting fat. She was ninety pounds now. Dr. Tisdale wanted her to get up to at least a hundred.

"At your height, a hundred and ten to a hundred and twenty would be appropriate, but I'll settle for a hundred pounds," he'd told her.

Some days she did better than others. Like, Tuesday she'd been *starved* all day, and she'd eaten so much she didn't even want to think about it. But today she could hardly look at food. Every bite choked her. Sometimes she just wanted to quit eating and say to her mother, "See? All I'm doing is what you expected."

Mostly she didn't want to go back to Bridges, with those Nazi guards patrolling the dining hall and sticking their heads in your room and eavesdropping on every conversation. Lots of the women and girls there had been back at least twice. They knew the whole routine.

Most of the time these days, she thought she'd take feeling gross and fat if she could also be *normal*. She wanted friends, and even a boyfriend. Some of the sophomores had been asked to senior prom, and they were all preening in the bathroom and bragging and talking endlessly about their dresses and the limo they'd be going in and where they'd be having dinner and about parties afterward. No guy had even *looked* at Emma, never mind asked her.

She was sixteen. Almost an adult. She just wished she could get her mother to treat her like one.

So, okay. She used to lie about whether she was eating. But she didn't anymore. Mom had seemed so cool about it when Emma first got out of Bridges, even letting her pick out food for herself and swearing that she'd let the whole issue of food be between Emma and her doctor and therapist.

Look how long *that* had lasted.

She was almost all the way around the block when she saw Logan's blue pickup truck turning onto their street. On impulse she stepped off the curb and stuck out her thumb.

He saw her, grinned and stopped.

She opened the passenger door and scrambled up.

"Need to get out of the rain?" he asked.

She scrunched up her face. "Away from Mom, more like."

"Uh-h," he said mildly. "Getting on each other's nerves, huh?"

"You mean, she's getting on *mine*." In the right side mirror, she noticed a car turning the corner and then hesitating, blocked by his pickup. "I saw a parking spot around the corner," she told him.

"Thanks." He started forward. "So, what's she doing?"

He was so cool! He'd been over, like, every other day since Emma got out, and he was so easy to talk to. He reminded her of Uncle Ryan, even though they didn't look at all alike. But he never seemed to get upset, never seemed in a hurry, never faked wanting to talk to her when she could tell he didn't, like some adults did.

She couldn't believe her mother was dating him. Uncle Ryan irritated Mom *so-o* much, even though they loved each other, too. As long as Emma could remember, Mom had claimed Uncle Ryan was lazy because he didn't want to be a bigger contractor, with more crews doing more jobs under him, instead of still doing some of the work himself. She acted like you couldn't always depend on him, and it just wasn't true! She was the one who wouldn't let him work on the house, because she said she was determined to manage herself. He was always offering. And every time they'd really needed him, like when they found out the bathroom floor was totally rotten, he'd come right away and worked hard. For free.

But he was the opposite of Emma's dad. And so was Logan. When Dad walked into a room, everybody noticed. He crackled with energy. He was a workaholic, too, and he didn't need much sleep, only five or six hours a night, so *everybody* looked lazy compared to him. He could hardly stand it when Emma slept in until nine or even ten o'clock. Dad never just *sat*. He paced, even when he was talking on the phone. He hated it when people didn't get to the point. Mom always said, "Dad doesn't *chat*."

He was also super handsome. Even when he came back from the health club in his sweats, he looked as if he should be in *GQ* or something. Dad liked the best. He wouldn't have been caught dead in faded jeans or a sweatshirt with a ripped elbow or with his hair shaggy. He wanted Mom and Emma to look good, too. Not that it was ever a problem for Mom, but Emma wished sometimes she could slouch downstairs in baggy pajamas to have breakfast, or that it didn't matter if she just threw on something to go to school.

The thing was, Logan wasn't like that at all. He *did* wear jeans with ragged knees or the outline of his wallet showing in the rear pocket even if the wallet wasn't in it. His hair *was* shaggy and sometimes he had to shove it back so it didn't fall in his eyes. Even though Emma liked his face—he had kind eyes, and the coolest smile—she had to admit he wasn't really handsome. He looked like a football player, almost too beefy.

And he did sit. Once he found out it was okay, he'd put his feet up on the coffee table in the living room and coaxed Pirate onto his lap. He was really patient when Mom was finishing something and he was waiting for her. The other night, he'd played Scrabble with Emma, and Mom finally wandered away to work on laundry.

Emma didn't think he'd rat on her if she told him how mad Mom was making her. So she did.

While she was talking, he'd parked and turned off the engine. But he didn't move, just watched her face and nodded his understanding every time she said, "You know?"

When she finished by saying, "She should trust me!" Logan was quiet for a minute.

"She worries about you," he said. Which she expected.

"I know she does. But I'm doing fine!"

He nodded. "It's been a long time since you did fine. And from what she tells me, you lied a lot. Is that true?" He didn't say it accusingly, just as if he wanted to know her side.

"I guess," Emma admitted.

"How's your mom supposed to know you aren't lying now, too?"

"Look at me! I'm getting fat! Sharon—my therapist—told her how much I weigh this week, and I'd gained a pound. So how can I be lying?"

If Logan knew about the way she used to trick the scale by putting weights in her shoes and the hems of her jeans, he didn't say. He just nodded thoughtfully.

"She promised she wouldn't be like this," Emma said passionately. "But *she* lied."

"Maybe she did."

Emma stared at him, shocked that he'd agree.

"Maybe she was lying to herself, too. Could be, she really thought she could back off on the eating, and she's finding it harder than she thought."

"But she *keeps* lying." Emma looked through the windshield, blurred by the misty rain. Some old woman was walking her dog, who was little and fat and probably old, too. He tried to turn and go back, but the woman tugged on the leash and made him keep walking. They toddled toward the pickup. Emma went on, "She claims she's not watching me or keeping track of how much I eat, but she is! And when I accuse her, she blushes. She always does when she lies. She's not very good at it."

A trace of amusement showed in his eyes. "I've noticed."

"Does she lie to you, too?" Emma asked with interest.

"Oh." He shrugged. "Little white lies. The kind everyone tells."

"Why won't she at least give me a chance?"

"Maybe," he said, "she's afraid to."

"Like… She thinks I might *die* or something?" Emma asked incredulously.

"Is that so impossible?"

"Yes! Maybe I was a little too skinny. But I slipped when I hit my head that time. I did not faint, like she keeps insisting I did! She freaked for no reason!"

"You look mighty skinny to me now. Like a puff of wind would blow you away. Your mom tells me I should have seen you six weeks ago. She said you had to rest when you went up the stairs to your bedroom."

"That's not true!" Except, Emma realized guiltily, it was. There'd been a time she had exercised to make up for every bit of food she ate. The past six months, she'd been too tired to do much but some leg lifts when she was lying down.

Logan laughed, but nicely. "You know, you blush when you lie, too."

Horrified, she pressed her hands to her cheeks. "Do I really?" They did feel warm.

"Yup."

"Oh, gross!"

"Try being patient with your mom," he advised. "Just remind yourself that she loves you, and that's why she's being irritating."

Emma let out a huff of air. "I've tried and I've tried…" She saw his face. "Okay! I'll try some more. But…would you talk to her?"

"I hate to get between you two."

"Not between. Just…maybe tell her you've noticed her watching me at meals, or something like that?"

"You want me to lie?"

She grinned at him. "*You* don't blush."

Logan laughed. "No, I won't lie. But I will talk to her. Is that good enough?"

"Yes!" She opened the door and started out, stopping to look back. "Thanks."

"Thank *you.*" His hand was on the door handle, too.

"For what?" Emma asked, puzzled.

"For being nice to me. For not resenting me dating your mother."

"But you're cool," she said in surprise. "Why would I resent you?"

"Your mom thought you might. She said you didn't like it when she dated after the divorce."

Emma made a face. "They were, like, creeps! You know. All smiley and insincere. But they didn't like me at all."

"Ah," he said. "I thought it might be something like that."

They both got out of the truck and she heard the locks snick closed. Rain dampened her face and clung in droplets to her lashes when they hurried toward the corner.

On impulse, Emma turned toward him. "Do you want to marry my mom?"

"I don't know yet," he said.

But she thought he blushed.

KATHLEEN LEANED AGAINST Logan and laid her head against his shoulder. "Mmm," she murmured. "It's so nice just to cuddle."

His laugh was a rumble under her ear. "I don't know if I'm flattered or not. Shouldn't you be pining for passionate kisses?"

Eyes closed, she smiled and rubbed her cheek on his flannel shirt. "I do pine sometimes. You know I do. It's just that…you're so peaceful. Sometimes I need that."

"Mmm." He kissed the top of her head.

Kathleen felt herself drifting. She was almost asleep, but not quite, loving his heartbeat and scent and hard muscles and…oh, just his company. Having him here, and apparently content with the silence, too.

He'd cooked dinner tonight at his place, just for the two of them. Afterward they had wandered out to the living room, thinking about watching the news, but somehow never turning it on.

They might have sat for half an hour, or an hour and a half. Kathleen didn't come sharply awake. Rather, she found herself worrying again, thinking, planning, and knew the peaceful interlude was over. With a sigh, she sat up, pushed her hair back from her face and tucked one foot under her.

"I needed that."

"Why?" Logan asked simply.

He didn't move. He lounged, feet on his coffee table, arm stretched across the back of the couch, and waited patiently.

"Work is the pits. I like my boss less by the day, and I'm starting to really resent doing more than my share of the work for less money than I deserve." Kathleen grimaced. "Bet you've heard that one before, huh?"

"And you've been working hard on stock-piling soap, haven't you?"

"Yes, but I enjoy that. I just hope…" She stopped. "Oh, I don't know. That this isn't a pie-in-the-sky dream. Helen has visions of us building this into a real business that at least pays the two of us a decent return. But what if it flops? Handmade soap is every-where these days. For most soap-makers, it's a cottage-industry. Part-time, brings in some extra cash."

"Your product is better than most."

"I'd like to think so." She hated feeling so discouraged, so lacking in optimism. But everything had conspired lately—her jerk of a boss, the endless rain and gray sky, a frustrating lack of new orders for soap and, most of all, Emma's snarls and slammed doors. "I guess this summer will tell," she said dispiritedly. "If summer ever comes. If it keeps raining, it'll kill the craft fairs."

"It's still only May," he said comfortably. "The tulips are blooming—"

"You mean, they're getting battered down by rain."

He smiled. "Maybe. Nonetheless, spring has sprung. It's just a damp one. You know it'll quit raining one of these days."

"Uh-uh."

Logan watched her, eyes perceptive. "Something else is bothering you."

"Oh…" She let out another gusty sigh. "Emma, of course. Things were so great for all of a week. Now, I can't do anything right. If I don't talk to her, I'm spying on her. If I do, I'm conducting an inquisition. She's being an incredible brat. No," Kathleen corrected herself. "It's worse than that. I think maybe, as she gains some confidence in herself, she's rejecting me."

"She loves you."

"Does she?" Her mouth twisted. "I'm not so sure anymore. I'm not even sure I blame her if she doesn't."

Creases formed on his forehead. "You're being too hard on yourself. You're a perfectionist. Is that a bad quality to pass on to your kids?"

"It is if they take it to an extreme."

"She's the one who took it to the extreme, not you. You aren't responsible for every one of her decisions."

"So I can just let myself off the hook?" Acid etched her words, burned in her stomach.

"No, but…" He frowned now. "You have influence, good and bad, but how the balance tips…" He shrugged. "That's not up to you."

"It's easier to be philosophical when you're not the parent," Kathleen said, a little too sharply.

He raised his brows, but said nothing.

She gave a crooked smile. "I'm sorry. That was awful. You're trying to help, and I'm telling you to butt out."

"Is that what you're telling me?"

Something in his tone made her wary. "What do you mean?"

"Emma asked me to talk to you."

For some reason, the very idea filled her with outrage. She put both feet on the floor. "Emma *what?*"

He smiled wryly. "You heard me."

"Emma actually asked *you* to intercede with me."

"Why's that so surprising?"

"She hardly knows you!"

"We've gotten to be pretty good friends," he said mildly.

"Friends."

His eyes narrowed. "You don't sound very happy about it. Were you hoping she'd hate my guts?"

"No! I just…" Oh, she hardly understood herself why it upset her so much to think of her daughter and Logan talking behind her back. Of Emma talking to Logan when she wouldn't to her own mother. "What were you supposed to talk to me about?" Kathleen asked.

"She thinks you haven't kept your promise to back off on the food issues. She thinks you watch every bite she eats."

Kathleen leaped to her feet. "That's not true! Did you buy into this? Do you believe her?"

He still hadn't moved, but tension radiated from him in waves. "Buy into it? All I'm doing is reporting what she said."

Anger and hurt tightened her chest. "It sounds a lot more like an accusation."

"It wasn't," he said shortly. "Don't you think you're being a bit paranoid?"

"No!" She paced away, swung back. "I think you don't have any business interfering between Emma and me."

He didn't say anything for a long time. So long, she felt her cheeks flush, painfully hot. Logan's expression never changed, but she felt his withdrawal nonetheless.

"I've been put in my place, haven't I?" he said finally, voice quiet, devoid of emotion. "In case I had any doubt of it."

"No!" she cried. "I didn't mean…"

"Didn't you?" He uncoiled from the couch. "I think we've both said enough tonight. Why don't I run you home now?"

"I…" A huge lump clogged her throat. "Logan…"

"Let's see. You have a coat, don't you?"

He left the living room and returned with it, holding it out for her to slip into.

He ushered her implacably to his pickup and drove her home without saying another word. Kathleen said nothing as she sat beside him, back straight, her eyes and nose burning with unshed tears. He was the best thing that had happened to her in years, and she'd blown it.

The pickup stopped on the street in front of her house. Two doors down, there had been an empty parking spot, but he'd made no effort to pull into it.

"Shall I walk you up?" he asked politely.

"No, I'll be fine. Logan…"

"Good night, then," he said with terrifying finality.

Kathleen nodded, clambered out, slammed the door and fled before he could see her in tears.

"WHAT'S WRONG?"

Kathleen started and wiped her wet cheeks. Thinking everyone else was asleep, she'd turned out most of the downstairs lights, grabbed an afghan and a box of tissues, and made herself comfortable on one end of the living room couch for a good cry.

She couldn't do it in bed, not unless she wanted to take a chance of Emma in the next room hearing her.

Bundled in a ratty pink chenille bathrobe that clashed with her disheveled fiery auburn hair, Helen moved into the small circle of light cast by the lamp.

"Nothing. Just…little things. Really." Kathleen tried for a weak smile. "I'm fine."

"Uh-uh." Warm gray eyes surveyed her face. "You don't look fine."

Kathleen wiped at wet cheeks. "I don't suppose I do. I hope I didn't wake you."

"Heavens, no!" Helen pulled the robe more snugly around her and came to sit on the couch as well. "I don't sleep well. You know that."

Distracted from her own troubles, Kathleen said, "I thought you were doing better."

"Oh, I am! But still…I worry about Ginny, and the future, and the past, and…" She laughed softly. "I think I've forgotten how to sleep like a normal person."

Kathleen scrubbed again at her tears. "And here I am feeling sorry for myself!"

Helen seemed to consider that. "Divorce is as hard as death, I think. Maybe harder."

Remembering the shell-shocked woman

and wraith of a child she had accepted as roommates less than a year ago, Kathleen shook her head. "No. How could anything be harder?"

A shadow crossed Helen's face. "Regrets. Regrets might be."

"My regrets go back further than my marriage. Way further."

Now, why had she said that? She didn't want to confess her petty sins of arrogance to one more person.

Helen surprised her by saying only, "It's Emma, then."

"And Logan. I was awful..." She was crying again! Kathleen sniffed and groped for a tissue. At least she had prepared when she sat down to weep.

Helen watched her with those kind eyes. "Awful?"

"Emma asked him to intercede with me."

"And?"

"I was jealous!" Kathleen blurted. "I am jealous! She hates me, but she talks to this guy I'm casually dating?"

Helen arched her brows. "Casually?"

"Yes! Casually!" She blew her nose and mopped her cheeks. "I'm not ready... I can't..."

Her roommate took her hand and squeezed. "You are, and you can."

Kathleen shook her head. "I don't even know myself anymore. I don't like who I was, and I don't know who I can be."

"Kathleen," Helen said firmly, "you are a very nice woman. You're a patient mother, a good friend and a hard worker. What's not to like?"

"I alphabetize the soup cans!" she wailed.

At least Helen didn't laugh at her. "That is a little weird," she admitted. "Yeah, you're a neat freak, but that's okay. Why wouldn't it be?"

A stillness came over her. "Because I taught Emma that everybody has to be perfect all the time. She almost died trying, and it's taken me this long to realize that it's my fault."

Helen wouldn't let go of her hand, although she tugged to withdraw it. "You know it isn't that simple."

"Maybe not," Kathleen admitted drearily. "But that's what's at the heart of her problems. Me."

Troubled lines creased Helen's brow. "She's doing well."

"Yes. I suppose she is. I think," it tore at

her to admit it, "she'd do better if she weren't living with me. Haven't you noticed? We fight all the time."

"She's just...feeling her oats."

"I don't know. She used to be so sweet."

"She still is. With Ginny, especially."

"I don't know what to do. She can't go to Ian, even if he was interested. And—aside from our relationship—you're all family to her. She needs you."

"And you." Helen's worried lines had deepened. "She does need you."

Kathleen shook her head, more in bafflement than denial. Numbness seemed to be creeping over her. Perhaps she was cried out. "I think I'm the one who needs her, not the other way around. Isn't that sad? I should be letting go—she's sixteen years old!—but I'm hurt when she turns to someone else for advice."

"Aren't you glad she likes Logan?"

"I don't know!" The spurt of anger seemed to come from nowhere, dying as quickly. "Yes. Of course I am. I just...didn't expect her to take to him so quickly. So wholeheartedly."

"Are you afraid she'll get hurt if you break up with him?"

Kathleen was ashamed to realize that hadn't even occurred to her. Just as a future without Logan hadn't occurred to her, despite her doubts and confusion.

She laughed, a pathetic, painful sound. "I'm pretty sure he broke up with me tonight. And who can blame him?"

"He's in love with you, you know."

Love? He'd called her that a few times, but he had never said, "I love you," or even hinted it, nor had she. And yet...

She pressed a hand to the ache in her chest. "Tonight, I told him he had no business interfering between Emma and me."

Helen winced.

Kathleen's mouth stretched into a painful kind of smile. "Yeah. As he said, I put him in his place. And after he's listened so patiently to my worries."

Helen sat silent for a moment. "Well," she said, "it seems to me that you have to decide whether you love him and want him to be a real part of your life. And if you do, you'd better tell him so."

"Tell him I love him?" Kathleen said, appalled.

"At least tell him you're sorry. Tell him why you lashed out."

A small moan escaped her.

Helen laughed. "You can do it. As for Emma…she's eating. Not a lot, but enough. Isn't that what really counts? So what if she screams at you and slams her bedroom door?"

Kathleen blinked. "When you put it that way…"

"Listen to wise Helen. Who—" she stood "—is now going back to bed."

"Helen… Thank you."

"You're welcome." Helen disappeared toward the hall, her soft, "'Night," coming from the darkness.

Kathleen wrapped the afghan around her shoulders and huddled inside it, aware again of the quiet and the creaks of an old house settling and the thump that was probably Pirate leaping to the floor from a bed upstairs to greet Helen. Thanks to her comforting visit, the house felt friendly around Kathleen.

Emma is eating, Kathleen told herself silently. *Helen's right. That's what is important.*

Her mind hopped, as if she'd thrown a pebble to the next square. *Do I love him? What if I knew—if I was sure—he loved me?*

How could she admit she'd been jealous? She had begged him once not to look deep, not to see the parts of her that she knew to be unworthy. And now she was supposed to confess something so ridiculous, so childish, so sad?

Do I love him?

Abruptly she scrambled to her feet, turned out the light and felt her way through the dark toward the hall. Her trailing fingers found the easy chair, then the wall, and finally the door molding. She crossed the hall to the kitchen, blinking against the light when she flipped the switch.

The canned goods were in a lower cabinet, to the left of the sink. Wishing she wore her slippers, nonetheless she plopped onto the floor, draped the afghan over her shoulders and opened the cupboard door.

Closing her eyes, she reached in and shoved cans around, willy-nilly. Let them fall where they may.

Do I love him?

CHAPTER ELEVEN

"Mom." Emma's voice was subdued. Worried. "The phone's for you. It's Dad."

"What?" A bar of soap fell to the pantry floor and Kathleen looked back up at her daughter, standing in the doorway with the phone extended in her hand. "It's your father?"

Emma nodded, her eyes huge in her face.

Now what? Muttering under her breath, Kathleen peeled off the latex gloves she'd been wearing to unmold soap—including the bar, still soft and uncured, that had squished into a useless blob on the floor. Even with the newly installed fan running, the mixture of scents in the tiny room was overpowering.

She stepped over the empty molds she'd been setting out of the way on the floor and followed Emma into the kitchen. There, she took the phone.

"Ian?"

"Hello, Kathleen." She knew his voice as well as her own.

"What is it?" Surely he wasn't going to insist yet again that she let him pay a settlement?

"I called to see how Emma is. I couldn't get more than a 'fine' out of her. Obviously she's out of that residential program."

"Yes, and she's doing very well." Kathleen grabbed for a chair and pulled it out so that she could sit. "She's still thin, but eating."

"I'm glad." He was quiet for a moment. "I'm hoping I can see her."

"See her?" Kathleen parroted.

Emma's eyes got even bigger.

"I'm her father."

Shock hadn't hit her yet. "May I ask what caused your change of heart?"

"I miss Emma." Pause. "I miss both of you."

She should feel something. Anger. A pang for their lost, happy years. Instead she remained remote, as if imagining a scene that hadn't happened.

She heard her voice, cool and far away. "You'll have to tell Emma that. Visits will be up to her, Ian. I won't force her." She didn't say, *Unlike you.*

"May I come over one of these evenings? Talk to you both?"

Kathleen hesitated. Sharon thought it was important that Emma reestablish a relationship with her father. Ian *had* loved Emma, and she'd loved her daddy. In her mind, he'd become a monster, a hideous image that blocked remembrance of the father who'd carried her on his shoulders and swept her around the dance floor and taught her to ice skate.

What would it hurt if he stopped by? Emma could choose to see him or not. But at least she'd have the opportunity, if that was what she decided.

"All right."

Emma's face contorted as she asked silent questions.

"Tomorrow night?" Ian asked.

"Fine."

"I'm looking forward to seeing you," were his last, quiet words.

Kathleen in turn pressed End on the phone and set it on the table.

"What did he say?" Emma burst out.

"He wants to see you. He's coming over tomorrow night to talk to us."

The teenager's voice rose. "And you said he could?"

"Emma, he's your father." Kathleen felt the tremor in her hands when she laid them on her thighs. "He's not a patient man, but he does love you."

"He tried to kill me!"

"He tried to force you to eat," she corrected. "He thought you were defying him by starving yourself. He lost his temper."

"It was…" Emma trembled all over. "It was horrible. I don't want to see him. I won't!"

"That's okay," Kathleen said. "But I think you should. Listen to him just this once. Then, if you don't want to agree to regular visits, I'll back you up. You heard what I told him—it's up to you. But…he is your father, and he used to be a good one. Remember that, Emma."

"You're taking his side!" Hysteria edged her daughter's voice.

"No. I will always take yours. But you know how Sharon feels about this. She thinks it's important for you to see him and, oh, put him in proportion. He's just your father, who cracked and did something scary. You're older and stronger now, and you can face him."

Face bleach-white, Emma cried, "I can't!"

"Don't let him have some kind of power he doesn't deserve."

"I hate him."

"Do you?"

Emma glared. "You sound like Sharon! I do hate him!"

"Okay. Tell him so. Maybe he deserves it." Everyone knew, Emma was quick enough to yell, "I hate you!" to her mother. It would be refreshing to have her hate someone else for a change.

"You can't make me see him!" Emma whirled and raced from the kitchen, her footsteps thudding up the stairs. Above, her bedroom door slammed.

Kathleen winced. The whole household probably had. Everyone else must be getting as sick as she was of that furious bang. Sometimes she wanted to take the door off its hinges. Emma should count her blessings that she wasn't living with her father now. If he'd gone off the deep end then, imagine how he'd react to her teenage tantrums now!

Ian. What would he think of this house, an elderly lady sagging and wrinkling? And of Kathleen's motley household of women and children and a half-grown cat who could eye two people at once? It was a world apart from the home Ian and she had shared, elegant, spacious, designed for entertainment more than for a family. He would look at her with pity and condescendingly offer the settlement again, Kathleen guessed.

I miss both of you, he'd said. What had *that* meant?

I'm looking forward to seeing you, he had closed with. Not, *I'm looking forward to seeing* Emma.

Surely he wasn't hinting at a reconciliation?

Kathleen got to her feet in agitation, then grabbed her latex gloves and hurried back to the pantry. She had work to do. Soap to unmold and set out to cure.

Ian could hint at whatever he liked. She wasn't interested. Not when another man's face appeared before her mind's eye in unguarded moments, when she felt a leap of hope every time she heard a pickup truck on the street, every time the phone or doorbell rang.

Of course, she should call Logan, not wait for him to call her. She would, when she worked up the nerve. When—if—she knew for sure that it wasn't best for things with him to end now.

Maybe, in a weird way, seeing Ian would help her decide. She wouldn't have him back even if he begged, not after what he'd done to Emma. Not after she had found out how much more tender a man could be. She didn't *want* the life Ian had given her.

What she *did* want was the question.

EMMA CUT HER LAST CLASS the next day. She was always the good little girl who would never do anything like that. But her stomach had been churning all day, and Ms. Peterson, her English teacher, had said in this irritated tone, "Emma, kindly pay attention!" while in Spanish, Señora McBride had dropped a book with a smack on Emma's desk, making her start and almost fall out of her chair as the class laughed. Emma couldn't listen! She just couldn't. She wouldn't go to math at all. So what if she had an unexcused absence? Mom was mad at her all the time anyway.

She walked fast, her head down, skipping the first bus stop and going an extra block before she stopped under the overhang in front of a little Italian restaurant to wait for the city bus. Arms crossed, she shivered and wished she could have gone to her locker for her coat before she took off. But then the bell would have rung and someone would have noticed her leaving campus.

Dad was coming tonight. To see her. And Mom was letting him.

Emma couldn't believe it. She hadn't thought she would ever have to see him again. She tried not to think about him. Sharon was always trying to get her to talk about him, but she refused. It wasn't like he had anything to do with whether she ate or not, except maybe in the first place when she'd believed losing weight would also make her beautiful so he'd be proud of her.

What a dumb kid's fantasy!

He'd been so mad. She cringed at her memory of his face. The very next day, Mom had packed up their clothes and they had moved out. Emma hadn't seen him since, although he had tried once, coming to the apartment Mom rented. Emma had hidden in the bedroom, listening hard, waiting for raised voices that never came.

Sharon said he was Emma's ogre under the bed, that she had to lift the bedskirt some-day and *look,* or she'd always be scared. And also that it was really, really important that she recapture the memories of being loved by both her parents.

Was Mom right? Could she face him, and even say, "I hate you for what you did?"

She didn't know.

Emma rode the bus all the way downtown and got off in front of Nordstrom. She walked, and looked in store windows, and tried not to think about tonight.

Finally, worried that Ginny would beat her home and be there all by herself, Emma caught another bus.

She was late, but Ginny wasn't on the doorstep. Anxiety rising, Emma let herself into the house. Immediately she felt a rush of relief and remorse. Looking small and scared, Pirate on her lap, the six-year-old sat on the bottom step of the staircase.

She stared at Emma. "You weren't home."

"How did you get in?"

"Mom gave me a key. In case. Why weren't you here?"

Emma dropped her book bag by the coat tree and sank down on the step next to Ginny. "I'm really sorry. I just…I was upset about something, and I took the bus all the way downtown, and then it took too long to get back home."

"What were you upset about?" Ginny asked, face tilted up. Her fingers kept working in Pirate's dense orange-and-cream fur, and he rumbled contentedly.

"You know how I've told you about my dad? The way he shoved food in my mouth and almost choked me to death?"

Ginny nodded gravely.

"Well, he's coming here tonight. He wants to see me."

"Oh-h," she breathed, eyes saucer-wide.

"Mom says I don't have to see him. I haven't decided yet. Sometimes I want to tell him how much he scared me, and how mad I am."

Ginny looked awed at the idea of Emma telling off a grown-up.

"But Mom says he loves me, and he just lost his temper that once, and…" She stopped. "So I don't know what to do."

Ginny nodded solemnly.

"You won't tell your mom or anyone that I was late today, will you? I'll get in trouble."

Ginny's forehead crinkled. "No, but I was scared."

"I know. I'm sorry. I won't do it again. I promise."

The little girl pursed her mouth. "Okay."

"Let's do something fun, so I don't have to think about Dad. Let's play a game, okay?"

They went upstairs and played Chutes and Ladders and even Twister, although they had to take their hands off the colored spots to spin the dial. Even so, it was fun. Despite being small, Ginny was better than Emma; she could twist like a pretzel without falling down.

At dinner Mom kept watching Emma, which wasn't new, but this time she didn't catch Mom assessing how much food was left on her plate. Afterward, when everyone was collecting dirty dishes to carry to the sink, Mom asked in a low voice, "You okay with this?"

Emma didn't know she'd made up her mind until she found herself nodding. "I guess."

Mom smiled. "Good girl."

"What if I do tell him I hate him?"

To her surprise, Mom just shrugged. "He can handle it. You do whatever feels right to you."

Behind them, Jo growled in frustration. "The sink is plugged up again!"

Mom hurried to see what the problem was. Emma knew what Uncle Ryan would say:

the plumbing was decrepit. But Mom had spent her budget, on the two bathrooms and the new cabinets for her soap-making business. So she kept a plumber's snake and a big bottle of that toxic stuff that was supposed to unclog drains, and she kept pouring it down and poking in the pipes with the snake. Emma bet Logan would fix it if she asked him, but he hadn't had dinner here since the problem started. In fact, he hadn't been around at all in several days. Maybe he was out of town or something. Emma wondered if he'd ever talked to Mom the way he said he would.

When the doorbell rang, Mom was viciously stabbing the snake down the drain. Her head came up, and she said, "Crap!"

She yanked the slimy coils out, dropped them in the sink and grabbed a dishtowel to dry her hands. Her hair was sticking up, and her face was red, and she'd gotten water on the front of her shirt.

"Emma, can you get that?"

Suddenly paralyzed, Emma didn't get up from the chair.

"Jo? Helen?"

"I'll get it," Helen called from somewhere

else in the house. She'd cooked, so she didn't have to clean up.

Mom peered at her reflection in the tiny mirror that was stuck with a magnet to the fridge. Poking at her hair, she muttered, "I look awful," then scowled as if she'd made herself mad.

Voices came from the front hall. Emma gripped the seat of the chair with both hands, as if someone had threatened to drag her out of it.

Mom came to her. "Are you ready?"

She shook her head hard.

"You know, your dad is a handsome, smart man who can be a jerk sometimes. Don't give him more credit than he deserves."

Emma didn't even know why she was so scared. She knew what Mom meant, and she knew it was true. But still, she saw him coming out of his chair at the dinner table with his face horribly twisted, felt him grip her head and squeeze her jaw so that her mouth opened as he scooped food from her plate and shoved it in, a huge handful of it. Saw the way he looked at her, as if he hated her.

But it wasn't just that. She almost wished it was, that she didn't have all this other stuff tangled up inside her. Because part of her *wanted* to see him, and kept thinking that maybe now, finally, he'd look at her with open astonishment and say, "Wow. My Emma has become a beauty." She'd see in his eyes that he meant it.

She hated knowing that she still cared what he thought. She didn't want to care. She didn't want him for a father at all. She wanted someone like Uncle Ryan, or Logan. Someone who would love her even if she *wasn't* beautiful, or the smartest girl in school, or the best dancer or actor or whatever.

Mom touched her lightly on the shoulder. "I'll go talk to him. When you feel ready, come on out. If you don't, that's okay, too."

Emma gave a choppy nod.

A moment later, she heard Mom's voice join her father's out in the entry hall. Their voices receded as they went into the living room.

Jo was the one stabbing the snake down the drain now. All of a sudden, there was a gurgle and she exclaimed, "Hallelujah!"

"Did you fix it, Aunt Jo?" Ginny asked, rising on tiptoe to try to see in the sink.

Jo scrunched up her face. "For now. Emma,

do you think your mom would kill me if ask Ryan to look at this?"

Emma made herself relax her hands, one finger at a time. "Uncle Ryan won't let Mon kill you."

"My hero. Well." She reached for the dish soap. "I guess I don't have any excuse not to wash dishes now, do I? Are you girls going to dry?"

"I will!" Ginny said. "'Cept I have to get a chair."

"I will after Dad goes." To her astonishment, Emma realized she was rising to her feet. "I guess I should go talk to him."

"Yeah." Jo flashed her this big smile. "You should. It'll be good for you."

Emma rolled her eyes. "I hate things that are good for me."

Jo laughed. "Don't we all."

Emma's feet carried her out to the entry hall. Through the arch, she could see Mom on the couch, seemingly relaxed and nodding at something Dad was saying.

Emma took a deep breath and walked into the living room. Mom saw her first and smiled much as Jo had. When Dad saw Mom's head turn, he stood.

"Emma."

"Hi, Dad."

"You look…" He changed his mind and gave a little cough. "It's great to see you."

Sure. Yeah. *You've become a swan. What a beauty my Emma is.* Uh-huh. That was going to happen.

Mixed with her sickening disappointment was a wave of relief, because Dad was…well, just Dad. Like Mom said. A man. Still good-looking, for a guy his age. His eyes were bright blue, and even Emma could see that the few lines beside them added character to his face. The little bit of gray in his hair was all at his temples. Mom used to tease him about turning gray.

He was looking Emma up and down with the same critical gaze that used to make her shrivel, but today she just ignored him and walked over to the couch, where she sat next to Mom.

"Are you sure she should be out of the hospital?" he asked her, as if Emma wasn't there. "She looks like a concentration camp survivor."

"Were you this tactless when you courted me?" Mom wondered aloud.

"I'm just concerned," he said stiffly.

Emma wanted to wave a hand in the air.

Hello! I'm here, too. "I've gained thirteen pounds."

He looked at her as if she'd just announced that she wanted to be a car mechanic when she grew up. "Thirteen pounds!"

"Actually—" Mom smiled warmly at Emma "—she's doing very well."

"Oh, right!"

Following his exclamation, there was this uncomfortable little silence. Nobody knew what to say. *How are you, Dad?*

The doorbell rang, making Emma and Mom, at least, jump. "Who could that be?" Mom asked.

"Maybe Uncle Ryan," Emma suggested. "Or Logan."

"Oh, I don't think…"

"I'll go see." She stood, then realized she was too late. The front door opened and Jo was talking to somebody.

Holding a dish towel, Jo appeared in the arched doorway, her expression a little anxious and a little amused. "Kathleen, Logan is here."

Dismay on her face, Mom mumbled something Emma couldn't hear and started to rise, but Logan appeared behind Jo. Face expressionless, his gaze took in Mom, Emma and then Dad.

Dad stood, too. "A friend of yours?" he asked Mom, with this slightly sarcastic tone.

The muscles in her jaw bunched. "That's right. Ian, this is Logan Carr. Logan, my ex-husband, Ian Monroe."

The two men nodded. Neither held out a hand to shake.

"I didn't mean to interrupt," Logan said. "I'll come back another time." He backed toward the entry hall.

"No! I mean…" Mom looked back at Dad, then at Logan. "Actually…can I call you?"

"Sure." He took a last look at Emma's father, then at Mom's face, dipped his head awkwardly and disappeared. A moment later, the front door opened and closed again.

Mom had this weird expression on her face, as if…well, Emma didn't know as if what. Only that something had upset her.

But she forced a smile and said, "Can I get you a cup of coffee, Ian?"

"Thanks," he said with a nod.

Emma almost panicked, knowing why Mom had offered. Of course, she meant to leave them alone. Emma bit her lip, then sat again.

Dad did the same. He waited until Mom was gone, then looked squarely at Emma. "This is way overdue, but I came to say that I'm sorry. I lost my temper. I hope you'll forgive me."

Emma swallowed. "You scared me."

"I know I must have. I scared myself."

"I didn't think I ever wanted to see you again." She could hardly believe she was saying these things. It was like someone else talking. "I hated you so much."

He flinched. "I suppose I deserve that."

"I wanted to be pretty," Emma heard herself say.

"What?"

"I thought maybe, if I got skinny, you'd think I was pretty."

"But...you are pretty. You always have been. You look like your mother."

"You never told me I was pretty. You just said, 'Quit stuffing your face.' Or, 'quit picking at your food.'"

"I'm sure I've told you..."

She shook her head. "No. Never. You wanted to know why I wasn't the lead in the play. And why didn't I inherit your athletic ability."

He flushed. "Are you blaming me for your eating disorder?"

"I don't know." Emma stood. "Maybe. No. I don't know," she repeated. "But you hurt my feelings."

He frowned. "I love you."

"How come you never showed it?" she asked, then turned and walked out.

Her father called her name, but she kept going. Up the stairs, down the hall to her room. She felt so bizarre as she went in and quietly shut the door. Numb on the surface, but churning inside. Happy and scared and sick to her stomach.

She stood in the middle of her bedroom and thought in amazement, *I told him. I actually did it. I told Dad I hated him, and that he hurt my feelings.* All the things she'd imagined flinging at him like poisoned darts, seeing them bite into his flesh and bring him to his knees.

He hadn't exactly crumbled to his knees, but Emma thought maybe she had hurt him. And she was glad. Maybe, if he really did love her, she could forgive him someday, but Mom was right: he deserved to hear what she really, truly felt.

And she, Emma Monroe, had been brave enough to tell him.

Her nausea subsiding but her heart still racing, she plopped onto the bed.

"Wait'll I tell Sharon!"

IAN WAS STANDING IN FRONT of the fireplace, looking at photos on the mantel, when Kathleen came back from the kitchen with a tray. She had almost forgotten how handsome he was, with dark hair, blue eyes, strong cheekbones and the lean, athletic build of a tennis player. Tonight he was dressed casually, for him, in chocolate-brown corduroy slacks, Italian leather loafers and a Shetland wool sweater she had given him for Christmas several years ago.

"Where's Emma?" she asked, looking around. As if he'd stuffed her behind the couch cushions.

He turned to face her. "Apparently I'm the bad guy now."

Surprised, Kathleen set down the tray on the coffee table. "What do you mean?"

Stiffly, he said, "She says she's hated me, and implied that it's all my fault she tried to starve herself to death. Something about my never telling her she was pretty."

Well, well. It would seem that Emma had worked up the courage to tell her father how she really felt. Kathleen wished she could have heard.

"Oh, plenty is my fault, too," she said. "And maybe she's even right."

Ian resumed his seat, reaching for the cup of black coffee. "No," he said, waving off her offer of creamer, "I'm cutting calories."

He must have detected a little softening in the gut one morning, she thought with amusement. Ian did detest every symptom of aging.

"What do you mean by that?" He frowned at her, reverting to the point. "How is her eating problem your fault?"

At least he hadn't denied that it might be his. Could there be hope?

"I'm a perfectionist. You and I were both very image-conscious. Did we put pressure on her to live up to a predetermined mold we'd cast for our child? Or at least express disappointment when she didn't? Probably."

"Oh, come on!" he said explosively.

She raised her brows.

He scowled at her. "Maybe this anorexia thing is chemical. Or in her genes. Why does it have to be our fault?"

"Oh, it may be physical, too," she agreed. "After all, every girl who diets doesn't develop an eating disorder. But in Emma's case…" She looked down at her cup, not wanting him to see too much on her face. "She's expressed quite a bit of anger to me," Kathleen said carefully. "It's pretty clear that she felt…inadequate. For whatever reason, she was afraid she didn't measure up to our expectations. I will never forgive myself for having any expectation at all about her appearance." She looked up, her voice gaining force. "What difference did it make if she was plump? She was a smart, cheerful kid. Beyond worrying about her health, why did we care?"

"Watching her eat turned my stomach."

"Then you should have quit watching."

The cup rattled when he set it down too forcefully. "My fault again?"

"*Our* fault," Kathleen corrected.

He didn't like it. He never liked any implication that he might be wrong.

"What now?" he growled. "Is she better?"

"You mean, all healed and will now be normal?"

"You know what I mean!" he snapped.

"No. Eating will continue to be a struggle

for Emma. She's young enough that there isn't yet significant damage to her body. But the vast majority of anorexics don't 'recover.' Like alcoholics, they face a lifelong battle. Emma is doing amazingly well. She may be one of the lucky ones. Right now, she *is* eating without any nagging on my part. Not as much as I'd like, but given the way she looks at her food before she puts it in her mouth, she really is doing fine."

He frowned again. "How does she look at her food?"

"As if…" She hadn't put it in words before, even to herself. "As if even something as basic as a bowl of cereal is some alien substance. Or maybe not alien. Maybe, intrinsically disgusting. As if I was expected to eat monkey eyeballs, and not only did I know how icky the texture would be, the very idea of eating them appalled me."

"Your imagination is getting a little carried away."

"No." Kathleen shook her head. "I think even the texture of lots of foods repulses her. It's been so long since she's eaten anything but a few lettuce leaves on a regular basis, she's having a hard time with just the act. But right now, she forges through three meals a day. Some days more successfully than others, but I'm proud of her for doing so well."

"Fine. Then she's better," he said impatiently.

Kathleen opened her mouth, but closed it. Why bother arguing? She'd told Emma the truth. For all his admirable qualities, he was a jerk.

"How are you?" he asked suddenly. "You look good."

Good? She'd have laughed, except it offended her that, after everything they'd talked about, he would still determine how she was doing in her new life by how she looked.

"I'm just fine. And you?" She sipped her coffee.

He grumbled about the economy, the housekeeper, his stockbroker's poor judgment, and how empty the house seemed. It was the longest he'd talked to her in years.

"I miss you. I thought you'd get over this," he gestured at the room around them, as if the house itself was part of her mad start, "and come home."

Whatever her struggles with money and

Emma, she had never missed him, Kathleen realized. How sad.

"I've learned quite a lot about myself and what I want out of life," she said. "I doubt you'd much like me anymore."

His mouth curled. "Was that a new boyfriend? Surely you can do better."

She tensed. "And you summed him up—how? You barely met him."

"Oh, come on, Kath!" he said scornfully. "What's he do for a living? Dig ditches?"

She set her jaw. "He's a very talented cabinetmaker."

Ian snorted. "He's blue-collar. Does he have any education? Or don't you expect conversation from him?"

His jabs went deeper than he knew, but she wasn't going to give him the satisfaction of seeing her wince.

"When's the last time you and I had a stimulating conversation? I'm afraid I can't remember." She set down her cup and stood. "Who I see isn't your business, Ian."

He laughed unpleasantly. "You'll dump him."

To think she had once loved this man. That she had been dazzled by his charisma and handsome face and ability to make money.

How could she have failed to notice how unkind he was?

Without a word, Kathleen walked to the front door. There, Ian took his expensive wool coat from the rack and shrugged into it. "I'll want to see Emma again."

"That's between the two of you. Feel free to call her."

"I'm entitled to visitation."

Bristling, Kathleen said, "Because you pay child support? Do you think you're *buying* rights?"

"She's my daughter."

"She's old enough to make her own decisions. I've encouraged her to consider seeing you. For better or worse, you're her father. I know you once loved her." She shook her head when he started to interrupt. "But if she chooses not to see you, I'll support her. All the way to court."

Ian looked at her with open dislike. "You have changed."

She trembled inside. Outwardly her gaze was calm. "I do hope so."

"I'll be calling," he promised. Or threatened. Without saying good-night, he stalked down the steps toward the street.

Kathleen quietly closed the door and turned the lock with a sensation of relief.

Why had Logan stopped by tonight? What had he thought when he saw Ian here?

And how did she interpret her own emotions on seeing him standing there? She'd felt so much at once: joy, embarrassment, awkwardness. She had wished he was dressed better. Why had he had to appear, now of all times, in his working attire of jeans and flannel shirt, sawdust on his knees, a new bandage on one callused, scarred hand? Why couldn't he have looked suave and worldly and handsome, Ian's match?

But she was so glad he *wasn't* like Ian, why did it matter what he was wearing? Or what Ian thought! She didn't care. But she did.

For just a second, she had looked through his eyes, and seen Logan the way she would have two years ago. She'd seen a blockish, homely, working man. Someone of another class.

Someone too much like her father.

For the first time in her life, she wondered if that was so bad.

Kathleen turned and started up the stairs.

She'd have to call Logan, once she knew what to say. But Emma needed her first.

She was glad of the excuse to delay.

CHAPTER TWELVE

MUSIC POUNDING HIS EARDRUMS through his
headphones and muting the whine of the
electric sander, Logan worked down in his
basement long past the time of night when he
would normally have hung it up. He needed
the distraction, the noise, the purpose.

Upstairs, his house was so lonely, he
couldn't stand it. The once peaceful silence
had turned, like wine to vinegar. The TV no
longer filled it. Music sounded thin, mourn-
ful, bagpipes wailing over the barren hills.

He had it bad. He remembered when
Emma had asked whether he wanted to
marry her mother, and he'd lied. Didn't know
yet, he'd said.

He knew.

Logan turned off the sander, peeled off his
headphones and goggles, and ran a finger
over the birch, pale and fine-grained. Smooth
as silk. Smooth as Kathleen's skin.

He shook his head violently to clear the

image. Think instead about the way she'd looked at him tonight, dismay stamped on her beautiful face, he ordered himself. There she sat, sipping coffee and chatting with a man who reeked of money and arrogance, and Logan had had the bad taste to come calling. Something had flashed in her eyes that for a dizzying moment he had believed to be delight. Then she had glanced at the arrogant man, who'd raised his brows as if a servant had tried to join the party. When Logan had met her gaze again, he'd seen the truth: she was embarrassed to have to acknowledge him.

He clenched his teeth so hard, pain stabbed his temples. Angry, he yanked down the goggles, clapped on the headphones and picked up the sander again, the whine mingling with the hoarse voice of Bruce Springsteen singing about glory days.

He had never understood why a woman as beautiful and elegant as Kathleen Monroe had looked twice at him. Apparently he had his answer; it had been no more than a whim.

Why couldn't he have fallen in love with the redheaded cashier at Home Depot who'd been flirting with him for the past couple months?

Looking down, he switched off the sander. He'd gouged a good board, taking out his hurt and rage on it instead of the woman who'd inspired it.

"Argh!" he said out loud, unplugging the sander. He wouldn't start on another board tonight; he was too worked up to be productive.

In his methodical way, he cleaned up, putting tools in their places and sweeping up the fine sawdust as best he could. It filled the air, the scent prettier than most perfume. He could taste the delicate particles, feeling them in his nostrils, knew he'd see a raccoon face when he looked in the mirror, as if he'd patted talc on his face and neck except where the goggles had covered.

Wearily he shut off the lights and climbed the stairs.

He had his foot on the first step when the doorbell rang.

Logan hated the lurch of hope that he tried to bury under irritation. What now?

He took a minute to wipe his face with a dish towel, grab a glass of water then flipped on the porch light and opened the door. Kathleen was on the doorstep, hunched inside a parka that had probably been designed for Mount Everest.

The hope solidified, then crystallized into a substance like granite, with shimmery flecks of longing encased in something a lot harder.

Anger.

"Yeah?" he said.

She looked almost plain when she met his eyes. "May I come in?"

Trust her to put it that way: *may I,* not *can I?* Well-bred. Prissy.

Without a word, he backed up. She stepped in, hesitated, then peeled off her parka. When he didn't offer to take it, she hung it over the doorknob.

He was suddenly very tired. He wanted a hot shower and bed, not more turmoil.

"Why are you here?" he asked bluntly.

"So that I could tell you I'm sorry for what I said the other day. I didn't mean it. I wouldn't have introduced you to Emma if I hadn't hoped you'd become part of our lives."

"Uh-uh." He picked up his glass of water and took a drink. "But that part didn't include my taking your daughter's side against you."

Strain showed on her face, in the fine lines around her eyes. "It wasn't that."

"Then what was it?"

"I was jealous." She said it so softly, he wasn't sure he'd heard right.

"What?"

She glared at him. "I was jealous! All right?"

Logan shook his head in bafflement. "Why would you be jealous? I don't get it."

Kathleen backed up a step, hugging herself. Distress radiated from her. "Because everything I do is wrong! But, you... You come along, she decides you're cool, and before I know it she's hanging out with you when you come over instead of sulking in her room, confiding in you, getting you to talk to me."

"You wanted her to hate me?"

"No!" she cried. "I wanted her to...accept you. I'm glad she likes you. It's just that the ease with which you two get along makes me feel inadequate." She laughed, although it didn't come out quite right. "Even more inadequate."

"But...you're different," he said.

"Sure I am." She did smile, but it twisted. "I'm her evil mother."

"Not evil. But you are her mother. She

loves you. She wants to be like you, but she's mad at you." In the face of Kathleen's uncomprehending stare, he struggled to explain. "I'm just a sympathetic ear. Emma doesn't really feel anything for me. For you… there's this simmering pot of emotions. You see? She can't talk to you because she feels so much she doesn't even understand. But me? I'm nothing to her." He shrugged. "Why would you be jealous of that?"

She looked smaller than usual, washed out, vulnerable instead of confident and vibrant.

"Because you know how to talk to her. I should but I don't."

"How?" Logan echoed. "There's no 'how.' You say what you mean, and she reacts. She'll work all this out, Kathleen. Think back to when you were sixteen. What did you do when your parents tried to talk to you?"

She let out a shaky laugh. "Slam my bedroom door?"

Logan waited.

"Yes. Okay." Tears brimmed in her eyes. "You're right. It was dumb of me. But right away I could see her responding to you. I have tried so hard…" She swallowed, sniffed and wiped her eyes. "I was an idiot. Okay?"

"Okay."

She wavered, confused. He was supposed to have swept her into his arms and said, *I understand.*

"Will you…forgive me?"

"Of course I will."

"Then…"

His voice grated. "You weren't very happy to see me tonight."

Her eyes dilated. "What do you mean?"

"Don't give me that," he said harshly. "I saw your face. You were wishing me anywhere but there."

"It…wasn't a good moment."

Unrelenting, he said, "Because you didn't want to introduce me as your boyfriend."

Her chin came up. "We hadn't spoken in three days. I didn't know where we stood! How was I supposed to introduce you?"

"But that wasn't it, was it?" He watched her face for the slightest betraying reaction. "What if I'd been a well-dressed attorney or doctor? I'm guessing you'd have been more eager to parade me."

She hid her wince, but not well enough. "What does that have to do with anything?"

Twice before in his life he had felt pain as crushing. Once, when he understood that his mother was ditching him, and the night when the call came.

Mr. Carr? I regret to tell you that your wife is dead.

This was more like the first time, because shame twisted inside it, born of his belief that he wasn't good enough. Not smart enough, not handsome enough, not something. As an adult, he'd come to understand that his mother's problems were her own, and had nothing to do with him. He'd been a kid like any other kid. He'd done nothing to make her reject him. But now, for the second time in his life, he'd been found wanting.

It was all he could do to stay on his feet.

"I'm too much like your roots, aren't I?" Even his tongue felt clumsy. "Your father and I'd probably hit it off. We'd recognize each other."

"No! No, it's not…" She was shaking her head hard.

"I don't like being used."

Her voice quavered. "I love you."

He should feel something besides this raging pain. The words should have meaning.

"Yeah? Here's the thing. I don't believe you."

Her eyes closed briefly. "What can I say to convince you?"

"I don't know." His fingers curled around his water as if he were trying to crush it. "I don't know if you can."

She whispered. "You don't…care about me?"

"Care?" Logan didn't even recognize that harsh laugh. "Sure I do. Is that what this is about?"

Kathleen seemed to shrink. "What do you mean?"

When he wrapped his arms around her he felt as if high-tension wires were zinging under his palm. "Is this what you're here for?" he asked, just before he bent his head.

He swallowed her small, startled cry in a kiss that was demanding, even angry. Did he care? What did she think?

He missed her so much he was sick with it. He fell asleep at night thinking of her, woke up in the morning with dream images of her slipping from his grasp. He'd thought, with her, that magic had sparked.

She kissed him back, seemingly helpless to do anything else. Once he lifted his head, he saw the track of tears down pale cheeks. Stiffening, despising himself, Logan pulled back. His anger was still palpable and it was hurting them both.

"I think you'd better go home."

With a muffled sob, Kathleen ran, her feet a clatter in the hall. The front door opened and slammed, with finality that hit him like an bolt of electricity, jerking his body.

She was gone.

EMMA HARDLY RECOGNIZED her own mother the next morning. Emma's school bus came half an hour before Mom had to leave for work, so Emma always got up first. Usually, the second Mom walked into the kitchen, her gaze would go to Emma's bowl or plate. Emma would see her calculating the caloric and nutritional value of her breakfast, how much she might have already eaten, how much she would undoubtedly leave. Then she'd say something bright and fake, like, "That toast smells good! Maybe I'll have that, too."

This morning, Mom walked into the kitchen like a zombie. Shuffle, shuffle, shuffle. Each step was mechanical, slow, as if she had to think, *Move the left foot. Move the right foot.* Her hair was a rat's nest. Hadn't she even looked in the mirror yet? Her face looked puffy, the skin under her eyes bruised, and her eyes themselves were unfocused.

"Mom?" Emma said uncertainly.

Her mother's gait checked. Her head turned slowly, as if with an effort. "Yes?" she asked without interest.

"Are you all right?"

"I'm fine." She shuffled on to the counter.

Coffee was brewing, started last night on a timer. Mom looked as if she really, really needed a cup.

"Are you sick?"

"No."

"You look…" Emma hesitated. *Awful* might be mean to say, but was true. "Um… tired."

"Didn't sleep much."

"Oh. Are you going to work?"

She didn't even summon her usual note of impatience or irritation that implied Emma was such a child, she didn't understand an adult's responsibilities. "Yes."

She lifted the pot and poured, missing the cup and splashing hot coffee on the counter and her bathrobe. She muttered, adjusted the angle, then smacked the coffeepot back down on the burner. She dumped a huge spoonful of sugar in it, then shuffled back toward the table without even wiping up the spill.

Alarmed, Emma asked, "Are you sure it's a good idea?"

"I can't afford to stay home," Mom said dully.

On a pang of guilt, Emma said, "Because of me, I suppose."

Mom's gaze wandered her way, as if she were some near stranger sitting at the breakfast table. "What are you talking about?"

"Nothing!" Emma felt suddenly breathless, anxious. "I've got to get ready."

She hadn't eaten much of her cereal. Mom didn't even notice. Which should have relieved her, but instead scared her.

What had happened? Had she and Dad had a fight? But she'd come upstairs after he left and sat on the edge of Emma's bed.

"He says he's going to be calling you," she'd said. "Whether you want to talk to him or see him is entirely up to you. Okay?"

"Okay." Emma had sat cross-legged, clutching her pillow on her lap. "Did he tell you what I said?"

"I think you stung him a little bit." Mom smiled. "If he thought he could stroll back into your life without hearing a few home truths, then he's a bigger idiot than I gave him credit for."

Now, as Emma brushed her teeth and then stuffed her binder and textbooks in her bag, she thought in confusion, *Mom was okay then.*

She'd left Emma's room, and Emma had heard voices from downstairs. Mom talking to Helen or Jo. She didn't think the phone had rung or anything.

So what had happened?

Of course, it was raining again today. Emma trudged to the corner where the bus came, and stood under a big tree that had leafed out for spring and kept all but some drips off her.

Maybe nothing happened. Maybe Mom just had insomnia, or a migraine, or an upset stomach.

The bus rumbled up, creaked to a stop, then belched as the door opened. With a shrug, Emma got on it. Mom would be okay later.

That afternoon, Emma didn't see her mother when she first got home from work. As soon as Ginny's bus dropped her, she and Jo started playing War. Emma went to her room to do homework. Not until Helen called, "Dinner time!" did she close her math book and go downstairs.

Mom was in the kitchen, still dressed for work except she'd changed her shoes for some fluffy slippers.

"Hi," Emma said.

Mom turned. She'd put on makeup and stuff, so the blue circles under her eyes weren't as obvious, but she still looked really tired. And, Emma realized, really mad.

"I got a call from the attendance office. They tell me you skipped a class yesterday."

"Um…"

"Don't bother lying. I called Mr. Wellborn. He said you weren't there."

"I was upset about Dad coming." She lifted her chin. "So I left school a little early. Is it that big a deal?"

"You know it's a big deal. Did you come home?"

Emma sneaked a glance toward Ginny, who already sat at the table. Had she ratted?

Mom noticed, and her eyes narrowed. "Where did you go?"

"Just…around!"

"That's not good enough."

"I went downtown. I looked in store windows. That's all!"

Mom's lips thinned. "I'm disappointed in you."

Emma's eyes filled with tears. "Aren't you always?" Mad at herself, she raced for the stairs.

Mom came right after her. "Don't try to evade this conversation! You knew how I'd feel about you cutting classes."

Halfway up the stairs, Emma turned. "One class!" she cried. "One! That's all. I never do stuff like that!"

Mom's expression altered. She suddenly looked very tired and very sad. "No. I know you don't." She sighed. "Come and eat dinner, Emma."

"Is that an order?"

"I'm asking…"

Burning with resentment, Emma said, "I don't *feel* like eating anymore."

Mom flinched. "Please don't use that, of all things, as a weapon."

What was she supposed to use? Filled with a sense of power, Emma said, "I can't eat when I'm upset."

Face pale, Mom gripped the newel post. "Please come to the table."

"I told you! I'm not hungry!" Emma yelled, and hurried up to her room.

She flung herself onto her bed, battling a sense of guilt that took the form of her therapist's face. Sharon was shaking her head in disapproval. They'd talked endlessly about why Emma used food as a way to have control over a corner of her world, as if it were castle walls not even her parents could storm.

But how could she just sit down and eat dinner, after her mother was, like, *screaming* at her?

Her stomach rumbled and she ignored it. She hated being hungry. It was as if she had lost control of her own body. She used to feel so strong and so pure, like she was rising above the mean demands of her physical self. Emma had read once about Northwest Coast Indian shamans, who fasted until they thought the light could shine through them. Sometimes she'd felt that way, like clear glass that didn't cast a shadow.

Only, she always did eat something, and then it was as if she'd caved in. She was weak! Fat! Ugly! She'd exercise and exercise until she recaptured that sense of purity, but she always lost it again.

Tonight she was ashamed to realize she wasn't striving for that sense of ultimate control and purity. She just wanted to hurt her mother.

Her anger fading—she'd *known* Mom would be mad about her cutting class—Emma lay on the bed debating whether she should go downstairs and say she was sorry.

Only then, a knock came on her door.

"Emma? Can I talk to you?"

She sat up. "Come in."

Mom looked old or sick or something when she came in. The sight of her face sent a stab of repentance through Emma.

Mom sat on the edge of the bed as if she was too tired to keep standing.

"I won't be seeing Logan anymore," she said.

Emma stared at her. "What?"

Mom's nostrils flared. "You heard me."

"But...*why?*"

"You liked him that much, huh?"

"He was cool!" She grabbed her pillow and squeezed it hard, not even understanding her own turmoil. "I thought you might marry him and everything!"

So quietly her words were almost indistinguishable, Mom said, "I thought I might, too."

"Then...why?" Emma asked again. Begged to know.

Pain showed on Mom's face. "He thought I was embarrassed by him."

Understanding flooded Emma. Understanding, and outrage. She flung the pillow aside. It fell off the bed. "Were you?"

Mom's head came up. "Of course not!"

"You were!" Tears burned in Emma's eyes. Logan was so cool! "It's just like with Uncle Ryan! And Grandpa. You wished he wasn't your dad!"

"That's not true!"

"That's what you said. He didn't go with your perfect life. Any more than I did." She scrambled from the bed. "So I bet Logan's right. You were embarrassed by him."

Mom stared, not at her, but at the wall. Very softly, she said, "It's hard to change all at once."

"I wish *he* was my dad!"

Her head turned and she met Emma's gaze. Her eyes were alive with pain, but her voice was dead. "And I wasn't your mother? I suppose just about anybody would be better. Maybe you're even right." She pushed herself to her feet. Without turning, she said,

"I'm sorry I lost Logan for you." Then she left, gently closing the door behind her.

A moment later, Emma heard her door, only a few feet away, shut.

CHAPTER THIRTEEN

KATHLEEN PARKED at the curb in front of the house where she'd grown up in West Seattle. For the first time, she was struck by the resemblance between her own house and this one. Oh, hers had been grander in its heyday, but both had been built in the same era, each on a sloping lot with the one-car detached garage at street level. Steep stairs led to small front yards supported by retaining walls. Her parents' house was sided with white clapboard instead of brick, but the porches were very similar, the peaks of the roofs, the leaded glass front windows.

Perhaps, she thought bemusedly, she had been trying to go back to her roots since the day she left Ian.

It was Saturday and her father had his morning bowling league. He'd told her to let herself in if she beat him here. She had made sure she did, wanting a few minutes to wander and maybe remember.

Mom and Dad had always kept Ryan's and Kathleen's bedrooms just the way they were. Dad didn't want a den, and Mom didn't sew, so why would they bother remodeling either bedroom? Now, Dad must rattle around in the house.

She went upstairs first, pausing to glance in Ryan's room with the plaid bedspread, blue walls and simple desk. He had taken more furniture when he left home. She recalled a bookcase he had built in high-school shop class, when he discovered his love of woodworking.

She'd curled her lip and said, "What? You want to be a carpenter or something?"

"Maybe."

She had let sarcasm drip from her voice. "Why don't you just become a welder like Dad?"

Her brother, unfazed as always by her disdain, said simply, "Because I like wood."

Shaking off the memory, she looked in the one upstairs bathroom shared by the whole family, with predictable battles once she and Ryan both reached teenage years. The grout was aging but the bathroom was spotlessly clean.

Her father hadn't lifted a finger to clean

house when his wife was alive, but after her death he'd taken over her chores without complaint, at least to his grown daughter.

When she had remarked one time on how he must have just waxed the wood floors, he had shrugged. "Don't have much else to do."

Her parents' marriage hadn't seemed a love-match to her youthful eyes, but now she wondered. Dad hadn't remarried; hadn't even seemed to consider doing so. Perhaps they had loved each other more than she'd realized. There was so much about them she didn't know.

Her bedroom was across the hall from theirs. Unlike Ryan, she had taken scarcely a thing when she left home. After college, she had married, and Ian had always had money. She hadn't needed the garage-sale desk her mother had painted white and trimmed with gold, or the twin bed with bolsters. At some point, Kathleen had taken down the posters on the pale pink walls herself, afraid—she supposed now—that they didn't support her image of who she was and always had been.

Funny how well she remembered the day she and her mother together had painted her room. She'd been…oh, twelve or thirteen.

They'd had fun, just talking and admiring the clean pale sweep of walls as they worked.

Of course, when she was sixteen she had decided pink was too silly and feminine, but her parents had balked at repainting so soon. Some of her friends had redone their bedrooms every year or so, and she couldn't believe her parents weren't willing to spend the money for a can or two of paint.

She sat on the bed and remembered hiding up here, reading and talking endlessly on the phone with her friends, dreaming of escape.

What if she'd known her mother would die so young? Would she have taken better advantage of the time they had as a family?

The front door opened downstairs and her father called, "Kathleen? You here?"

"Upstairs, Dad." She smoothed the bedspread with her hand, stood and went to the stairs. "Don't come up," she protested at the sight of his foot on the first step. "I'll come down."

He backed away and watched as she descended.

"How was bowling?"

His seamed face brightened. "Bowled a 240 today." He mimicked a swing. "No bad for an old man, eh?"

"You're not so old."

"Seventy," he reminded her. "That's no spring chicken."

She kissed his cheek. "Forty is looming for me, you know."

"Happens."

"Are you hungry yet? I brought lunch."

Usually when she came she took him out—or he took her, insisting on paying. Today she'd liked the idea of them staying home. She hoped he didn't mind.

He exclaimed over the thick sandwiches she'd made and the homemade minestrone soup she set to warming.

"Helen made it," she said over her shoulder. "She's the best cook of all of us."

"You, living with a bunch of women." Her father shook his head.

Laconically, she imitated him. "Happens."

He laughed and popped open a soda from the refrigerator. "Want one?"

Kathleen shook her head. "Why is the idea of me living with a bunch of women so strange?"

"You weren't the artsy type." He shrugged shoulders that were still strong, although he'd retired several years ago. "You wanted a fancy condo in Belltown or what you got, a rich husband and a mansion."

"Got and threw away."

His eyes were shrewd. "You never did tell me what happened."

She hesitated, then sat down at the table. "Ian had no patience with Emma's anorexia. He tried to force-feed her one night. I had to drag him away. It was a horrible scene, and the last straw."

Her father nodded. "I never liked him, you know."

She knew. He hadn't tried to hide how he felt. Her father was a blunt-spoken man who had undoubtedly sensed Ian's condescension.

Dad reached for the sandwich. Chewing, he said, "How's Emma?"

"Good." She smiled with difficulty. "Constantly mad at me, but eating."

He shook his head. "Teenagers."

So everyone said. Kathleen thought— knew—that Emma's feelings toward her mother were far more complicated than the usual teen angst. But she only nodded.

Her father still wore his brown bowling-team shirt with dark blue polyester slacks, snagged in a couple of places and sagging in the knees and rear, but still in good shape, he'd tell her, if she suggested shopping for new ones. He had apparently shaved this morning, which was something. Most days he sported gray stubble.

Trying to look at him objectively, she decided he had probably been a good-looking man when he was young, strongly built and the possessor of a devilish smile. By most people's standards, he hadn't been a bad husband. She couldn't imagine he'd ever strayed from his marriage bed, for example. He'd brought home a paycheck most weeks, unemployment in down times. Neither had paid for extras, but they'd owned a house and managed bills and raised kids. He was surviving now on his retirement and a little he'd "put away" once those kids were grown.

"I've been a lousy daughter." Her eyes filled with tears.

He pushed back from the table in alarm. "What are you talking about?"

"I've never had you over often enough. I'm always so busy with my own life."

"I've got my friends." He nodded toward the sink. "Paper towels over there, if you want to blow your nose."

She gave a choked laugh and fetched one. "I'm sorry. I've just been...looking back at my life and discovering I don't much like myself. I cared about all the wrong things."

He looked wary. She and her father never talked about things like this. And he'd never wanted anything to do with women's tears.

"You were a good enough kid. Just set on having a life better than your parents', that's all."

"Better? How?" she asked bitterly.

"Not scratching for money to pay the bills. So you could have nice things."

"It's not as if Ryan and I were deprived. Why was he happy with our life and I wasn't?"

She didn't expect an answer, and was surprised when she got one.

"Your mother."

"What?" she exclaimed.

The lines in his face deepened. "Your mom wanted better for you. You were so pretty and so smart, she always said, you could have it. She was so proud of you. The friends you had, going to college, your wedding being so fancy. That's what she wanted for you."

"Mom?" she said, dumbfounded.

"Your mother, now, she was a real pretty woman. You look a lot like her." He gazed into the past with a mix of grief and joy that answered her question about how much he had loved his wife. "Didn't have the chances you had. If she could have finished school, your mom'd have done better than me." He shook his head. "She always said she didn't mind working, but that's not what she wanted for you. 'Being on your feet for an eight-hour shift, that's hard,' she used to say. And having to smile even when some jerk didn't leave a tip or complained to her boss about her or pinched her…" He cleared his throat. "And then she took care of me, too."

"I never knew…"

"That she was proud of you?"

"I knew that." Kathleen fumbled through memories as clumsily as if she held a fat pile of snapshots in her hand. "But not that she encouraged me to be the 'princess,' as Ryan liked to put it."

"I wasn't sure she was doing the right thing, making you believe you were too good for your own parents." He shook his head. "But she'd have her way."

You can make nicer friends than those. Mom shut the door firmly behind departing playmates, her expression disappointed. *You can be one of them popular kids.*

You don't belong here with us. Mom stood at the foot of the stairs and watched her come down in her prom dress. *You look like a princess tonight, honey. Don't you think, Dad? Like she oughta live in some palace?*

Setting down her half-eaten sandwich, feeling queasy, Kathleen asked, "Didn't Ryan mind?"

"What would he care?" her dad said in surprise. "He was a boy. He'd just make fun of you when you got too uppity."

She smiled ruefully. "Yeah. He did. He still does."

His eyes were grave and even anxious. "Your mom meant well."

"I know she did." Kathleen blinked away a prickle of tears. "She gave me confidence in myself. I just wish I'd used it to tackle a career instead of believing I was entitled."

Princess. She'd stood in front of mirrors and posed endlessly, tilting her head this way and that, smiling graciously for the adoring masses. *Mommy said...*

Kathleen sighed deeply, then reached across the table and gave her father's hand a quick squeeze. "Ryan and the kids are coming over for dinner tomorrow. Can you come, too?"

"Short notice." He frowned, but failed to hide that he was pleased. "What time did you have in mind?"

"Oh…noon. One o'clock? I'll bet Ryan would pick you up."

Dad drew himself up. "Nothing wrong with Harriet." Harriet was a massive Buick he'd been driving for fifteen years or more. "Or my driving."

"I didn't say there was." Taking a sniff, she said, "Oh, no! I forgot the soup! Do you have room for some, if I didn't burn it?"

"Just as soon save it for dinner." He pushed away from the table. "Won't have to cook, that way."

"Baseball game on?" she judged, from his sidle toward the living room.

He looked abashed. "It can wait."

"Don't be silly. I'll pop the soup in the fridge and be on my way. You go ahead and watch your game. I'll stick my head in and say goodbye."

"That's fine," her father said in relief, and escaped, as he had for most of her childhood.

But not before he'd told her what she wanted to know.

She looked around her mother's kitchen and thought, *Mommy, I wish you'd told me to become somebody important. Not somebody who was most famous for who she married.*

SUNDAY DINNER WAS predictably chaotic. Emma thought it would have been perfect if Logan had been here, too.

This spring, Sundays had become a day to gather, usually in this house, but sometimes at Uncle Ryan's. Uncle Ryan and Jo wanted to be together all the time anyway, but they were waiting until summer to get married.

"When I'm out of school, and can be completely free-spirited," Jo claimed, but Emma knew that really she and Uncle Ryan were waiting so that Melissa and Tyler had their dad to themselves for a while.

They'd come to visit him for Christmas, expecting to go back to Denver where their mom lived, now that she had remarried. Only she'd called and asked if they could stay with Uncle Ryan.

"Her marriage is in trouble," Uncle Ryan had said, looking grim around the mouth. "She doesn't want to involve the kids in any uproar."

Emma had overheard Jo telling Mom that he was being charitable, that Wendy had chosen her new husband over her kids.

Emma had shivered at the thought. Having your parents divorce was scary enough, but being ditched by your mom? Wow.

Emma could tell that Tyler didn't mind as much, that he'd rather live with his dad anyway. But Melissa had seemed really sad at first.

Today Emma grabbed her and said, "Want to come up to my room? I downloaded some new music."

Melissa's exaggerated expression of relief was funny. "Thank you! Tyler is driving me *crazy!*"

The girls flopped on the bed and listened to music, but mostly talked.

"I can hardly wait to start middle school," Melissa confided. "The boys in my class are so *juvenile*. Maybe the eighth graders will be cooler."

Emma doubted it. Dances in middle school really weren't that much fun. A few couples wrapped their arms around each other and swayed, and otherwise girls danced in clumps because boys never asked them. But she remembered how excited she'd been, too. By sixth grade, you were so tired of being treated like a little kid. Middle school, with different teachers and classes all day, was

more like high school. You could hang out
with friends between classes, and you had
a locker and there were dances and sports
teams and a choir—Melissa, Jo had said
proudly, was an incredible singer.

She was pretty, too, delicate and blonde
and blue-eyed, looking, Uncle Ryan said,
like Emma's mom when she was a girl. Like
Emma, too, he'd added, really quick. It was
nice of him to say so, but at eleven, Emma
had not exactly been delicate. Those were
the days when she stuffed her face all day
long and wore, like, a size thirteen or fifteen
when her friends were all in ones or threes.

"Do you miss your mom?" Emma asked.

Melissa rolled onto her back and stared at
the ceiling, where Emma had glued stars that
glowed in the dark. "Sometimes. She called
this morning."

Emma waited, sensing she wasn't done.

"She and my stepfather are moving again.
He was transferred. They're going to Sacra-
mento. In California, you know?" She made
a face. "We're supposed to go spend a month
there this summer. I wish he'd gotten transferred to L.A."

"But it's close to San Francisco, isn't it?"

"Yeah, I guess." She was quiet again for

a minute. "She calls every week. She ask
about stuff—you know, what we're doing—
but then she doesn't remember what I've tol
her. Not like Jo does. Or Dad, of course."

Emma nodded, although Melissa probabl
didn't see her. "I saw my dad this week. Fo
the first time in over a year."

Her cousin rolled onto her side and
propped her head on her hand. "Really? Were
you scared to see him?"

Emma grimaced. "Kind of. But it felt good
to tell him how mad I've been. I don't think
he liked it. He hasn't called again."

"Do you want him to?" Melissa asked,
wide-eyed.

"I don't care." She frowned in turn up at
the ceiling. "Yeah, I guess maybe I do. I don't
know. I'm mixed up about him."

"I am about my mom, too."

The two girls lay side by side and listened
to the singer with a deep, scratchy voice that
gave Emma goosebumps sing about loving
one girl and remembering another.

"Girls!" Mom yelled up the stairs. "Dinner!"

"I'm starved!" Melissa exclaimed, scrambling up.

I am, too, Emma realized.

The kids all ate in the living room, sitting

on the floor around the coffee table, while the grownups—Mom, Helen, Jo, Uncle Ryan and Grandpa—ate at the table in the kitchen. Emma wished she could hear what they were saying, but she liked hanging out with her cousins. And Ginny, of course. Ginny was like a little sister.

Emma had been surprised to see Grandpa. He mostly came on holidays. And, he'd just been here for Easter. But Mom hugged him and kissed his cheek and he patted her on the back when he came in. Mom looked out the window then and shook her head over his parking job—Emma came to see, too. Grandpa drove the biggest car she'd ever seen except for hearses and limos, and it barely fit their street. The front wheel was smack in the middle of the sidewalk and the rear bumper stuck out in the street.

"I guess the neighbors won't mind," Mom whispered.

"If they can get by," Emma said doubtfully.

"I can't ask him to move it. He'd just say," she deepened her voice, "'You trying to tell me how to park? When I've been doing it for fifty-four years?'"

Emma giggled. "I think it's okay."

Mom turned from the window. "Dinner

smells good, doesn't it? I love turkey and the works." Her mouth formed an O when she remembered Emma wasn't eating meat. "I did make some stuffing separately. For you."

She probably knew to a fraction of an ounce how much there was, Emma thought now as she dished up from her own special foil-covered casserole dish. Which meant she'd know exactly how much Emma ate.

She wondered if Logan had a chance to talk to Mom before they broke up. He'd said he would, and she just knew he would keep a promise. Emma kept thinking he'd call, even though he and Mom had apparently had a big fight, but the week had passed without Mom saying anything. Maybe he *wouldn't* call, she thought gloomily. Finding out that Mom was secretly embarrassed by his clothes and what he did for a living and everything must have really hurt.

Mom had been weird all week. Somebody had mixed up all the cans in the cupboard, and Mom hadn't straightened them out. She'd gone to the grocery store with a list, and still forgotten stuff. One night, she didn't remember that it was her turn to cook, and Jo had to do it. Mom overslept one morning, and swore when Emma woke her and she leaped out of bed.

She'd been making soap in a frenzy, every evening. Emma hated going in the kitchen, with Mom wearing a mask and goggles and stirring lye in a huge pot. The smell was gross!

She and Helen were doing their first craft fair next Saturday and Sunday. This soap wouldn't be cured by then, but they were both hoping they would sell their inventory and need lots more by July and August, when they would be doing fairs almost every week-end.

While Mom worked, melting and blending oils to mix with the nasty lye solution, Helen sat at the table cutting regular-size bars from the giant ones Mom made, then bundling some and tying them with a couple of colors of raffia. She'd slip a label under the bow, one she and Mom had designed together and that they printed off on the computer onto this heavy, pale amber paper. They had also found a cheap source for small baskets, and she arranged other bars artistically in them and tied them up with big lengths of the raffia. The pantry was totally stuffed now, and so were the shelves and cupboards Logan had built specially for soap.

Emma hoped they would sell a bunch. Either that, or she'd still be using all this up when she was ready for a nursing home.

After a while, Grandpa left. Emma knew he liked to watch sports on TV. He'd said something about turning on the Oakland A's, but not even Uncle Ryan seemed interested, and when he saw the living room full of kids, he said goodbye.

Helen declared that she was going upstairs to take a long, luxurious bath.

Emma grinned at her. "At least we have soap."

"We do indeed have soap," she agreed, making a horrible face that made the girls laugh.

After she left, Tyler asked, "Wanna play Uno?"

Melissa and Emma looked at each other. Emma shrugged. "Sure."

Mom glanced in once they were sitting around the coffee table again, Tyler dealing. "Yell if you want cocoa or anything," she said, and went away.

Ginny played "with" Emma, who hadn't noticed she'd left until she came back, plopping on the couch next to where Emma leaned.

"They're talking about you," she announced. "Auntie Kath said, 'I've been waiting for the chance to talk to both of you together about Emma.'"

Both of you? Jo and Uncle Ryan, Emma realized. Why did Mom want to talk to them about her?

She shot to her feet. "You stay here," she hissed at the others, when Tyler started to rise, too. "And don't cheat."

Still holding their cards, they stared wide-eyed as she left the living room. She wore only socks, so she moved silently on the hardwood floor. Upstairs she heard water draining; Helen must be getting out of the tub.

Low voices came from the kitchen. Emma stood to one side of the open doorway and strained to hear.

"...talked to Emma about this?" Uncle Ryan asked.

"No," Mom said. "The idea just came to me." Then she must have moved, because her voice became muffled. "...you first," she finished.

Anxiety squeezed Emma's heart. They

sounded so serious, not as if they were discussing a cool trip Uncle Ryan and Jo might take her on, or something like that. More as if… She didn't know, but she was scared.

And then she heard it: just a few words from Jo.

"…while she's living with us…"

Living with them?

And then Emma knew. Mom was getting rid of her.

JO AND RYAN DIDN'T SEEM totally opposed. They listened with grave expressions as Kathleen explained her rationale, nodded, asked questions. Neither of them said, "You've got to be kidding! You want *us* to take on *your* problem teenager?"

Kathleen didn't know if this was the answer, but the idea had been niggling at her for a few weeks and finally surfaced yesterday.

What if Emma had the chance to concentrate on getting well, if only for a few months, while still living with people who loved her? She wouldn't have the day-to-day conflict with her mother, but Kathleen could easily call or see her as often as Emma was willing. Ian wasn't an option, but Emma's uncle was.

"We'd have to talk to Melissa," Ryan said, frowning as he considered. "Let's face it. We don't have an extra bedroom. The two girls would have to share. That's asking a lot of 'Lissa. She'll have to be okay with it."

"I do understand that," Kathleen agreed.

Jo waved away his worry. "Melissa worships the ground Emma walks on. Of course she'll go for it. I'm more concerned about how this will affect our relationships with her. While she's living with us, we'd be the bad guys."

"Honestly, she's very responsible," Kathleen started to say.

Her daughter's angry voice came from behind her. "How long have you been planning to ditch me?"

Kathleen closed her eyes in horror. Emma had overheard. If this wasn't the worst way to bring up the idea, she didn't know what was.

Jo and Ryan rushed into speech together. "Honey, we were just talking."

"We thought you might like..."

Kathleen turned and met her daughter's eyes, blazing with betrayal.

Over the top of the other two adults, she said, "I was going to talk to you tonight, if Ryan and Jo agreed. I'm *not* ditching you. I'm looking for a living situation that will make *you* happy."

"Me?" She laughed wildly. "I can't believe it, after the way you talked about Aunt Wendy! You're doing the same thing, aren't you? If the kid's too much of a hassle, get rid of her. Right?"

The hurt on her daughter's face pummeled her. "This is not the same thing…" she tried to say.

Emma cried, "My mom doesn't want me. How's that different from 'Lissa's mom not wanting her?"

"It's not that I…"

"It is!" Her face contorted. "Fine! I'll go pack right now." She stormed from the kitchen.

The silence she left behind resounded in Kathleen's ears.

"You'd better go talk to her," Ryan said mildly.

Kathleen nodded. "I…excuse me."

She saw the other kids staring at her from the living room. They'd heard, and in their eyes was judgment.

What have I done? she thought.

Upstairs, she brushed by Helen, who had emerged from the bathroom in a robe with her hair wrapped in a towel. She turned in astonishment to watch Kathleen hurry down the hall, face her daughter's bedroom door, raise her hand to knock…and then let her fisted hand drop to her side.

She was too shell-shocked to cry. Too dismayed at her own stupidity in taking the awful risk she had today. No, not just stupidity, her *condescension,* in letting Emma be the last to know. Of course she felt betrayed!

Finally Kathleen made herself knock.

"Go away!"

"I can't." Her voice hitched. "Emma, I have to talk to you."

"No!" her daughter screamed. "I'll talk to Uncle Ryan!"

Kathleen turned the knob and walked into Emma's room.

Emma, curled on the bed hugging a pillow, rolled the other direction. "Go away!" she cried again, in a tear-thickened voice.

"I love you," Kathleen said. Whispered. Tears rained down her cheeks. "I love you so much."

"You don't!"

"I do." She sat on the bed and laid a hand on Emma's thin shoulder. "I would do anything in the world for you. Including let you live with someone else, if that would make you happier."

Emma scooted away from her hand. "You don't care what makes me happy."

Vision blurred, Kathleen said, "All I know is, I can't seem to. I won't let you kill yourself because I'm being selfish. I'm not ready for you to grow up. You're my little girl, and you always will be."

"Then why…" Emma whispered. She rocked, still lying with her back to her mother. "Why?"

"Because all of your eating problems are my fault, aren't they?" She gazed dully at her daughter's bedroom wall and felt the tears fall. She didn't recognize her own voice. "I don't blame you for not loving me anymore. I don't even like myself very much. But I need you to know that I have always, and will always, love you."

Kathleen felt movement beside her. She turned her head to see Emma rolling over and rising to her knees.

Her face looked as awful as Kathleen

knew her own must, wet with tears, her eyes red and swollen and her hair wild.

"It's not your fault."

A sob shook Kathleen. "I was…so arrogant…"

"I love you, Mommy." Emma flung herself at her mother, and Kathleen's arms closed around her.

She buried her face in her little girl's hair and cried, even as Emma cried against her chest.

CHAPTER FOURTEEN

KATHLEEN WENT DOWNSTAIRS long enough to tell Ryan and Jo that everything was okay and thank them.

"She'll be staying home," she told them, accepted their hugs, then went back upstairs as Ryan gathered the children to leave.

She and Emma talked for hours, eventually going downstairs when they heard Helen tucking in Ginny.

Both washed their faces and changed into pajamas on the way. They sat at the kitchen table, sipping cocoa until the dregs turned cold.

"I think, if my wanting so much to be slim and pretty is anyone's fault, it's Dad's," Emma insisted. "I mean, I wanted to look like you, but it was him who always said stuff. And just looked so disgusted or disappointed in me." She reminded her mother what he'd said when she started to diet, about how maybe now he'd have *two* beautiful women. "Except, no matter how skinny I got, he never said, 'Emma, you look beautiful.'"

That jerk, Kathleen thought.

"I know I'm not," Emma said. "Beautiful, I mean. But wouldn't you think he could have *lied?* Since I'm his kid?"

"But you are beautiful!" Kathleen exclaimed. "Sharon says you have a distorted body image, but I wish you could trust me on this one."

Her daughter wrinkled her nose. "You're my mother."

"Yeah? So?"

"You lie."

Kathleen couldn't help laughing, in a choked kind of way. "About this, I'm not. Just…look at yourself. Honestly."

Emma's forehead puckered. "Then how come no boy ever asks me out?"

"You have been awfully skinny, honey. Also…" Kathleen hesitated, then chose honesty. "Until recently, did you notice or care? You've seemed really self-absorbed. All you thought about was not eating and whether you were fat. Did you ever just talk and laugh with other kids?"

Emma bowed her head and stirred her

cocoa vigorously. "Maybe not," she mumbled. "I guess... I mean, I don't really have any friends."

"You did. Until you started to diet."

Her head came up. "They were jealous of me."

"Are you sure?"

Emma opened her mouth as if to make a heated retort, then closed it, frowned fiercely and finally said, "I don't know. I did sort of brag about how much weight I was losing. I mean, I wanted everyone to see how strong I was being!"

"Being, um, self-righteous is not the path to friendship."

Her shoulders slumped. "I guess not. Now, it's like, I don't know *how* to make friends anymore."

"And yet, Ginny and Melissa adore you," Kathleen pointed out.

"That's different," Emma grumbled.

Kathleen stirred her own cocoa, reflecting. "You know, I lost most of my friends when I left your dad. Did you notice?"

Her daughter frowned, her eyes thoughtful. "Yeah. Sort of. But...why?"

"I can't be sure. Then, I thought they'd just dismissed me because I didn't have enough

status anymore. Now, I think it was partly
that I was unavailable. I couldn't have lunch
with them, I wasn't at the health club, I didn't
even call some of them to let them know
my new phone number. But I also realize in
retrospect that none of them was especially
close. We were friends because of circumstances. We didn't share real problems or
feelings. For example, when I started worrying about your eating, I didn't tell anyone."
She snorted. "I had to maintain our image,
you know."

"The perfect family?"

"Something like that."

"Why did you *care?*" the sixteen-year-old
asked, gazing at her with honest puzzlement.

Kathleen tried to explain everything she'd
been learning and thinking lately, about
her mother's dreams for her and her father's almost complete lack of involvement
in her day-to-day life. "But honestly," she
concluded, "I don't know. Maybe at some
point I found the 'right' friends, and Mom
was pleased, and then I let myself be swept
along. My father just shrugged, and he says
my mother was thrilled that I no longer belonged with my own family. Ryan was the

only one who ever gave me a body check and I resented that, of course."

Emma was quiet. "Um, do you miss Logan?" she asked after a long moment.

"Yeah. But I'll survive." Kathleen tried to smile in reassurance.

But after tonight, and everything with Emma, and her grief about that last scene with Logan, she didn't know if smiles would ever come naturally again. Her whole face felt stiff, her eyes puffy.

"Can't you talk to him?"

"I think maybe we passed that point." Despite the rivers of tears she'd shed tonight, they threatened again. She cleared her throat and said briskly, "I'm feeling like it's bedtime. What about you?"

A yawn stretched Emma's face. She laughed, picked up her cup and pushed back her chair. "I guess I am tired."

They flipped out the lights and started up the stairs.

"You know," Emma said, "the can cupboard is a mess. Do you want me to straighten it out tomorrow?"

Kathleen found she could smile after all. "I messed it up myself," she told her daughter cheerfully. "Let's just leave it that way, okay?"

Looking awed, Emma nodded. "I guess. I mean…sure."

"Can I tuck you in?"

Emma nodded, a little shyly.

The ritual had mostly been abandoned in the past few weeks. Always, on the nights when Emma's door slammed, punctuating their most recent fight.

Kathleen waited while Emma brushed her teeth and climbed into bed, then smoothed the covers up under her chin. Kissing her forehead, she said, "We may fight again tomorrow, but promise me you won't forget I do love you."

Emma nodded sleepily. "Me, too. I mean, you, too."

"For better or worse, we're a team."

"For better…" Emma repeated, the words slurring as her eyelids drifted shut. Her lips kept moving, but Kathleen couldn't tell if she'd finished.

Going on to bed herself, Kathleen thought, in defiance of the inevitable tomorrows, *Who needed the rest of the vow anyway?*

PRIDE WAS AN UGLY THING, Logan discovered. The woman he loved had come to him, against all odds, and said, "I'm sorry. I love you." What had he done? Taken her at her word?

No! He'd sent her away. As a result, he was alone in a house that no longer felt like home without her. He could see the nights stretching ahead of him, quiet but for the tinny blast of the television set. Alone with his bitter knowledge that he was responsible for his own aching loneliness.

He couldn't imagine that Kathleen would accept an apology. He owed her his head on a platter. But chances were, she'd dump it in the garbage and carry the sack right out to the street.

The truth, Logan had realized, was that she had been momentarily dismayed to have him show up when her ex-husband was there. That was all. She hadn't been thrilled to introduce him to Monroe. Maybe, if he had been "somebody"—a city councilman or a partner in a law firm or a television personality—she would have been happier about saying, *See how much better than you I can do?* Yeah, okay, that was petty. But who wouldn't be, under those circumstances?

Back to pride, he realized. Not just his, but hers.

Of all people, he ought to understand. His, he had come to understand after long, sleepless nights, had been scalded because it was already sensitive. His mother had abandoned him. On some unnamed level, he had expected Kathleen to do the same, to see what he had always known: that he wasn't good enough for her. If his own mother hadn't wanted him, who would?

He did know better. But stuff had been simmering beneath the surface without his awareness. Maybe it had when he met and fell in love with Brynn, too, but nothing had ever happened to cause the simmer to become a full, rolling boil. Or maybe, because Brynn was a gentle, humble woman, pretty to him but nothing spectacular, she hadn't triggered his deep-rooted sense of inadequacy. He didn't know; never would. Because she'd been stolen from him in another way.

But he had a suspicion that he had just been waiting for Kathleen to notice that he wasn't worthy. All it had taken to scare him was that one look in which he had read, *Why is* he *here?*

And, hey, it was better to reject her than to let her hurt him more, right?

Logan trudged down the hall to his bed. *Right.*

Lying between cold sheets, his arms crossed under his head, the moonlight and the wind-swayed branches of the maple outside his bedroom casting uneasy patterns on the wall, Logan came to a decision.

He owed her an apology.

He didn't expect anything in return. How could he, after seeing the expression on her face. But he had to say, "I'm sorry. You didn't deserve that."

Then, if she wanted to slap him, he'd turn the other cheek.

He couldn't figure how to get her alone. He wasn't much of a writer, or he might have put his regrets on paper. No, that wouldn't do, anyway. He wanted her to see his face, to know that he meant it.

Morning wouldn't be good, when she was rushing out the door to work. Coming home tired at six in the evening wasn't any better.

He finally decided to hope she went out to lunch. The next day, Logan drove over to the chiropractic office where she worked and sat in wait. She never emerged.

Ditto the next day. She must bring a bag

lunch. Her money was tight; maybe she always did.

But he was, he thought wryly, a patient man, whatever his other failings. So he went back Thursday and parked on the street, where he could see the door leading to the parking lot.

He'd been sitting there maybe ten minutes when she came out. His heart thudded.

Logan straightened, then got out and walked toward her. "Kathleen."

She stopped, her back to him, then turned so slowly, he knew she was reluctant. "Logan?"

He shoved his hands in the pockets of his jacket. Gruffly, he said, "I...wonder if we could talk for a minute."

She studied him for an agonizingly long moment, as if weighing the pros and cons. He gritted his teeth. What if she wouldn't listen?

"Okay," she finally said, with a tired nod. "I was heading out for lunch."

"I can take you. Or we can buy drive-through."

Kathleen nodded again and followed him to his truck.

I'm sorry rode his tongue, wanting to jump

out, but he started the engine and put the pickup in gear. If he spoke now, she might listen, say, "Too little, too late," and hop right back out. Away from here, she was a captive listener. Maybe he could make her understand.

His hands gripped the steering wheel so hard, his knuckles ached.

"Any place in particular?" he asked, trying real hard to sound casual.

"Oh…how about that bakery near Spud's on Green Lake? It's almost warm enough to sit at a picnic table," she said wryly.

Well, it wasn't raining, which was about all he could say for the day. Still, peonies and the first roses had replaced tulips in bloom, while late rhododendrons blazoned their glorious, gaudy colors. Despite the weather, summer was near.

He managed to park half a block away, around the corner from the bakery. When he killed the engine, neither of them moved. A pair went by on Rollerblades, on their way to the paved trail that went around Green Lake, but Logan didn't even turn his head.

Looking straight ahead through the windshield, he said, "I was an idiot. Nothing I can say is adequate, but I wanted you to know how sorry I am. You didn't deserve that."

"No. But I hurt you, and I'm sorry for that."

Out of the corner of his eye, he saw her hands, knotted on her lap.

He sat quiet for a moment, working up the guts to bare his soul. "I don't know what I wanted." The words were wrenched from him. "For you to spit in that man's eye and say, 'See? This is a better man.'"

"You are a better man." Kathleen lifted her head, revealing blue eyes shimmering with tears. "That's exactly what I should have done."

Her contrition ripped at his heart. "No! I didn't have anything to do with you and Emma and him. It was a bad time. So what? I overreacted."

She sniffed, and the first tear rolled down her cheek. "But you're right. For just a second, I saw you through his eyes. You aren't rich. You don't manipulate the stock market or people's lives every day. You work with your hands. So you aren't worthy, in Ian's world. I hate his world!" she said passionately. "But I've spent so many years letting him and all our 'friends' dictate what I valued, for a second I let myself be sucked in again. I swear that's all it was! And then you were gone, and I could hardly wait to get rid of him, so I could go apologize to you."

"Which I refused to hear." Logan dared to touch her cheek, catching tears with his thumb.

"I thought…you hated me," she whispered.

His chest seemed to be cracking open, baring his heart to her scalpel. Shaking his head, he said rawly, "I love you. I loved you then. And I was scared."

"Scared?" Kathleen raised drenched, puzzled eyes to his face.

Still rubbing his knuckle over her satin-soft cheek, he said, "I've been doing a lot of thinking."

She turned her head just slightly to nuzzle his hand. A shaft of pleasure pierced him, so sweet it hurt.

He talked then, telling her what he had realized about the aftereffects of having his mother walk out on him when he was a child.

"And then, you'd said enough things about your father to send up a flare for me. I could tell he was just a guy who'd finished high school, like me. Earned a living. You know?

And in the back of my mind I kept wondering what you saw in me."

"You're kind and handsome and smart."

Would he ever believe that's how she really saw him? He hoped so.

"I'm homely and ordinary."

"But didn't you just tell me your self-esteem is lacking?" She smiled through her tears, looking as beautiful as he'd ever seen her. "Obviously you're not capable of judging your own worth, Mr. Carr. If *I* say you're handsome, you're handsome. Got it?"

"You're sure?" he asked with sudden intensity.

He didn't care whether he was labeled "handsome." Well…yeah, he did, when she was doing the labeling, but that wasn't what he needed to know. He was asking for some kind of guarantee that he wasn't just a whim for her. This past ten days had been hell. If he had her, and then lost her again… He didn't know if he could take it.

"Surer than I've been about anything in years," Kathleen said, letting him gaze deep into her eyes. "Although I don't know how you can love me, with everything you know about me."

She made it sound as if she'd spent her life

defrauding senior citizens or abusing small children. Logan gave a choked laugh. "You haven't done anything so awful. In fact, what I see is a gutsy woman who gave up a lot to protect her child. These days, you're pretty much working two jobs, but you still have time to care about the people you live with, and even me, amazingly enough. With the stress from Emma's illness and her anger added to the mix, I don't know how you've stood up." Letting his tone become just a little playful, he concluded, "I'm thinking, Ms. Monroe, that you aren't so good at judging your own self-worth, either."

"It could be you're right," she admitted.

He wrapped his hand around her nape. He wanted to kiss her. He bent his head, then stopped a hairsbreadth from her mouth at the sound of laughter.

A gaggle of women were window-shopping. He'd parked right in front of an antique store, with a gift shop next door and a Mexican restaurant beyond that. The sidewalk was as busy as Times Square. Nobody was staring at the two people sitting in the pickup truck, but he didn't like knowing they could.

He looked the other direction to see that the path around Green Lake was clogged with bicyclists, joggers, inline skaters and mothers pushing baby carriages. When the rain stopped, Seattleites burst from cover. You'd have thought it was seventy-five degrees out there.

"I guess this isn't the place," he muttered, and straightened.

Kathleen had looked around when he did. "Probably not and I want the chance to talk this out with you...without an audience. Um...my house should be empty. Until Emma gets home at two."

"Mine is closer." He reached for the ignition, then started the truck.

Halfway there, Kathleen said suddenly, "Are *you* sure?"

He took a hand off the wheel to grasp hers. "I have never in my life felt about anyone what I do for you."

"But..."

"I loved Brynn," he tried to explain. "But it was different. More...expected. We met and dated and reached the point where it was time to get married. I guess it was a comfortable kind of love, not one that grabs you by the throat."

"Comfortable," Kathleen mused, "sounds nice."

"Maybe we'll end up old, staid and comfortable. You never know."

He pulled into his garage and when the door closed behind them, he turned to her. She untangled herself from the seat belt to fall into his arms. He kissed her, and everything felt right again.

"I don't deserve to be so happy," Kathleen stated, as they settled on the couch in the living room a few minutes later.

"You're wandering into that self-esteem thing again," Logan warned.

"Oh, dear. Okay. I didn't *expect* to be so happy. I didn't think I ever could be."

"Something's happened with Emma," he guessed. Maybe he should have been wounded to realize that he alone wasn't responsible for her joy, but, strangely, he wasn't. He really liked her skinny, pretty, sad daughter.

She told him about her decision to offer Emma the choice of staying with her or living with her brother Ryan, and about the awful scene that had erupted when Emma overheard her discussing the possibility with Ryan and Jo.

"I should have talked to her first, but I guess I didn't want to raise her hopes if Ryan and Jo weren't willing. Anyway, she was so hurt, it scared me. I didn't think she'd ever believe how much I love her. We were both scared. It brought things in the open that we should have said before. I think maybe we'll be okay."

He stroked her back, feeling the ripple of reaction as her muscles quivered beneath his hand. "Is she going to be okay with us?"

"Are you kidding? She chewed me out for being so stupid as to lose you."

"Really?" Ridiculous to be so pleased. But, hey. It was nice to know he had a fan. Especially since, if he had his way, this particular one would be his stepdaughter.

He went still inside. He'd said, *I love you.* He'd been thinking wedding rings and ever after.

What if she wasn't?

Kathleen had a cozy living arrangement now. She wasn't that long out of her marriage. Now she had her own house, good friends to share it with, a budding business. Sure, Jo was marrying and moving out. Which only meant that Ginny, going on second grade, would have her own bedroom. Where did *he* fit in?

"Are you listening?" She poked him right in the breastbone.

Logan jumped. "What?"

"You weren't!" She was trying to look indignant, but failing, her laughing eyes giving her away. "I could tell!"

"I'm sorry. I was thinking." This wasn't how he'd ever imagined proposing to a woman. You did that by candlelight. He should keep his mouth shut. "Will you marry me?"

Her eyes widened; the pupils expanded. It was her turn to go still. "Marry you?"

A sick knot formed in his belly. "I love you."

"You really want to marry me?" Her doubt reared like Mount Rainier over Seattle on a clear day.

He had to unclench his teeth. "I take it the thought hadn't occurred to you."

"Well, of course it occurred to me!" She scrambled to sit straight. Maybe she couldn't imagine receiving a proposal in his living room. "I love you, Logan."

His shoulders relaxed a fraction. "Then…"

"Yes." She sounded utterly composed.

"Yes?"

"I'll marry you."

Flooded with exhilaration and relief, he kissed her. He felt her smile against his mouth.

"You scared me again."

"I'm sorry." Her eyes were huge pools of blue. "You just took me by surprise."

"I should have waited. Done this right."

"No. I needed to know that you want me for good," she whispered, nuzzling his cheek.

"I guess we'll have decisions to make."

"I could rent my house to Helen," Kathleen said tentatively.

"Yeah." He wouldn't mind bringing her and Emma home. But another idea had occurred to him. "Or I could sell this place. You do have a basement that could become a workshop."

Worried creases formed between her brows. "But…I can't ask Helen and Ginny to go. Helen doesn't make that much."

"I wasn't suggesting you do." He smoothed her hair back from her face, his thumb working at the worry lines. "Call me crazy, but I was thinking I'd just move in." Almost apologetically, he added, "I like your household."

"You mean that?"

"Yeah. We'll have Emma anyway. What's a couple more people?"

Kathleen giggled. "You have a point."

"One condition."

"What's that?" she asked warily.

"You have to let me work on the hous And spend *my* money on it."

She blinked. "But…it'll be *your* hous too. Why wouldn't I let you work on it?"

"Just checking," he murmured, and kisse her.

How lucky could a man get?

* * * * *